"How did a thoroughbred like you ever grow up to be cowboy?"

"I'm not a cowboy," she said, sounding miffed. "I am what is known as—" she coughed and intoned "—'a range technician.' Impressive, huh?"

Jason shook his head. "All I know is, I thought I was supposed to meet some beat-up old cowpoke. S. J. Stewart, chief wrangler for the Salmon River District. What would *you* think?" When she didn't answer, he asked, "What does the *J* stand for? Jane? Joy? Jeanette?"

She sighed. "Jaimison. It stands for Jaimison."

There was a long silence while Jason played that over in his mind. So that was the ghost in her closet, he thought. Well, it was certainly one hell of a ghost. He took a swallow of wine and asked carefully, "So, are you *that* Sandra Jaimison Stewart?"

The look on her face told him the answer even before she nodded and said, "'Fraid so."

Dear Reader,

This is a special month for Silhouette Intimate Moments, and those of you who have been with us from the beginning may know why. May 1988 marks our fifth anniversary, and what a lot has happened since May 1983, when we launched this new line with no idea how it would be received.

If we'd hoped for the best scenario we could imagine, we still might not have been able to come up with all the good things that have happened to these books and their authors. Silhouette Intimate Moments is selling better and better each month, thanks to you. And in return for your loyalty, we give you award-winning authors, books that consistantly win the highest praise from romance reviewers, and a promise for the future: We will always be proud of everything we have done, but we will never rest on our laurels. In coming months, look for new miniseries from authors like Parris Afton Bonds and Emilie Richards, innovative books from longtime favorites like Kathleen Eagle and newcomers like Marilyn Pappano, and, of course, books that take no new chances at all but always live up to the standards we've set for this exciting line.

One last thing: Silhouette Intimate Moments has always been a line designed by the readers. It came into being because you told us you wanted stories that were not only longer but also bigger, larger than life, stories with mature characters, atypical plots and a strongly sensuous romance. Through the years you've never been shy about writing to me with compliments, complaints and suggestions. Now I want to renew our commitment to bringing you the books you want and to ask you, once again, to please keep writing to me. If we keep those lines of communication open, there's no telling how far we can go together.

Leslie J. Wainger
Senior Editor
Silhouette Intimate Moments

Kathleen Creighton
Rogue's Valley

Silhouette Intimate Moments

Published by Silhouette Books New York

America's Publisher of Contemporary Romance

SILHOUETTE BOOKS
300 East 42nd St., New York, N.Y. 10017

ISBN: 0-373-07240-6

First Silhouette Books printing May 1988

Books by Kathleen Creighton

Silhouette Intimate Moments

Demon Lover #84
Double Dealings #157
Gypsy Dancer #196
In Defense of Love #216
Rogue's Valley #240

KATHLEEN CREIGHTON

has roots deep in the California soil and still lives in the valley where her mother and grandmother were born. As a child, she enjoyed listening to old-timers' tales, and her fascination with the past only deepened as she grew older. Today she says she is interested in everything—art, music, gardening, zoology, anthropology and history—but people are at the top of the list. She also has a lifelong passion for writing, and recently began to combine her two loves in romance novels.

For my grandmother, Hattie Merriam Hand;
she always kept a special place in her heart
for horses, black sheep and lonely people.

Chapter 1

The stallion approached the spring with caution, stepping delicately across the muddy ground. Every now and then he lowered his head to blow puffs of vapor at the ice-rimed pools in the shallow depressions left by the hooves of earlier visitors to the water hole.

Once he paused to snort and paw the ground, stamping and tearing at the turf with his hooves until it was a pulpy mass of oozing brown mud. The predator had been here, and though the spoor was an old one, the stallion was taking no chances. Lifting his head, he shook it furiously, then sent a shrill challenge skyward. A challenge, and a warning: Don't mess with me, or with anything that is mine! I am ruler here!

The stallion shook his shaggy black mane once more and then stood still, ears pricked forward, listening. A shadow flicked across the ground; he danced nervously and again trumpeted his warnings to the skies. The reply came back to him on the wind—the high, thin cry of the raptor, a hawk, or perhaps an eagle. Reassured, the stallion lowered his muzzle to the ground and made a series of low grunts and whickering sounds.

The answering whinny came from farther up the valley. The stallion stood motionless, watching his little band of mares emerge like creatures of myth from the ground fog near the hot spring. Seven mares and four foals, three of them spring foals, sturdy and well grown.

The fourth, last to arrive at the water hole, suggested a reason for the stallion's caution. This one was a new foal, a few days old at most, still spindle-legged and knobby-kneed, scampering self-consciously at his mother's flank. His stubby mane and tail were black, and his shaggy coat red gold, lighter than his sire's, though it would darken in time to the same burnt crimson. If he lived long enough. A colt born so late in the year would have a rough time of it when the winter blizzards came to the central Idaho wilderness.

But now it was only early September, and though there was frost on the meadow grass in the mornings, the sun was warm on the colt's back, the air smelled of earth and pine, and his belly was full. He seemed a naturally curious and venturesome rascal, snuffing at spotted frogs, kicking up his heels and gamboling off after the little yellow butterflies that abounded in the meadow. But when his mother whickered anxiously he raced back to her side, holding his tail aloft like a fuzzy black flag.

The stallion drank while keeping a watchful eye on his mares. His ears were in constant motion, twitching and rotating, alert to the sounds of danger. Whenever a mare or foal strayed too far from the band, he was off at a gallop, head lowered, ears flat, to bring the wanderer back.

For the most part the mares accepted his harsh discipline as the natural order of things, but when the stallion came too close to the new foal, his mother squealed and drove her lord and master away, nipping at his flanks with her teeth. Perhaps the stallion knew instinctively that the wobbly-legged youngster might someday challenge him for leadership of the band; certainly the mare knew that a stallion was not above doing away with a future rival. In her baby's defense she would stand up against any enemy, whether man, mountain lion or the colt's own sire.

Suddenly a faint, faraway sound reached the stallion. He stood still, head up, nostrils flaring, ears pointed straight ahead, flanks quivering. Listening.

The sound grew louder. A shadow flitted across the uneven ground, a shadow that was neither raptor nor scavenger. The stallion reared, flailing the air with his hooves, and then, bugling his defiance, with bared teeth and slashing hooves he drove his little band toward the safety of the trees.

The Bureau of Land Management's chief wild horse wrangler for the Salmon River District kept one hand firmly on the helicopter controls while she lifted her camera and snapped several quick pictures of the fleeing horses.

"*There*—got you that time, you great big red rogue, you!" Sandy Jaimison Stewart muttered; then she laughed out loud and leaned over to scribble a note on the clipboard above the chopper's control panel. She'd been wondering where that big bay stallion's band had gotten to. They'd been eluding her all summer. She was a little surprised to find them this high in the range, but the canny old devil did seem to have found a nice home for his harem. It had everything—water, plenty of forage, good cover. A little high-altitude Eden.

The herd had reached the trees. As Sandy watched the last of them disappear with a wave of his stubby black tail, she chuckled. "No doubt about *your* sire, you little rascal."

But something else had struck her about that colt, and she wasn't smiling as she kept the chopper hovering a moment or two longer, trying to see through the thick evergreen canopy below. It was hard to tell—she'd only had a glimpse of a little red-gold rump, and she would have to wait for the photos to be able to say for sure—but that colt had seemed awfully young for this time of year. Unless the stallion moved his band to the lower ranges before snowfall, the odds were against the colt surviving the winter. Unless, of course, she could manage to pull him in during the roundup....

With a mental shake of her head, Sandy scribbled a note to that effect on the clipboard. It would be a lot easier said than done. That stallion had eluded capture so many times that he knew all the wrangler's tricks. Sometimes it almost seemed to her that he knew what she was going to do before *she* did. Like that time over near the Yellowjackets, in Silver Creek Canyon.... Sandy had been so frustrated and angry that day, she'd wanted nothing so much as to nail that animal's scruffy red hide to her door! But she couldn't help but respect him, too—even admire him—and if the truth were known, she wasn't sure she even wanted to catch him anymore. Like the angler who finally hooks the granddaddy trout he's been after for years—and then sets him free.

The colt, though, was another story. She'd definitely be looking for the little guy, come November. If she could pull him in off the range and find him a good home through the Bureau's wild horse adoption program, with decent nutrition, some TLC and training, and that big bay's bloodlines, that colt could turn out to be a pretty fine horse.

Sandy gave a mild snort of chagrin, laughing at herself. Here she was again, imagining the colt sleek and fat in her family's stables, pampered and groomed to within an inch of his life, enjoying the very advantages she had renounced for herself. She didn't know why she did that sometimes. It wasn't as if she missed it, any of it. Well . . . except maybe the stables. She did miss the horses. The thoroughbreds, skittish and fine boned, with coats that gleamed like silk. And her own black hunter, Rasputin. How different they all were from these ragamuffin mustangs with their sturdy, compact bodies, rough coats, and wild, tangled manes.

Wild. That's what they were, and she couldn't afford to let herself forget that—ever. She knew that in their hearts, these wild-born horses bore as much resemblance to the beautifully groomed animals in her father's stables as a timber wolf does to a cocker spaniel.

Still, most of them were tameable, with patience and time. The foal had a good chance, provided he hadn't inherited too much of his sire's stubbornness and indomitable will.

Smiling again, Sandy checked her watch and abandoned the stand of timber. No sense hanging around—that red rogue wasn't going to let any of his brood poke so much as a whisker into the clear as long as she was there. Just as well. It was time to go meet that prospector the BLM had decided to saddle her with. *Damn.* She sure wasn't looking forward to that.

It wasn't that she had anything against the man personally—she'd never even met him. For all she knew he could be a real peach of a guy, although she doubted it; most of the geologists she knew were bookish sorts, tedious in the extreme. It came, she supposed, from spending so much time billions of years in the past. What she resented was the fact that she hadn't been given any choice in the matter. At least, that was what she'd tried to tell herself. The truth was that she resented him because he was a threat to her beautiful, unspoiled, undeveloped wilderness, and she didn't give a hang if he looked like something right out of a Western movie.

Having reached a good cruising altitude, Sandy paused and hovered, taking a moment to look back at the valley. Completely surrounded by jagged, snow-capped peaks, from this high up it resembled an emerald set in silver and platinum. Such a beautiful place. She hated to think of it as a possible site for a thermal energy power plant. Briefly, she wondered what it was called and made a mental note to look it up when she got back to her home base in Silverville. For now, though, and probably for always, she would think of it simply as Rogue's Valley.

"That's probably your ride comin' in now," the kid in the blue coveralls said. He ducked under the wing of the small private plane he was servicing and squinted up at the sky. "Sounds like the BLM chopper." He transferred the one-eyed squint to Jason, who was sitting in the shade of a corrugated tin building. "Sandy's always a little late. I'm goin' to the soda machine; can I get you anything?" There was an eager light in the kid's eyes.

Jason shook his head and exhaled smoke from the cigarette he'd just lit. Actually, the guy wasn't really a kid; it was just that everybody seemed like a kid to him these days. He thought it had started a couple of years ago, right about the time he turned thirty-five. Coming home after fifteen years hadn't helped, either. Fifteen years. Just thinking about the fact that such a big block of his life had passed in what felt like the blink of an eye made him feel old.

The kid—Mike, damn it, his name was *Mike*—headed off to the redbrick terminal building at a jog trot. Jason watched him for a minute, then took the cigarette from his lips and placed it carefully on the ground beside his boot heel. While he ground it to dust he watched the chopper move in, hover and settle into the heat shimmer like a dragonfly alighting on a wind-rippled pond.

The rotors slowed, the sound they made changing from the characteristic thump-thump to a lazy swish. Jason got stiffly to his feet, but didn't move away from the hangar. It was just too damn hot. He figured if he and the wrangler were going to exchange pleasantries they might as well do it in the shade.

When he saw the tall, slim figure climb out of the helicopter he uttered a sibilant expletive under his breath. This one really *was* a kid. He'd kind of been expecting the wrangler to be a wiry old ex-cowboy with bowlegs and a hide like saddle leather. The kind of guy who rolled his own cigarettes and shaved once a week whether he needed it or not. This dude looked wiry, all right, but he was straight as an arrow and moved with that particular kind of efficiency associated with natural athletes. Not a big man—around six feet, Jason guessed, even in cowboy boots—but definitely *young*. He wore his faded jeans like comfortable old friends, and in spite of the heat was sporting a denim jacket with a sheepskin collar, a black cowboy hat and aviator shades.

Mike the mechanic loped past Jason, looking pink and sheepish. He held up a can of diet soda as he passed and muttered, "It's for Sandy," by way of explanation. Jason lifted an eyebrow, but didn't say anything. He'd seen a lot

in his lifetime; there wasn't much that surprised him anymore.

A couple of moments later, though, he got one of those
rare surprises, and it was a doozer.

Out by the chopper, in the blazing midday sun, the
wrangler was indulging in a good stretch, arching his back,
rotating his shoulders, rubbing his neck. When he heard
Mike come running up he turned around, giving Jason a
glimpse of white teeth in a tanned face. And then, while
Mike held the can of soda and shifted from one foot to the
other, the wrangler took off his jacket and tossed it into the
chopper. The cowboy hat sailed after it. And then a braid
the color of vanilla ice cream uncoiled, snaked down and
slapped against a blue denim rump.

The wrangler took the soda, lifted it and drank. A long,
graceful throat, gleaming with sweat, rippled with a series
of swallows. A lean brown hand rested on one slender hip.
Breasts pushed against the white fabric of a tank top, made
of something soft looking and clingy. Nothing spectacu-
lar, but definitely... breasts.

Jason swallowed, too, and wished he'd let the mechanic
get him that drink. He hadn't been prepared for anything
like the bolt of physical response that had just hit him.
Response, hell, it was pure unadulterated *lust*. He felt as
if he'd been hit by a swinging door; it was downright em-
barrassing for someone his age.

Mike was talking, pointing his way. The woman—the
wrangler?—lowered the can and looked over at him, tilt-
ing her head slightly, not smiling, just sort of taking his
measure. Jason acknowledged the look by touching his
temple with the first two fingers of his right hand. He
supposed there was a bit of mockery in the salute—self-
mockery, but the wrangler wasn't going to know that.

Sure enough, her somber appraisal deepened to a frown. And then, still watching him, she pulled a bandanna out of a pocket and used it to wipe the sweat from her chest, her throat, the nape of her neck.

Jason didn't know when he'd ever seen a gesture so completely, unselfconsciously *sensual*. Once again, his response was immediate and powerful.

Jeez, he thought, what *is* this? The woman was like an unshielded reactor; even twenty yards away he could feel sexuality radiating from her like heat from the sun. He had an uncomfortable feeling that she could be hazardous to his emotional health if he didn't figure out how to protect himself, and pretty quickly, too. Being attracted to a woman was one thing, but this felt like something that could tie him in knots if he let it.

And he didn't need any more knots. Not today, thanks.

He knew she was waiting for him to come over to her. He knew he *should* go over, for good manners' sake, if nothing else. But for some reason it seemed important that she come to him instead. He needed the reassurance, he supposed, that he could control both her and his own impulses. So even though he knew it was probably going to get him off on the wrong foot, he just lit another cigarette and deliberately leaned back against the hangar, making it clear that he intended to stay there.

The expression on the woman's face changed again; Jason thought it seemed half annoyed, half puzzled. He locked his gaze with hers, putting all the force of his will into it, and saw her head come up slightly. She'd definitely recognized the challenge now. He wondered what she was going to do about it.

It occurred to Jason that this little duel of wills he'd initiated was childish, the kind of macho posturing he thought he'd outgrown in adolescence. It occurred to him

that it wasn't exactly a great way to begin a working relationship—or any relationship at all, for that matter. But it
didn't occur to him to stop.

He kept his stance relaxed, almost lazy, but inside he felt
tense, keyed up, excited. It was the way he always felt when
he knew he was about to do battle with a resourceful and
highly respected opponent. When he knew it was going to
take everything he had and a little something extra if he
was going to come out on top. So far he'd always managed to do so, but he had a feeling he'd never met an "opponent" quite like chief BLM wrangler Sandy Stewart.

Arrogant, macho jerk, Sandy thought, sizing up the
government geologist in one glance.

"Wonder what he's waitin' for." Mike was scratching
his head and looking puzzled. "I told him it was you
comin' in."

Sandy frowned as she mopped at the sweat on her neck
with her handkerchief. It got pretty chilly in the chopper
at high altitude, so she tended to forget how hot it could be
on the ground at midday in September. She never had done
well with heat, it made her cross and edgy.

She didn't know why the man was just standing there
smoking his cigarette and watching her the way a hawk
watches a rattlesnake. She didn't know why that look
should make her feel shivers of uneasiness, but feel them
she did; her arms were roughening with goose bumps in
spite of the heat. There was *something,* some kind of
magnetism, something that raised her hackles and kicked
all her defenses immediately into overdrive. She could feel
it even from this far away, and though she never liked to
admit being afraid of anything, she knew she wasn't in any
hurry to close that distance.

He was so *big,* for one thing. That wasn't an observation Sandy made very often about anyone, since she pushed six feet pretty hard herself, wearing her hat and boots. It was impossible to tell by just how much this man would top that, seeing him standing alone and at a distance, but she had an idea it would be plenty—at least half a foot. And he wasn't lanky. There was power in the width of his shoulders and the depth of his chest, a suggestion of cat-quickness in the slim flanks and well-muscled thighs. In his standard government-issue boots and khakis, with his shirt sleeves rolled to his biceps, all he needed was a knit cap, Sandy decided, and he'd look like Paul Bunyan.

And then she thought, No. Paul Bunyan was a sweet, gentle giant. She had a feeling this man wouldn't be that benign. She knew it was probably only his black hair and beard that gave him such a fierce and dangerous look, but to her he resembled nothing so much as a pirate. Blackbeard!

Blackbeard, indeed. She almost giggled. That schoolgirlish notion amused her and might have jolted her back to a more practical perspective if she hadn't at that moment realized that the man was treating her to the same intense scrutiny she'd been giving him. His dark gaze swept over her like the unexpected touch of a cold breeze, and once again, in spite of herself, she shivered.

"Well," she said, covering her reaction with a light laugh, "if the mountain won't come to me..." She swallowed the last of her soda and gave the can back to Mike, along with a radiant smile. "Give it a quick once-over for me while I go talk to the man, would you please?"

The mechanic responded with an eagerness that made her feel guilty—she hated using charm to manipulate people—but for reasons she couldn't explain she wanted to confront this guy alone, one on one. *Confrontation.* She didn't know why she should think of it that way. All she was doing was meeting a man with whom she was supposed to spend the next couple of weeks, acting as guide and adviser. It was a professional courtesy to someone who worked for the same government agency, nothing more.

And yet she knew that a certain amount of the adversarial attitude between her and the geologist was understandable, given the Bureau of Land Management's policy of multiple use of public lands. The timber interests were always at odds with the mining interests, the recreation people complained loudly about the cattlemen and the wildlife people were at odds with everybody else. Interdepartmental jealousies, sibling rivalries; those things were pretty universal.

But this was different. This was something she felt in her guts, a hard, tight throbbing in the pit of her stomach. As she walked toward the dark figure lounging against the hangar, Sandy felt herself moving more and more slowly, muscle and sinew instinctively resisting the force of the man's personality the way an unbroken horse resists the pull on his halter.

Reminding herself that she was an intelligent woman, not a horse, Sandy firmly squelched her antagonistic impulses. A lot of people had tried to intimidate her, without much success; she wasn't about to let this guy undermine her self-confidence and authority. She was chief wrangler in this district. This was *her* territory, not his.

With a firm step and a steady gaze, she marched up to the man, put out her hand and said, "Hi, I'm Sandy Stewart."

The geologist straightened without haste, took a last drag on his cigarette, dropped it to the ground and stepped on it. "Rivers," he drawled, taking her hand. "Jason Rivers."

Sandy had expected his voice to be a bass rumble, and it was. What she hadn't expected was that it would caress her auditory nerves like something warm and furry—mink, perhaps, or sable. Mumbling, she repeated the name, feeling anything but intelligent, anything but confident.

Up close, Jason Rivers was even bigger than she'd estimated, and far more intimidating. He made her feel fragile and vulnerable, and for someone who'd had to fight as hard as she had for her own space and independence, those weren't comfortable feelings. Somehow this man made her feel fraudulent, as if she knew deep down in her heart that everything she'd worked so hard to achieve had foundations of sand.

And he did look like a pirate. The neatly trimmed beard did nothing to hide the strong, angular bones of his face, the arrogant hook of his nose, the duskiness of skin that suggested the ruthless scourings of sun and wind. There were pale lines radiating from the corners of his eyes—from squinting, Sandy thought; he didn't look like a man who smiled easily or often. It occurred to her that his mouth might be sensuous if it were softened by a smile, but instead it looked set and unyielding. It was, she thought, the mouth of a man who didn't believe in compromise. A man who'd face any odds—and win.

Oh great, Sandy thought. This is all I need.

But her dismay was tempered with something else, something she couldn't name. She found Jason Rivers *disturbing*. As she stood there, her hand completely lost in his, she felt her heart begin to struggle with a new and unfamiliar rhythm. She felt its thunder in her stomach, in her throat and in the places where his flesh met hers. Then she forced herself to meet his gaze, and found that the most disturbing thing of all. It was bold and steady, but there was something brooding behind it, as if those obsidian eyes had already seen far too much.

Though it made no sense to her, Sandy knew suddenly that she was frightened. It was an odd kind of fear, seemingly without object or focus. Certainly this man wasn't about to do her in; for all his size and savage looks, Jason Rivers was only a geologist. As if saying it would cement that reality more firmly in her consciousness, she stated flatly, "You're the geologist."

Because she'd said it for her own reasons, she was faintly surprised when he replied, "That's right."

"You don't look like a geologist."

"You don't look like a wrangler."

"Touché," Sandy said, and thought, I was right. He doesn't smile.

Disengaging her hand, she widened the distance between them by taking a step backward and immediately felt the thumping in her chest ease. "And now, if you're ready... Is that duffel bag all you brought with you?"

"That's all." He swung the bag onto his shoulder.

A man of few words, Sandy thought; aloud she said, "Okay, then, shall we go?"

Mike came out to meet them, wiping his hands on the front of his coveralls. "She's all ready for you, Sandy. Needs a good servicing, though, and your radio's out. You gonna be able to bring her in sometime soon?"

"Not until after the roundup," Sandy said. "Sorry, Mike, I'll do it as soon as I can afford the time. Looks like I'm going to be tied up for a while."

The mechanic glanced at the man beside her and smiled uncertainly. "Yeah, well . . . I guess I'll see you in a couple of months, huh?"

"Right. I won't forget, I promise." She smiled and saw the familiar blush in response. She liked Mike. He really was a sweet kid, and a genuine genius with any kind of engine.

Her passenger was already stowing his bag in the chopper. Sandy waited for him to clear the doorway, then climbed into the pilot's seat, leaving him to lever his big frame into the space that was left. His presence seemed to fill every cubic inch, making her feel claustrophobic and anxious to be off the ground. At least in the air there would be the endless sky and distant horizons, and all that glorious uncrowded wilderness unfolding below them.

"Isn't this a little unusual?" Having finished adjusting the seat and fastening his safety belts, Jason threw a look her way. "I wouldn't think too many wild horse wranglers fly their own helicopters."

Sandy snorted, but didn't look up; she was busy going through the preflight checklist, listening to the engines and monitoring the rhythm of the rotors. Feeling more like herself now that she had something to focus her attention on, she said dryly, "How do you suppose I got this job? I'm a certified pilot, and I have a degree in animal science. That's all it took to counteract the fact that—" she threw him a glance "—I don't look like a wrangler."

A rumble of laughter surprised her. She looked up quickly, barely in time to intercept a wry smile. So, she thought as she looked out at Mike and gave him a thumbs-up signal, I was wrong. Blackbeard *does* smile.

Mike returned her signal and followed it with a wave. Sandy nodded and lifted off. She thought her passenger seemed a little tense, so she turned to him and, raising her voice above the racket of the motor, inquired, "Queasy stomach?"

Jason Rivers shook his head, but didn't relax. Sandy shrugged and set a course for home.

From the air the ski resort looked quainter than it did from the ground, like a toy alpine village in an elaborate electric train setup—toy houses and toy roads with little toy cars, and tiny signal lights that really worked. Without snow, the ski runs looked like scars.

Sandy followed the river north into the mountains, the shimmering gold of aspens giving way to the somber blue-green of pines. And then the helicopter was sweeping over the Galena Summit and out across the Valley of the Sawtooths, where the upper reaches of the Salmon River, barely a creek here, lay like a piece of blue yarn carelessly dropped onto a green carpet.

There she paused for a moment, hovering like a golden eagle riding a thermal updraft. She loved the Sawtooths, that jagged, steel-blue ridge, so aptly named, so raw, so newly born. These were mountains in their infancy, barely worn by scouring winds and bitter snow. To Sandy, looking at those ragged, virgin peaks, the whole world seemed fresh and new, all hopes and dreams attainable.

Impulsively, she turned to Jason and said, "Welcome to Idaho."

He didn't answer. He was staring through the window with narrowed eyes, and there was a moist, shiny look to his skin. Thinking he might be a nervous flyer after all, Sandy was about to ask if he was all right when he abruptly sat back in his seat. She felt his big body relax and heard the soft hiss of an exhaled breath.

"Thanks," he said in a perfectly normal-sounding voice, "but I'm not exactly a newcomer."

"No? You've been here before?" She wondered then if she'd imagined his unease.

He looked at her, smiled slightly, then turned back to the distant peaks as if, Sandy thought, he couldn't help himself. "You might say that," he said quietly. "I was born here."

Chapter 2

Jason had been wondering when it was going to hit him. On the plane from Salt Lake City he'd caught himself staring out the window, waiting for his first glimpse of the Snake River, dreading it. But that awesome rent in the earth had given him no feeling of homecoming, no gut-tightening sense of déjà vu.

Of course, come to think of it, he'd never seen the river from that perspective before. He'd left Idaho on a Greyhound bus. And in the fifteen years since then he'd seen a lot of rivers, deeper, wider, meaner rivers....

It had taken the mountains to bring it all back to him. These particular mountains—so incredibly unchanged. It was as if he'd never left, as if he were still twenty-two years old, and Jared just fourteen, and they were fishing for cutthroat trout in the shallow rapids of the Salmon River. *The River of No Return*....

Wishing he'd had the sense to face this alone, Jason braced himself for the inevitable questions: No kidding, you were born here? How long have you been away? Why did you leave? Glad to be back?

When he didn't hear them, he glanced at the woman beside him and found her frowning. If she felt his eyes on her, she didn't show it, and all she said was, "In that case, welcome home."

She sure isn't a gabby woman, Jason thought as he muttered some sort of acknowledgment. He liked that.

He decided there were a lot of things about Sandy Stewart he might like, which was as good a reason as he knew of for keeping conversation between them strictly business. Things could get complicated otherwise, and Jason didn't allow that kind of complication in his life. As far as he was concerned, there were only two kinds of people in this world: those he liked, and those he didn't. The ones he didn't like, he avoided. The ones he liked, he put into neat categories: those he had business dealings with, those he called friends and those he took to bed. He made it a point never to mix up the categories, and so far it had worked pretty well. He'd enjoyed some productive business relationships, some lifelong friendships and some truly memorable sex—all without ever once putting his heart in jeopardy.

That was the way he wanted it. He'd learned a long, long time ago that his heart was the most vulnerable part of him, the only part he couldn't protect with his strength, reflexes and brains. He'd learned the hard way what can happen to an unprotected heart, and he'd made up his mind he'd never endure that kind of pain again. To ensure that, he'd wrapped up his heart and stowed it away, and now he made sure no one ever got close enough to him to find it.

Beside him, Sandy was stirring, putting on her jacket, her shades. Jason studied her without looking at her, trusting his memory's eye to explore the long golden lines of her arms and throat, the neat upthrust of her breasts as she'd stood, head thrown back, drinking. The nipples had been noticeable under the tank top, he remembered, even though it had been so hot. He wondered why.

At that point he put an end to his mental exploration.

No doubt about it, Sandy Stewart was going to stretch his willpower to its limits. The problem was, she would fit very nicely in all three categories, if he let her. She intrigued him, made him want to know more about her, maybe see if they might become friends. And he certainly wouldn't mind exploring that long, lean body of hers with more than his imagination. But since the business connection was preordained, he didn't have much choice about where to fit her.

He allowed his mind one more brief memory of the way her throat had rippled when she swallowed, the way the tanned skin across her collarbones had shimmered with perspiration. And then, with only a slight twinge of regret, he slipped Chief Wrangler Sandy Stewart firmly into the slot marked Business.

"I'm not going to do it," Sandy announced to Bert, the cocktail waitress at the Silver Horseshoe Saloon and a good friend of hers. "I just decided."

"I thought you said you didn't have any choice in the matter," Bert drawled. She was just coming back from putting money in the jukebox. Later on, when the place filled up with Friday night locals and ranch hands, there would be people standing in line to drop quarters in the thing, and there would probably be a discouraging word or two exchanged over the choices, not to mention the occasional good fistfight. When it was slow, though, Bert liked to keep the background noise level up.

"Everyone's always got a choice," Sandy said morosely, then winced. "Did you have to pick Johnny Rivers?"

"What's wrong? I thought you liked Johnny Rivers."

"I used to. That's the guy's name, you know."

"No kidding? Johnny—"

"No, Jason. Jason Rivers." Sandy wiped a hand over her face and sighed.

"No kidding. Jason Rivers. You don't suppose he's any relation, do you?"

"I doubt it," Sandy muttered, staring down at her diet soda. "I don't think this guy's got much music in his soul. I'm not sure he's even got a soul." She didn't know why she'd said that, but after playing it back in her mind, she didn't feel like retracting it.

"He didn't look that bad to me," Bert said with a silent whistle. "In fact, I'd say he was . . . definitely hunk city."

"Jeez, Bert, you, too?" For some reason, that irritated her. "I swear, the whole town must have come out to watch us pass through on the way up to Mrs. Clancy's."

"That's where he's staying? Mrs. Clancy's?"

"Yeah, two houses down from me. Isn't that great?"

"Well," Bert pointed out, "it's pretty much the only place in town, unless you count the dump upstairs." She jabbed a finger at the ceiling. "And I wouldn't wish that on a dog. So, tell me what he's like."

"You mean you didn't see for yourself? I'm not kidding, you'd think Barnum and Bailey had come to town this afternoon. I saw people today I don't ordinarily get to see except maybe on election day. Wanda over at the Mint Café was out sweeping the sidewalk, can you believe that? So what were you doing? I don't remember seeing you."

"I was washing the front window," Bert said unabashedly. "From the inside. I got to stare to my heart's content. So tell me, what's wrong with the guy? How come you don't like him? He make a pass at you already?''

"No, nothing like that. Just the opposite in, fact." Sandy shifted in her chair, suddenly remembering the way that huge hand had swallowed hers. "He seems . . . he just makes me nervous, that's all. It's something about his eyes." Eyes that had seen too much.

"I thought he had gorgeous eyes," Bert said dreamily.

Sandy looked at her for a minute and decided not to pursue the subject. "Plus, he's just so damn *big*," she said instead, shuddering.

"I'd think you'd like that. Be kinda nice not to tower over somebody for a change."

"I do *not* tower over everybody. Larry's taller than I am."

"Half an inch. Speaking of Larry, I haven't seen him for a while."

"He's over in the Tetons," Sandy said. "Counting mountain goats." She should have been grateful for the change of subject, but she wasn't. Lately Larry had begun wanting to be more than friends, and Sandy wasn't sure how she felt about that.

Three guys from the auto parts store came in just then. They waved at Sandy and said "Hi, how's it goin'?" and Bert went off to take care of them. It was closing time up and down Main Street, and the Silver Horseshoe was starting to fill up, so it would be a while before she got back to Sandy. In the meantime, Sandy got herself a second soda from the bar and munched pretzels while she thought about why she didn't want Jason Rivers flying around central Idaho with her in her helicopter.

If she'd been having trouble explaining it to Bert, it was probably because Bert wasn't a very complicated person, and this was a very complicated issue. So complicated

Sandy hadn't figured it all out herself yet. On the one hand there was the fact that Rivers was a geologist—a prospector. That alone would have made her hackles rise; she was pretty protective of what she considered *her* wilderness. All she had to do was think of that lovely little valley she'd seen today desecrated with a power plant and she practically breathed fire. But as much as she would have hated playing chauffeur to the man, she would still do it, because she was an adult and a professional, and it was a fact of life that people sometimes had to do things they didn't want to.

That was the simple part. It was the other thing that had her confused and not feeling much like either a professional or an adult. It was making her feel pretty foolish, in fact, like imagining the bogeyman under your bed when you were old enough to know better. It made her reluctance feel a lot like self-preservation.

"Whew! Busy tonight." Bert dropped into the chair opposite Sandy and took out her cigarettes. "I'm on my break," she explained through wafting smoke when Sandy lifted a questioning eyebrow, then picked up their conversation right where she'd left off to digress about Larry.

"Is that why you don't want to take him around? Just because he's big? Are you scared you couldn't handle him if he tried something?"

Sandy, who was used to having interrupted conversations with Bert, just shrugged. How could she explain that just being around Jason Rivers gave her cold chills? How did a grown woman explain the bogeyman under the bed?

Bert grinned. "Sandy, I wouldn't worry about it if I were you. For one thing, if it was me, I wouldn't mind if he tried something. And for another, I've seen you handle yourself, and I'd say *he's* the one who should be worried. Oh damn, speak of the devil."

"What, he's *here?*" Now Sandy tried to explain to herself why her heart had just jumped like a startled rabbit. She didn't have any better luck with that than she'd had explaining any of her other reactions to Jason Rivers.

"No, I wish. It's those two guys from the Rocking-W who were hitting on you last week, remember? Keep your voice down. Maybe they won't see us." Bert scooted down in her chair and started talking in a whisper, which didn't make much sense, considering the place was already so noisy you'd have trouble hearing a shout from across the room.

"They don't bother me," Sandy said.

"Well, good, because they're coming over," Bert drawled, stubbing out her cigarette. "I really hate to run out on you like this, but you won't mind if I get on back to work now, will you?" She patted her strawberry-blond perm and pushed back her chair. "Sandy, honey," she said plaintively, "just do me one favor. If you have to get physical with those jerks, please do it outside, okay?"

Sandy laughed and started singing along with the jukebox. A few moments later she was suddenly enveloped in a cloud of beer and cheap after-shave fumes.

"Well, hey, lookit here," a Texas-sounding voice breathed into her ear. "If it ain't Blondie! Hi, beautiful. Sandy, right? Hey, it's Buddy and Wayne, remember us?"

Sandy sighed. "I'm afraid so," she said.

Mrs. Clancy's Rooming House was off Main Street on the uphill side of things, clear across town from the BLM office and the meadow where Sandy had set the chopper down. Which wasn't really saying a whole lot. A sign just beyond the BLM's driveway announced: *Silverville, Idaho, Pop. 899.* Jason was still chuckling about that. Why in hell hadn't they just said 900? Judging by the new summer homes he'd seen hidden away in the pines on the outskirts of town, it was a few more than that by now, anyway.

He'd been in smaller towns, both before he'd left home and in the years since. In size, he'd guess this one fell about halfway between the little farm towns he'd known as a boy—which usually consisted of a gas station and a grocery store, a feed store, maybe six houses and a Baptist church—and the county seat and resort towns, where these days you could probably even get franchise fast food, if you wanted it. As far as he'd seen, this town didn't have a hamburger joint on Main Street, but it had both a café *and* a saloon. Jason wasn't sure what the difference was, but he was about to find out.

He could have eaten in the rooming house dining room. Mrs. Clancy had asked him right off the bat if he would "be dining in this evening," but personally, Jason found all that fragile china and polished cherrywood more than a little bit daunting.

Mrs. Clancy reminded him of his second grade teacher, tiny, with soft gray hair and pink cheeks and a deceptively benign look. She taught piano. Jason had made that discovery when, hearing the halting strains of "Für Elise" as he was unpacking his bag in his second-floor room, he'd gone investigating and come upon a scene straight out of Norman Rockwell: an old-fashioned parlor, filled with dust motes shimmering in a late-afternoon sun; a kid in pigtails sweating on a stool in front of an old-fashioned upright piano; Mrs. Clancy standing by, gazing dreamily into the distance and futilely beating the correct time with a pencil. When she'd interrupted the lesson to ask Jason if he would be joining the other tenants in the dining room that evening, he'd felt as if he were seven years old and had just been caught with a pocket full of frogs. He didn't know exactly what he'd replied, but he was pretty sure he'd called Mrs. Clancy "Ma'am." He hadn't called anybody that since grammar school.

Anyway, the upshot was that he was about to explore the town and get some fresh air and a bite to eat, and maybe a cold beer. And anything else he could think of to postpone the moment when he'd finally have to lay his head on a pillow and close his eyes.

Silverville had been around a while, Jason judged from some of the buildings he passed on the way down to Main Street. It had probably had a silver mine or two in its history, some rowdy times and glory days. There were several big Victorians like Mrs. Clancy's, though none as well kept up as the rooming house, with its fresh white paint, its turrets and cupolas and big, wide veranda, and its picket-fenced yard full of peonies and weeping willows. The town hall occupied a small redbrick Victorian, and the firehouse was of yellow clapboard, with green shutters and a weather vane on the roof.

Back down on Main Street, Jason paused in front of the Mint Café while he tried to make up his mind what he wanted to do. A chalkboard in the window announced that the day's special was fresh Idaho trout, and the smells coming from inside made his mouth water. On the other hand, judging from the noise and music coming from the Silver Horseshoe Saloon across the street, that was where the Friday night action was. And right now action was what he needed—bright lights, loud music, noisy people—so he wouldn't have to be alone with his thoughts. Or his memories.

His stomach rumbled loudly, and that decided him. Food first, action later. But as he was about to turn into the café, some of that "action" across the street happened to catch his eye. Three people—a woman and two men—had just come out of the saloon and were heading his way. The woman had come out ahead of the two men, and when they caught up with her it was obvious that she wasn't happy about it.

None of my business, Jason told himself firmly. One of the best ways he knew of to get into bad trouble was to stick your nose in a domestic dispute or a lovers' quarrel. And anything involving a triangle was the worst kind of dispute of all. The closest he'd ever come to getting killed, not counting Central America, had been a little misunderstanding with two merchant seamen over a barmaid in Singapore. No thanks, that much action he didn't need.

He actually had his hand on the door of the Mint Café when he looked over his shoulder at the trio across the street one more time and caught the glint of a long silver braid.

I'll be damned, he thought, and against his better judgment, decided to watch a while longer.

The first thing that struck him about her was the way she walked, with that kind of ungainly grace usually referred to as "coltish." Funny, he would never in a million years have supposed he'd consider that kind of walk sexy.

She's business, strictly business, Jason reminded himself, but he went on watching.

The second thing that struck him, once he'd made himself stop thinking of her walk as sexy, was that it seemed to indicate that she was stone-cold sober. And it was pretty obvious that the two guys with her *weren't*. They kept tangling with her and getting in her way like a couple of puppies. She kept shaking them off, and they kept persisting, and the more she shook them off, the more persistent they became. Watching them gave Jason a funny feeling in his belly, a cold hard knot that couldn't in any way, shape or form be called businesslike.

Sandy had stopped walking. She seemed to be trying to reason with the two guys, but Jason could see it wasn't doing much good. They weren't in a reasonable mood, and they pretty much had her surrounded. Fact was, they had her cornered.

Still none of my business, Jason told himself, but he started across the street anyway.

He was getting close enough to hear what they were saying now, and what he heard didn't please him. That feeling in his belly got colder and harder, and he started moving faster. Sandy Stewart was tall, and she looked to be in pretty good shape, but she was still a woman, and there were two of them.

For some reason, even though he knew it had nothing to do with business, he found himself thinking about her mouth and the way the lower lip was sort of soft and pillowy and turned up at the corners, while the upper lip was shorter and came to a peak. Vulnerable, that was what it was.

He was just about to break into a dead run when he found out how vulnerable she *wasn't.*

It happened so fast that he had to reconstruct the action after the fact. One minute those guys were all over her, and the next minute one of them was sitting on the ground holding his middle, and the other was hopping around on one foot, cussing mad. Jason thought he knew what was coming next—the guy still on his feet was going to go for Sandy like a wounded bull. Jason figured he'd arrive on the scene just in time to intercept him, but he needn't have troubled himself. Just before he got there, Sandy took care of things all by herself with a hard left cross.

"Not bad," Jason said appreciatively, coming up behind her.

Only his reflexes saved him from the fist she'd aimed square at the middle of his face.

Sandy stared past the huge hand clamped around her wrist and saw the face of a buccaneer—glittering eyes and a hawk's nose, and the cold, pale flash of teeth. She thought, *My God he's quick!* How could someone so big move so fast? He had been faster than her eye could register, faster than a snake's strike. She had been left with hammering heart and boiling blood; she felt both hot and cold at the same time, and knew that any second now she would start to shake. A moment ago, facing two drunken cowboys and the possibility of assault, she hadn't been the least bit afraid. But she was afraid now.

"Don't even think about it," Jason said very softly.

Sandy whispered, "Think about what?" In his grasp, the bones of her wrist felt as fragile as eggshells.

"The obvious countermove to what I just did is a knee to the groin. I wouldn't advise it."

"I wasn't. I wouldn't."

"Good." Was there amusement in his soft voice? "Because I come in peace."

"Then could you let go of me?"

His grip eased, but he didn't let go of her wrist. His thumb began to move across the delicate sinews instead, lightly stroking. "You're shaking," he observed, his voice so low it seemed almost like a tiger's purr.

"No I'm not."

"Yes you are."

Abandoning a second denial, since it was obvious to both of them that Jason was right, Sandy looked up past the junction of their hands into eyes that reflected light like polished stones. Shaking? Yes...and shaken. "I guess I am," she said. "I don't know why."

"Don't you?" He lowered her hand, and she eased it out of his grasp. "Would you like to sit down?"

She nodded and looked around. "Yes, but not here." Wayne and Buddy were both still sitting there looking disgruntled, and it didn't seem likely they'd be moving anytime soon. Sandy held up a hand, palm out, and took a step back. "Look, I'm just fine now, so why don't you go on ahead and do whatever it was you were doing—" She stopped, because the ground had suddenly tilted. She felt trembly, light-headed, weak. And her hand was beginning to hurt. She really should have picked a softer target than that cowboy's jawbone.

"Are you all right?"

Jason's hands closed around her elbows. She shook her head, then nodded. It seemed worse when he touched her; every instinct in her told her to run like crazy, but instead she found herself clutching his forearms and hanging on for dear life. She'd never felt anything like those forearms—as hard and unyielding as blocks of wood, but warm, pulsing with life and strength, silky smooth beneath her damp palms, the hair crisp under her fingertips.

"You're not fine," Jason said.

"Yes I am."

"Are we going to do this again?"

Sandy sighed. "I don't know what's wrong with me."

"Delayed reaction?"

"I don't know. It doesn't usually bother me."

"This happens often, does it?" This time there was definitely a hint of laughter in that deep voice.

Sandy cleared her throat. "Look, it's really okay. I'll be fine."

Then there was silence while they both stood very still, staring down into the small space between their bodies. To Sandy, the air around them seemed to hum, like the singing of high-tension power lines. She could feel her heartbeat clear up in her throat. Once again she had a futile impulse to break and run.

One of the cowboys groaned and said something loudly profane. Sandy looked down at him; she'd forgotten all about him and was surprised to see him still sitting there at their feet.

"Come on," Jason said. "Let's get out of here. I was about to get a bite to eat at the café across the street. Why don't you join me? Unless you've already eaten?"

"No," Sandy said. "I haven't." That's what it is, she thought. I'm just hungry. Low blood sugar combined with excess adrenaline. "All right, that sounds good." That's better, she thought, nice and businesslike.

Remembering suddenly where her hands were and what they were doing, she lifted them away from Jason's arms. He kept his hold on hers just long enough to steady her as she stepped over the cowboy's outstretched legs.

As they started back across the street, Sandy stuck her hands in the back pockets of her jeans and looked up at Jason's rugged profile. "How come you're not eating at Mrs. Clancy's?"

Jason glanced at her and snorted. Sandy clapped a hand over her mouth, but wasn't entirely successful in stifling a gust of laughter.

"I feel like a bull in a damn china shop," Jason muttered, throwing another black look Sandy's way. "Did you do that on purpose, to get back at me?"

"Me?" Still chuckling, Sandy clapped a hand over her heart and gave him a wounded look. "I didn't have anything to do with arranging your accommodations, I swear. Anyway, if I *had* wanted to get back at you, I'd have put you up in the Silver Horseshoe." She jerked a thumb over her shoulder toward the saloon, from which, with perfect timing, came a burst of laughter and loud music.

"Hmm," Jason said, looking back.

"I'm sure you could move if you wanted to."

"I'll have to think about it. Did you know Mrs. Clancy gives piano lessons?"

Sandy nodded, but her mind had skipped backward. She frowned at him as he held the door of the Mint Café for her. "Get back at you for what?"

Wanda called out, "Hi there, Sandy, I'll be right with you folks. Just pick any old place."

Sandy smiled and said, "Hi, Wanda," but she kept looking at Jason as they settled into a booth. He took a menu from behind the napkin holder and handed it to her. She waved it away. "I'm just going to have a hamburger. What do you mean, get back at you? I just met you."

"I'm going to have the trout," Jason announced, scanning the menu with the practiced eye of a man who eats most of his meals in restaurants. He tucked the menu back in its slot and lit a cigarette, while Sandy watched his hands and remembered the way they'd felt on her arms. Her heartbeat did a little stutter-step, then steadied again. She leaned carefully back in the booth, rubbing the places where Jason's hands had touched her and studiously avoiding his level black gaze.

"Let's get something straight." His voice was as soft and deep as before, but it had acquired something—not an edge, exactly, but something more like *density*. Purpose.

Sandy dragged her eyes back to his, bracing herself as if for a collision; instead she found herself sinking into something dark and heavy, like quicksand. She sat up straight and transferred her gaze to the middle of his face. "By all means."

"I'm pretty well aware of how you feel about me."

"Oh?" It took an effort, but she kept her voice cool. "And how's that?"

"Well..." He took a drag of his cigarette, exhaled and surveyed her through narrowed eyes. "To put it bluntly, I'd say you'd rather I left the state altogether, and you for damn sure don't want me riding along with you in your chopper. I'd say what you'd probably like to do is tell your district supervisor to either find me another pilot or himself another wrangler. Am I right?"

She hadn't expected to hear it put so baldly, but she wasn't about to let him see that he'd surprised her. She said, "How did you know?" She kept her tone mildly curious, asking the question only to give herself time and to cover the jittery, unstable feeling in her insides. It didn't matter how he knew what she was feeling. What she found so unsettling was the mere fact that he knew, the fact that those penetrating black eyes had already seen so much. The man was intelligent and perceptive. How could she protect herself from him if he had the power to strip away her mask with a glance?

Jason shrugged. Sandy saw the hint of a smile behind the cigarette. "Body language. Common sense. Does it matter?"

"It's nothing personal," Sandy said.

"Isn't it?"

She forced herself to meet his eyes. "No. Of course it isn't. How can it be? I just met you."

"That's true." He looked down at the cigarette as he stubbed it out. Sandy felt her breath escape as if he'd just released her from a hard and painful grip. When he looked quickly back at her, she was caught with her mouth open, unprepared for his next quiet question. "So why do I get the feeling you're afraid of me?"

She said, "I—" and shook her head. "That's silly."

"I agree." His voice and smile were gentle, disarming.

Sandy felt her heartbeat slow to a hard, steady thumping. She kept silent, determined not to let him see how he'd rattled her.

"Look, Sandy, I know neither one of us is quite what the other expected. Personally, I expected someone a little bit more..." He waved a hand and left the sentence unfinished.

Sandy smiled wryly. "And I expected someone... a little *less*...."

There was unexpected charm in his soft chuckle, an appreciative twinkle in his black eyes. Okay, Sandy thought, relaxing a little, so he still isn't quite Paul Bunyan. But at least if he were a pirate he'd be a relatively civilized one. Like Francis Drake, maybe?

As if he'd read her thoughts and was hastening to confirm them, Jason said, "Hey, I'm harmless. From what I saw a little while ago, *I'm* the one who should be worried. Where'd you learn to handle yourself like that?"

Sandy lifted a self-deprecatory shoulder but was saved from having to come up with a reply when Wanda showed up to take their order. Wanda all but genuflected when Sandy introduced her to Jason, which, coupled with Bert's assessment of the man, left Sandy feeling obscurely piqued. She was beginning to feel like the only person in town not of the opinion that Jason Rivers was a cross between Abe Lincoln and Rhett Butler!

When Wanda had departed, Jason leaned forward, adopting a stance Sandy recognized. Nonthreatening power, that was what it was; she could read body language, too.

"Look, Sandy, we both have jobs to do. You believe in yours, I believe in mine. I also respect what you do. Now, if you can bring yourself to have the same respect for what

I do, I don't see any reason why we can't work together."
Sandy's silence was eloquent, and after a moment Jason
went on in a voice that was even softer than before. "Just
because our jobs are different, it doesn't mean our goals
are. Let me ask you something. Which would you rather
see, a few thermal power plants tucked away in those
mountains out there, or those same mountains in a haze of
fossil fuel smog?"

Damn him. Damn him for being intelligent, perceptive
and articulate. Sandy remained stubbornly silent, hiding
her resentment behind a look of cool appraisal. How she
hated being lectured to. She always had, especially when
she knew there was a good possibility she was in the wrong.

"I understand your reservations about development,
believe me I do. But, Sandy, there's room in that wilderness out there for everybody, provided it's managed right.
That's our job—both of our jobs. You manage the horses
and cattle so there'll be room for the elk—"

"Don't tell me my job," Sandy snapped, tasting the
brassy tang of anger.

Jason nodded and sat back. "All right, I won't. I know
you know your job, and that's why I know we can work
together." His tone was bland. "You're too much of a
professional to let your personal feelings get in the way."

"I don't have any personal feelings about you," Sandy
said. "None whatsoever."

"Good," Jason murmured, showing even white teeth.
"Then we should get along just fine." The smile he gave
Wanda as she set his dinner in front of him should have
raised the room temperature by degrees. "Boy, this looks
good. I'm sure hungry."

Sandy regarded Jason's plate with extreme distaste. The
crisp-fried trout on its bed of rice stared back at her with
a baleful eye. She knew when she'd been manipulated;

she'd had her strings pulled by some of the best manipulators in the world, and she knew she'd just been outplayed, landed and netted, just as thoroughly as that wretched fish. Jason had neatly boxed her in. She couldn't refuse to take him with her now without looking churlish, childish and unprofessional.

Am I? she asked herself. Am I being ridiculous? As she ate her hamburger, she kept throwing surreptitious glances at Jason, trying to get a fix on the man behind the black beard and hard, unreadable eyes. Am I the only one who feels this...whatever it is, that feels so much like fear? she wondered.

Sandy sat absently rubbing the goose bumps on her upper arms. Her instincts were trying to tell her something. She didn't know what it was yet, but she knew one thing for sure. There was a lot more to Jason Rivers than met the eye.

Chapter 3

Jason was pleased with the way things were going. A few
moments had given him trouble, but he'd managed to re-
store order. He was confident that he had Sandy Stewart
right where he wanted her, which was cooperative, but
distant. *Business, J.R., strictly business.* That was what he
told himself. Anything else with this woman and she'd tie
him in knots.

As for the rest of it, he figured he'd already cleared the
biggest hurdle just by coming back, by seeing the mountains again. There would be other hurdles, but he'd clear
them, too, one at a time, and when this job was finished... What about when the job was finished? He hadn't
really thought beyond that to what he was going to do with
the rest of his life; he supposed it pretty much depended on
how well he took those hurdles.

The only thing he knew was that he was tired of running. He'd spent a large part of the last fifteen years running from a dark cloud, only to discover that it was his

own shadow. Time and time again he'd tried to extinguish the shadow by immersing himself in darkness. He'd found it easy to do at first; there certainly seemed to be an abundant supply of darkness in the world. Sooner or later, though, he'd always come face to face with daybreak, and the shadow had always been there, waiting for him. There had even been times in the early years when he'd considered eternal darkness as the only permanent escape, but for some reason he'd never gotten serious about that. He wasn't sure why, or whether it was strength or weakness that had kept him from it; he just knew he'd had a bellyful of darkness and of running from shadows.

Right now, though, he was feeling pretty good. His emotions were under control, his stomach was full, and there was a feeling of satisfaction in knowing that this day—the day of his homecoming—was finally behind him. He was keyed up, and the night was young.

And the woman sitting across the table from him was blond, beautiful and sexy as hell.

Jason could allow himself the luxury of that observation because he was confident he had the situation firmly in hand. He'd established that Sandy Stewart was business; that made her no more real to him, sexually speaking, than a TV personality or a picture in a magazine. In fact, she was even starting to look a little bit familiar to him, like someone he might have seen in those contexts. He liked looking at her the way he liked looking at a beautiful woman on television, just for the enjoyment of it. So why not?

Right now he was watching her push ketchup around on her plate with the last of her French fries. He noticed that she had long-boned hands, long fingers with short, square-cut nails. He noticed, too, that there was some redness and swelling across the knuckles of the left one, from their recent contact with that cowboy's jaw. Not exactly your typical feminine hands, true, but surprisingly, considering the kind of work she did, they weren't masculine, either. He wondered if she wore gloves to protect their softness. If she did, it wasn't all the time, because her hands were as tanned as her arms—a deep, rich golden color. And the hair on her arms was pale; she was obviously a natural blonde.

Her hair. That was something he hadn't let himself think about much. She had an uneven hairline, and he liked the way short, pale wisps sort of floated around her face, framing it. But beyond that, to imagine what that wrist-thick braid of silvery hair would look like loose on her back, brushing her buttocks...to imagine what it would be like to bury his face in it, to feel it washing like cool water over his skin... Jason backed away from that vision the way he would tiptoe around quicksand.

"Hi, you folks gonna have some dessert?" Jason looked up at the smiling waitress and shook his head. She looked disappointed. "How 'bout some pie?"

Jason gave a replete sigh. "None for me, thanks. Sandy? How about you?" She hadn't said much since the food arrived, but then, neither had he; they'd both been pretty hungry.

She looked up at him and shook her head. Her eyes were a smudgy gray-green; he would have called them smoldering, except it didn't seem like a good idea to refer to a business associate's eyes in those terms. Not if he intended to keep the relationship strictly business.

"Just the check, I guess," he said.

Wanda sighed and popped her gum as she totaled their bill. Sandy handed Jason five dollars to cover her share, then waited by the door while he took care of it. When he gave her the change from the five dollars she stuck it in a pocket of her jeans without looking at it and went out ahead of him while he held the door for her. Outside, hunching her shoulders in the night chill, she looked at him briefly, then away.

"Listen . . . thanks." Her voice was edgy and a little rough, as if it had rusted during her silent spell.

"What for?"

She shrugged, still not looking at him. "For coming to my—for helping me a while ago. You know, with those two cowboys."

"You didn't need me."

She shrugged again. "I might have. Anyway, you didn't know that. I just wanted you to know I appreciate it."

"You're welcome," Jason said. "Any time."

She nodded, hesitated, then started up the street. "Going home?" Jason asked, wondering why. It wasn't any of his business.

"Yeah, I think so." She paused to look back at him, and he caught the wry tilt of her smile. "I think I've had about enough excitement for one evening. How about you?"

He jerked his head toward the Silver Horseshoe. "Think I'll check out the nightlife in this town."

"Good luck." She laughed and started walking again.

Jason stood watching her for a minute or two, then turned and headed up the street toward the saloon. He'd gone about ten feet before he about-faced again. Sandy was out of sight. She'd already turned the corner into the dark, chuck-holed street that angled uphill toward Mrs. Clancy's. For some reason, his heart gave a lurch. He broke into a run.

Long before he caught up with her, she'd heard him coming and had turned, looking like a scared rabbit in that instant before flight. "Oh," she said, sounding breathless, "it's you. What are you doing here? I thought—"

"You thought the same thing I did," Jason said, breathing a little erratically himself; he wasn't accustomed to sprinting uphill after a big meal. "It occurred to me that those two guys might still be around, a little more sober by this time, and maybe harboring a grudge or two. Thought maybe I'd better see you home."

She started walking again. "You don't have to do that. I can take care of myself."

"Probably." Jason fell into step beside her. "If you don't mind, though, I'd rather not risk losing my pilot."

She threw him a look that was both measuring and wary, but didn't say anything. After a bit she muttered something under her breath. Jason said, "What?"

She coughed and said, "Thanks. Again."

"Don't mention it. You live near Mrs. Clancy's?"

"Two houses further on."

"Ah." Jason nodded, and for a while they walked in silence, just strolling along. It was a nice night. Cold, the way he remembered it could get in the mountains in September, but with a half moon and enough starlight so they could see their way. He noticed a clean, fresh fragrance he thought at first was wind-borne, until he realized it was coming from the woman at his side. He wondered what it was. Not perfume—it was too natural, too much a part of her. Shampoo, maybe; the top of her head was almost level with his nose, and the breeze was stirring those pale wisps of hair around her face.

She walked with a long, easy stride. Jason began to think how nice it was to walk with a woman who could keep pace with him, a woman whose head actually came above the level of his shoulder. In fact, he thought she'd probably fit him nicely, and he couldn't say that about very many women. He wouldn't have to be afraid of crushing

her with his weight, or getting a crick in his neck bending
down to kiss her.

Just what the hell do you think you're doing? he asked
himself, annoyed.

"Nice night," he observed, startling Sandy, so that she
stumbled over a chuckhole. When he caught her hand to
keep her from falling, she gave a cry that reminded him of
some small, hunted night creature. The sound pricked
Jason's heart like a thorn, and his reaction to it was re-
flexive; he brought her hand to his lips and touched the
bruised knuckles in mute apology.

She gasped and pulled her hand away.

"Sorry. I didn't mean to hurt you." What was the matter with him, anyway? His voice was rough and his throat
tight; his responses were running amok. "Maybe you
should have that hand looked at."

"It's okay." With little eddies of shock still rippling
through her, Sandy tucked her hands into the warm place
between her arms and body and walked on. She kept her
head down, muffling her voice so Jason wouldn't hear the
tremor in it. She tried a light laugh. "That'll teach me not
to use my fists, I guess."

"Just aim for a softer spot next time," Jason drawled,
falling into step beside her.

"The voice of experience?" She couldn't risk looking at
him, even though she knew it was too dark for him to be
able to see her face, so she only felt him shrug.

"I've had a little."

Something about the dry way he said it made her certain it was an understatement of grand proportions. Which
was why it had been such a surprise to her—the softness.
And that was all it was, she told herself, that was why she
was reacting like this. It had just been such a surprise. The

unexpected softness of his beard, and then that brief, tender warmth.

"Well, personally, I'd rather not have any m-more." The tremors coursing through her body had grown too violent to conceal; her teeth were chattering.

"Cold?" She heard a rustling in the darkness as he turned his head toward her.

"No," she muttered. "I'm fine."

"You aren't either. You're cold."

"I am not."

Jason sighed and testily muttered something profane. "Here we go again. What's the matter? Are you afraid I might try to warm you? Afraid I might give you my shirt or—God forbid!—put my arm around you?"

He laughed, but there was a sharp edge of irritation in his voice, and something else, too. Sandy chose to respond to the anger, it seemed safer. "All right, so I'm a little chilly. Are you satisfied? I admit it—I should have brought my jacket, but I don't think I'm likely to freeze to death between here and my house!"

There was a long silence, and Sandy felt the ebbing of Jason's anger as a kind of withdrawal. She knew she ought to feel relieved, but what she felt instead was a vague sense of loss.

"Would it make you feel more comfortable with me," he inquired finally, sounding cold and distant, "if I told you you aren't my type?"

She gave a short, humorless laugh. Mrs. Clancy's white picket fence loomed out of the darkness; a frond of weeping willow brushed her face. She stopped walking, and Jason turned to face her.

"I meant what I said, you know," he said softly.

"Thank you, that's reassuring," Sandy said. "I'll try to keep it in mind." *You're not my type either,* she thought, with the kind of panicky resolution with which children tell themselves there's no such thing as ghosts. She didn't know what her type was, but it certainly wouldn't ever be the likes of this black-bearded, hawk-nosed mountain of a man! She liked a man she could laugh and dance with, a man who made her feel safe and relaxed and in control.

"Not about you not being my type—although I meant that, too. I mean what I said a while ago, in the restaurant. We have to work together, Sandy. We need a working relationship based on cooperation and mutual respect. A little trust wouldn't hurt, either." His voice was dry and soft, devoid of emotion.

"I trust you," Sandy said. *Trust him?* Here they were, standing together in the darkness among the swaying fronds of Mrs. Clancy's weeping willows, she and this man she'd barely met. He was an awesome presence; she could feel his warmth and bulk, hear him breathing, smell the clean man-scent of him, along with a hint of tobacco. And he made her feel anything but *safe*.

"Do you?"

"Yes." But it wasn't true! If she trusted him, why were those shivers still coursing through her body, wave after wave of them? Why was her heart racing like a frightened stag? Why did she feel hot inside when the night air was already holding the promise of frost?

"Well," Jason said. "Good."

"Look," Sandy said in a kind of desperation, "you don't have to come with me any farther. It's just two houses from here, and I don't think anybody's lurking in the bushes."

She expected him to give her another argument, but to her relief, he didn't. He just nodded and said, "All right then. I guess I'll see you tomorrow. What time do you like to get started?"

"Not tomorrow," Sandy said. "Tomorrow's Saturday. I have things to do. Monday. I'll meet you at headquarters at eight."

He hesitated, then said, "All right, Monday." He sounded almost disappointed. "Eight o'clock."

"Right. I'll see you then." But now, for some reason, it was hard to move away from him, like leaving a warm stove on a very cold night. With a small sense of shock, Sandy found that she'd put out her hand and almost touched the front of his shirt. Hastily, guilty, she pulled her hand back and walked away from him, murmuring, "Have a good weekend."

"Good night." His voice sounded muffled; a moment later she heard a cigarette lighter click. Turning to look back, she caught only a glimpse of his face in the flame's glow before the lighter was snuffed out, leaving them both in darkness again.

"Good night." The words caught in her throat and emerged as a whisper. Until that moment she'd forgotten how harsh and rugged his face was...how like a buccaneer's. In the darkness his voice had been so deep and warm, his touch so incredibly gentle.

She knew that he stayed there in front of Mrs. Clancy's until she reached her own front gate, because when she paused there to look back one last time, she saw the orange spark of his cigarette arc through the darkness and make a starburst where it hit the ground. She heard the scrape of gravel as he ground it out beneath his shoe, and then the crunch of heavy masculine footsteps fading away down the hill, toward the lights of Main Street.

Sandy had always hated dark houses. Whenever she knew she'd be coming home late, she made it a habit to leave a light burning in her apartment on the second floor of the modest Victorian she shared with a retired couple from California. She liked the welcoming glow in the window when she was coming up the street; she liked feeling, when she opened her door, that the rooms beyond were warm and lived in.

Tonight, though, the first thing she did when the door had closed behind her was to turn off the lamp. Rubbing her arms in an absentminded way, she crossed to the window and leaned against it, looking out across town to the dark mountains beyond. For some reason she felt restless, driven by a needling kind of dissatisfaction that was particularly frustrating because she didn't have any idea what it was she wanted. It was a familiar feeling, but one she hadn't been troubled with in years. She'd had it quite a bit as a child, and almost constantly as a teenager—the certainty that something was missing in her life, that there was something else out there waiting for her, if only she could find the courage to go and look for it. That feeling had left her the day she'd decided to leave her home and family and all of the pressures and responsibilities that went with them, and strike out on her own in anonymity. It had been the right decision; she'd never regretted it for a second. She'd made a place for herself, one she was happy in, one in which she knew she truly belonged. She'd thought she was done with that sharp, painful yearning. Until tonight.

She didn't know why it should have hit her tonight, of all nights, or whether it was just coincidence that it had happened on the same day a certain government prospector with a face like a bandit had come into her life. She knew there wasn't any point in trying to put her finger on what was missing; the answer would come when it came, and in the meantime all she could do was try to find surcease from the frustration and the hunger.

As a girl, more often than not her restlessness had driven her to the stables, where she had found comfort in the horses and in the hard physical labor they demanded of her. Where could she go tonight? This wasn't her family's estate; there were no stables filled with hunters and thoroughbreds whickering their soft welcome, no white-fenced paddocks and riding trails through sunlit glades. This was Idaho, and beyond her window there was only a dark and tumbled maze of mountain wilderness. Wilderness so vast and untamed that there were places that had never felt the imprint of a human foot. A wilderness of uncharted streams and unnamed valleys...

Unnamed valleys. A picture slipped gently into Sandy's mind, a memory picture of a beautiful little valley set in a circle of rocky, snowcapped peaks. A valley of meadows filled with wildflowers, forests of white pine and aspen, snow-fed streams, hot springs, and a little band of wild horses running free. A harsh but peaceful kingdom, unthreatened by man and machines, surveyed only by the hawk and the golden eagle, and ruled by a wild red rogue of a stallion.

The picture comforted Sandy and stayed with her when she finally turned, smiling, from the window.

Jason closed down the Silver Horseshoe that night. Not that he drank much; he just nursed a couple of beers, played some darts, poured quarters into the jukebox and flirted with a friendly, redheaded waitress named Bert. He kind of had the feeling the waitress would have been happy to prolong the evening with him, if he'd asked her to. He hadn't, for the same reason that he'd held himself to two beers. He'd learned a long time ago—the hard way—that some of the easiest solutions to his problem weren't worth the complications he'd have to face the next morning.

So it was alone and cold sober that he finally climbed the hill to Mrs. Clancy's rooming house. The moon had set;

it was fully dark now, and if the breeze ever died down there was going to be frost. Somewhere a dog barked, but that was all. It seemed that except for him and that dog, Silverville, Idaho—all eight hundred and ninety-nine souls—was sound asleep.

Mrs. Clancy's was silent and dark, too, but there was a light burning in his room, and on his nightstand he found a small decanter of brandy and a glass tumbler. He picked up the brandy and looked at it for a few moments, then uttered a soft exclamation and set it back down. His estimation of Mrs. Clancy was undergoing a few alterations.

He dropped his keys on the nightstand and unbuttoned his shirt sleeves, then poured a medium-sized measure of brandy into the glass and sipped it while he wandered around the room, emptying his pockets, turning down the bed, pulling the curtains to shut out the view of dark mountains.

When he was all ready for bed he poured himself another brandy, a bigger one this time, and drank it down like medicine. With the fire of it searing his throat and chest, he got into bed and pulled the comforter up to his chin, then lay staring at the ceiling, dreading the moment when his eyes would close and the dreams would overtake him.

To forestall the darkness, he thought of sunshine things: bronzed bodies on white sandy beaches; dolphins frolicking in the wake of a tramp steamer; wind surfers at sunset. And he thought of a tall woman with a coltish walk and a sultry look, wiping sweat from her golden throat while her hair rippled like pale silk down her long, naked back....

Eventually, of course, the dreams closed in on him anyway. They began as they always did, with laughter—a child's laughter and a man's. Jared's laughter and his. He saw Jared roughhousing with the dogs, racing hell-for-leather down a hillside knee deep in wildflowers, leaping stark naked into a sun-dappled lake. And then, as always, the looming mountains closed in, suffocating him; the noise, the roaring, began as distant thunder, then grew until it drowned the laughter and became an explosion inside his skull. As he always did, he heard Jared's voice, calling him through the rumble of a thousand freight trains, calling him in the terrible, silent emptiness, calling and calling.... And, as always, he was unable to answer, unable to escape from the dream until someone or something—a voice, a sound, or morning's light—finally released him, and he awoke with his throat raw and aching with silent screams.

The sound that woke Jason late on Saturday morning was one he had a little trouble identifying. It had been a long time since he'd heard the erratic, intermittent whir of a hand push lawn mower. He lay in bed for a few minutes, letting the bucolic racket, the smell of cut grass and the promise of sunlight seeping in around the edges of the curtains dispel the last remnants of the dream. Then he got up, brushed his teeth, pulled on his pants and a shirt, and went downstairs.

Sandy felt a little guilty about staying home Saturday. Most Saturdays she took the pickup truck and went out to check fence lines or salt licks. In fact, she really should have been checking on those new livestock waterers she'd installed last spring. This late in the season, water supplies could get low in some places, and when thirsty animals went wandering in search of a drink they usually played havoc with the delicate balance it was her job to maintain. She'd already had reports of some mountain lion trouble in the south, over near Phantom Creek.

Sandy didn't like lying. She'd lied to Jason because she'd wanted to put off as long as possible the moment when she had to get into a pickup or helicopter with him and go off into the wilderness...alone. It hadn't been a premeditated lie; it had just sort of slipped out. A defensive reflex, like putting out your hands to break a fall. She kept telling herself she was being irrational, but it didn't help much. Which was, she supposed, what being irrational meant.

At any rate, she tried to make herself feel less guilty by catching up on some of the Saturday jobs she rarely took time to do. After an industrious, if not terribly inspiring, morning spent dusting and vacuuming and doing laundry, she decided to walk down to Gleason's Market and stock up on groceries.

As she was passing Mrs. Clancy's rooming house, Harvey Schmidt, the gardener, who was lopping dead blossoms off the peonies along the fence, waved to her and called "Good morning!" Harvey was a retired tractor salesman from Boise who rented the garage apartment from Mrs. Clancy and did odd jobs. He'd once repaired Sandy's refrigerator for nothing, so she really couldn't pass by without stopping for a friendly chat.

She told Harvey that it was a nice day, and he agreed that it was. He asked how her refrigerator was running, and she told him it was humming like a top.

She went on, "I think I'm going to have to have you come take a look at my washing machine, though. It's developed this funny noise...." And then she stopped, because it had just occurred to her that she was hearing a noise right now that she shouldn't be hearing. "Harvey, isn't that the lawn mower? Have you got a new helper?"

Harvey chuckled. "Yep, I guess you could say that. Mrs. Clancy's new boarder came down a while ago and asked if I'd mind if he cut a lick or two. Well, shoot, I never turn down a helping hand freely offered, so I said, 'Sure, go ahead.' He's been at it ever since—finished the front and now he's doin' the back, I guess. Strong as an ox, that young fellow.''

But long before Harvey got to that point, Sandy had stopped paying attention. Because about the time he said "Mrs. Clancy's new boarder," the lawn mower came around the corner of the house, propelled by Jason, who was wearing jeans and a good, healthy layer of sweat. Period.

It was an incredible sight; anyone would have been forgiven for staring. He was just so frankly masculine, the way a stag is, or a stallion. He had a kind of grandeur, like a bigger-than-life-size statue of Zeus—awesome power in the neck and shoulders, and grace in the smooth, rippling muscles of his torso and back. And yet there was something so... *earthy* about him, something about the warm duskiness of his skin, the sultry sheen of sweat, the masculine pattern of dark body hair, and the way it arrowed down the center of his belly and disappeared into the waistband of his jeans.

To Sandy's dismay, that natural, unvarnished sensuality began to stir primitive responses deep within her; she felt her body becoming as heated as his, felt her breathing time itself to the in and out movements of his belly. Her pulse hammered in her throat, and when she passed her tongue across her lips she tasted the salty tang of her own sweat. She wanted to pull her eyes away; just looking at him had become an act of unbearable intimacy. Shaken, she made a small sound, like a cough.

"Well," Harvey said, looking over his shoulder to see what had claimed her attention, "speak of the devil. Run out of grass, did you, son?"

"All done," Jason said. "Where do you want the mower?" He was looking at Sandy. She knew it was only a quirk of the sunlight, but for a moment his black eyes seemed to flare with inner fires, like live coals.

"Oh, don't worry about it. I'll take it back to the shed. I'm going that way anyhow." Harvey was urgently motioning Jason forward. "Jason, come here a minute, I want you to meet my neighbor. This is Sandy."

"We've met." Jason's voice was a rumble, like thunder in the distance. "Hello, Sandy."

"Hi." It came out a breathy whisper. It took all the willpower Sandy had to keep her eyes glued to Jason's face, but she was so intensely aware of his body that she could see it anyway. She *felt* it.

"Sandy brought me in yesterday in her chopper," Jason blandly explained to Harvey. "She's going to be hauling me around with her for a couple of weeks."

"Well now, isn't that nice?" Harvey looked just as pleased as if he'd arranged it all himself. "I'll tell you what, since you two already know one another, you don't need me around to keep up conversation. I'm going to put the mower away and then I believe I'll go see what Helen—Mrs. Clancy—'s got on for lunch. Nice to see you, Sandy. Just let me know when you want me to come look at that washing machine. Jason, thank you again for your help."

"My pleasure," Jason said. "Anything to pass the time," he added in a dry murmur to Sandy as the gardener disappeared around the corner of the house with the lawn mower. "I think it was a tactical error on my part, coming into a strange town on a Friday. What do people in this town do on weekends, anyway?"

Guilt made Sandy blush. She looked at the ground and shrugged. "Same things they do everywhere, I guess—mow lawns, do laundry, clean house, go shopping."

"That where you're off to?"

"Yeah . . . groceries."

Jason nodded. After a moment he said softly, "What about at night? What do people find to do at night?" There was a wicked, teasing gleam in his eyes. "Besides visit the Silver Horseshoe and brawl in the streets, of course."

Sandy opened her mouth, then closed it again. The obvious answer to that question had popped into her mind—the obvious glib, flirty, cocktail party answer. *They do what people everywhere do at night....* It was the kind of answer that would sound only a little daring against the clink of ice cubes in highball glasses and the rackety thump of live rock music. But it was the kind of answer that was completely impossible at high noon, when the air was heavy with sunshine and redolent with the scent of new-cut grass, and she was standing too close to a half-naked man with the body of a Greek warrior and the face of a buccaneer!

Sexual awareness folded her in like a warm, suffocating blanket. She couldn't bear to look at Jason, yet she couldn't look away; she felt a desperate need to say something—anything.

"Sometimes," she heard herself say, "they have dances at the Elks' Lodge in Phantom City."

"Oh, really?"

"Yeah." Oh God, what now? She felt hot . . . so hot. "I think there's one tonight," she said and then, incredibly, "Would you like to go?"

Chapter 4

I can't believe I said that," Sandy said to Bert half an hour later in the kitchen of the small house Bert shared with her parents and her seven-year-old son. "I don't know *why* I said it."

Bert gave her a look across the cocktail waitress's uniform she was ironing, but all she said was, "Well?"

"Well, what?"

"What did he say?"

"He said yes, damn him. Bert, I'm going to a dance tonight with a guy I don't even want in my helicopter. What am I going to do?"

Bert said, "You're afraid of this guy, you know that?"

Sandy said, "I am not." She opened the refrigerator and took out a can of diet soda.

"Help yourself," Bert said.

Sandy ignored the friendly sarcasm. "You know perfectly well I can take care of myself. And anyway, he actually came to my rescue last night when Buddy and Wayne were giving me a hard time. Not that I needed it."

"He didn't know that," Bert pointed out.

"I know," Sandy said, frowning. "We had dinner together at the Mint Café, and afterward he walked me home, just to be on the safe side."

"So? I told you he seemed like a nice guy." Bert put the uniform on a hanger and unplugged the iron. "You know, though," she said thoughtfully as she sat down at the table, "I see what you mean about his eyes."

Sandy set her soft drink can down very carefully, hoping her voice would betray only casual interest. "When did you get a chance to see his eyes?"

Bert shrugged, unaware of tensions and undercurrents. "He came in last night—kinda late. Must have been after he'd seen you home. Stayed until closing time. Didn't drink much, though, just a couple of beers. He was real nice, real friendly. I flirted with him like crazy, when I wasn't busy. Well gee, I figured . . . shoot, why not, right? But I remembered what you said about his eyes, so I was trying to see if I could see what you were talking about."

"And?" Sandy prompted when Bert frowned and fell silent.

"And . . . you were right, there is something about his eyes. I just didn't get the same reaction you did, that's all. They didn't scare me or anything. His eyes made me feel . . . I don't know. Sad."

"Sad?"

"I don't know. Maybe."

Maybe. Sandy got up and carried her drink can over to the sink. The window there looked out on the river and the mountains beyond, and she gazed out without seeing them at all, seeing Jason's face instead. Bert wasn't the most articulate person in the world; maybe "sad" was as close as she could come to describing the bleakness that always seemed to lurk behind the hard, obsidian glitter of his eyes. Sandy found that bleakness frightening, because it gave her such a terrible sense of isolation.

"I thought maybe he was lonely," Bert said, unknowingly echoing the thought. "It seemed like he might have been, the way he stayed around, like he just wanted the company. But I don't know...I'll tell you this much, if the man is alone, it's because that's the way he wants it."

"What do you mean?"

"I mean, I made darn sure he knew he didn't have to go home alone if he didn't want to, and he didn't take me up on it."

"Bert!" Sandy said, laughing at the look on her friend's face, and also to cover the odd little jolt that had just hit her in the general vicinity of her heart.

"Well...?" Bert said irrepressibly, and shrugged. "So anyway, I don't think you have anything to worry about."

"Who said I was worried?" Sandy said lightly. "I keep telling you, I am not afraid!"

"Not of him, maybe." It was an unusually perceptive thing for Bert to say, and it caught Sandy by surprise. She opened her mouth and abruptly looked away. Bert said softly, "Aha. You *are* attracted to him, aren't you? I knew it. So what's the problem?"

Sandy shifted her shoulders. "No problem—and that's the way I want to keep it. Look, I just don't want to get involved with anybody right now, that's all."

"You're involved with Larry, sort of. Or is that why it bothers you so much, being attracted to Jason? Hey, look, Sandy, it's perfectly natural—"

"Larry and I are just friends," Sandy said flatly, evading both the argument and the question. She really didn't want to think about Larry right now.

"Yeah, well, from what I hear, that's not the way he wants it. And that's another thing—"

"I just don't want to get into anything complicated, okay?" Because she felt defensive, she sounded angry. "And anyway, I'm sorry, but it isn't any of your business."

"Okay, maybe it isn't." Bert started to say something, stopped, then released an exasperated breath and plunged on. "Sandy, don't get mad at me for this, but sometimes I don't understand you. We've been friends for—how long? Ever since I came back to this dumb town to live with my folks after my divorce, right? Now, me, I figure I don't have any choice. I can't afford to live anywhere else, and besides, it isn't a bad place to raise a kid. But sometimes I think I'm going crazy, burying myself in this dead zone. I'm not getting any younger, and I feel like life is passing me by, you know what I mean? But like I said, I don't have much choice. You, though—I can't figure out what somebody like you is doing in a place like this. As long as I've known you, you've never told me anything about yourself, or your folks, or where you're from, and I've never asked, have I? I figure maybe you've got reasons for being here, same as I have, and you're just the kind of person that doesn't like to talk about it. That's okay, I don't mind. But damn it, Sandy, you know you can only run from yourself just so long. Sooner or later you've got to face up to who you are, because that's all you've got, when you get right down to it. Isn't it?"

The silence was full of lazy sounds: a fly buzzing in the late afternoon sunshine on the windowsill; the tick of the cooling iron. Sandy saw that there was a spot of bright color in each of Bert's cheeks, and a look of appeal in her eyes. She felt a sense of shame, a tightness in her throat, and an even greater tightness around her heart. But she didn't know what to say, or how to relieve either one.

Isolation. Resentfully she thought, If anyone is isolated, I am. I wonder why it doesn't show in *my* eyes.

She wondered then if the thing that frightened her so much in Jason's eyes was only her own reflection.

"Bert," she said huskily. "Hey, it's all right." She wasn't usually demonstrative, but she gave her friend a quick, impulsive hug, which was easier at that particular moment than saying, *Thank you...and I'm sorry.* "Look, I've got to go, okay? Got to stop over at headquarters and pick up some transportation for tonight."

Bert nodded and looked away, touching her nose with the back of her hand. "Right. Listen, you have a good time tonight, you hear?" Her voice had a raspy quality to it. "I want to hear all about it!"

Sandy laughed. "Quit making it sound like a date."

"Well, isn't it?"

"No!" Sandy shouted, and slammed the door on her way out of the house

At a quarter past eight, Mrs. Clancy knocked on Jason's door and informed him that Sandy was waiting for him downstairs in the parlor. Jason had to chuckle about that; it sounded so prim and old-fashioned. However, a few minutes later when he walked in and saw her standing there beside the piano, he realized that "old-fashioned" was not a word he was ever going to be able to connect with Sandy Stewart.

She had one knee propped on the piano stool and was picking out a melody that sounded vaguely familiar to him, but which he couldn't quite place. She was wearing jeans, as usual, but as a concession to the occasion and to the chilly evening, she had put on a long-sleeved cream-colored sweater with silvery threads woven through it. She'd looped and tucked her braid into a coil at the nape of her neck, and there were silver hoops at her ears. That combination of dressy and casual shouldn't have worked so well, but somehow on her it was right. She looked as sleek as a thoroughbred, and as out of place among that clutter of Victorian knickknacks as a Ferrari at a tractor pull.

Out of place. That was it, Jason thought, the thing that he'd been aware of all the time, but which hadn't really struck him full force until now. She didn't belong here, didn't fit.

What was someone like her doing in this high-altitude backwater town, anyway? Where was she from? What was she doing working as a chopper jockey, riding herd on range cattle and wild horses? *Who the hell was she?*

With a sense of resignation, he watched all his resolutions about keeping her neatly cataloged under Business Only fly right out the window. No sense fighting it—Sandy Stewart had piqued his interest. And after last night he thought it was probably just as well; if he was going to avoid more nights like that, he needed a good distraction. If fate had taken pity on him and provided him with a puzzle like Sandy Stewart to occupy his mind, who was he to argue?

He was in a pretty blithe mood as he moved into the parlor.

When she heard his step, she stopped what she was doing and turned to face him. Jason nodded toward the piano and said, "What was that you were playing?"

She shrugged and looked at him in that way she had, sort of up through her lashes. No way around it, he could only call it sultry. "Oh, nothing…just something I learned a long time ago. It's a sonatina. Clementi, I think."

"You play?"

Her snort was eloquent. "How can you ask, after hearing me? I had lessons when I was a kid. Doesn't everybody?"

"I didn't," Jason said.

"Well," Sandy said after a little silence, "I guess we should go."

"Fine, I'm ready." When she hesitated, Jason waved her ahead of him and murmured, "After you...."

As they were going out the front door, Mrs. Clancy came out into the hall to call, "Bye-bye, now. Drive carefully," just as if they were teenagers leaving on a date.

Sandy reached the front gate before Jason did and opened it for herself. Then she hesitated. "Do you want to drive?"

It struck him as a funny question, considering their working relationship, but all he said was, "No, that's fine. You know the way." They got into the BLM pickup truck, and she started up the motor. He asked her if she minded if he smoked, and she said no, so he lit a cigarette.

"Buckle up," she said, and waited while he did, then put the truck in gear and headed down the street just a little too fast, jouncing over potholes.

"How far is it to Phantom City from here?" Jason asked. Although he knew approximately how far it was already, he thought maybe some chitchat would calm her down. She seemed so nervous that he was beginning to wish he'd taken her up on her offer to let him drive.

"About fifteen miles." They squealed around the corner onto Main Street and headed south, out of town. "Thought you were from around here." She looked at him long enough to make him feel edgy about the fact that she wasn't watching the road.

"Farther south," he said, and then after a moment, "A ranch, actually. Over near the Sawtooths."

"Your folks still there?"

"No." He shifted restlessly. "They live in California now. Bakersfield." They hadn't sold the ranch, though, just leased it, hoping that someday he'd come back.

He felt Sandy give him another look. "You been gone long?"

"Fifteen years."

She uttered a low whistle. "That's a long time. What have you been doing in the meantime?"

"This and that," Jason said vaguely, looking out the window. "I've been around a bit."

"Uh-huh." Her tone said plainly, I'll bet you have. And then, with more than just idle curiosity in her voice, she asked, "And you've never been back?"

He shook his head. "Nope."

"Why did you leave?"

Jason studied her dark profile without answering. After a moment or two he said, "Maybe a better question is, 'Why did you come?'"

"What do you mean?" She spoke lightly, but with a certain wariness, and it suddenly struck Jason that, for small talk, this conversation was generating an awful lot of tension.

"You aren't from around here." It was a statement of fact, not a question, and she just shrugged, not trying to deny it. He persisted. "Where are you from?"

Her voice was flat, dismissive. "Back East."

"Your folks?"

"Still there."

"Ah." And then, "You're a long way from home."

"Yes."

"And you've never been back?"

"Nope." She flashed him a look; he caught the pale gleam of her grin, but he knew a dead end when he heard one.

"Just a couple of vagabonds," he said, returning her smile.

"Except," Sandy said pointedly, "that you've come home."

She sure knew how to put an end to a probing conversation.

"I hope you weren't expecting rock music," Sandy said.

They were standing in the doorway of the Elks' Club Hall, watching the band, which consisted of a hefty red-headed woman on accordion, a bass player in overalls and a bald man with scrubbed pink cheeks and a round pot belly, who played the fiddle and tapped out the beat with the toe of a well-worn cowboy boot.

Jason just smiled and didn't answer; he was feeling pretty nostalgic. He didn't tell her that he'd been to more dances exactly like this one than she was ever likely to see in her life. It had been a long time, but he knew it all so well: the big, brightly lit dance floor; the smell of floor wax and old wood and sweat; plump, happy-looking older couples fox-trotting energetically around the room while little kids with orangeade moustaches tried to imitate their elders, giggling and falling all over each other. The band looked so familiar that he wondered if it could possibly be the same one he'd danced to during his high school summers. He bet he even knew what songs they'd play: "Mona Lisa," "Your Cheatin' Heart," "Tumblin' Tumble-weeds" and "Tennessee Waltz." And the last one would always be "Good Night, Irene."

"Want some punch?" Sandy asked him. She was looking uncertain, as if she wasn't quite sure how he was taking it all.

"No, thanks," Jason said. The punch would be pure sugar. "You don't suppose they'd have any beer?"

"They don't serve alcohol." Which, Jason thought, probably explained the little groups of people, mostly men, they'd seen standing around in the parking lot as they drove in. Doubtfully, she said, "I could probably get you a soda."

"No thanks, I think I'll pass."

They eased on into the hall. The band was playing something Jason recognized, though the name of it momentarily escaped him. He started to whistle, then stopped himself and said, "Would you like to dance?"

She looked at him as if he'd suggested a walk on the moon, but she couldn't have been any more surprised by the question than he was. Dancing with this woman, holding her in his arms for any reason whatsoever, sure hadn't been on his business agenda.

They were both saved from whatever answer she might have come up with when a couple of guys walked by, waved and said, "Hey, Sandy! Where you been keepin' yourself? Where's Larry tonight?"

"Hi, Chuck...Hi, Dave. Larry's still over in the Tetons counting mountain goats."

Some good-natured joking followed that, which Sandy didn't really seem to enjoy, Jason noticed.

After the two guys had moved along, Jason asked casually, "Who's Larry?" At least he hoped it was casual; it sure as hell wasn't any of his business, and he didn't have the slightest idea why he'd asked.

She gave him a funny look—sort of quick and guilty—before waving off the question with a vague, "Just a friend. He's with the Forest Service. So were those two guys. They're all . . . just friends.'' And then suddenly, as if the question hadn't already come up, as if it was something she'd just thought of, she blurted, ''Would you like to dance?''

She looked as if she wanted to bite her tongue. Jason knew she would have taken it back if she could, and for a second or two he thought about letting her off the hook. He thought about it even while he was saying, ''Sure, why not? It's what we came for, isn't it?''

He thought about it when he put his hand on her waist and felt her body heat melt through her sweater and flow into his fingers and right on up his arm. It gave him a good, warm feeling, like a cup of hot coffee on a cold morning.

He thought about it when he turned her to face him and she looked at him in that way she had, smoky-eyed and sexy as hell, but uncertain. He saw the gold-dust sheen on her skin and heard the sharp little catch in her breathing. And he wondered what he might have said or done to make her afraid of him.

He thought about what he could say to her that might lighten things up a bit, put her at ease. A few comments came to mind, but he didn't employ any of them. He didn't say anything at all. Instead, he increased the pressure on the small of her back and brought her into his arms. She walked into him, his arms went around her, and then they stood there for a few beats, thinking about it. She fitted him as well as he'd thought she would.

The band was playing ''Tennessee Waltz,'' but the waltz part was only a technicality; the tempo was so languid it wasn't necessary to pay much attention to the step. Which was a good thing, Jason decided, because he was having to concentrate hard in order to remember he even had feet.

He'd known it would be a mistake, allowing himself to get this close to her. He'd made quite a few mistakes with this woman, beginning when he'd underestimated the strength of the physical thing between them. He thought the reason it had hit him so hard was because he hadn't had a chance to prepare himself for it; she'd literally dropped in on him like a bolt out of the blue. And now he was laughing at himself for ever thinking he could ignore it, for thinking all he had to do to control the lightning bolt was turn his back on it. He should have known that turning his back on a bolt of lighting was a dangerous thing to do.

Now he was so aware of her that his body felt electrified, as if it gave off a static charge wherever she touched him. He wondered if she could feel it in him, as he felt the waves of tension coursing through her. And if she felt it, he wondered if she knew and understood what it was.

Then he remembered that look of uncertainty and fear in her eyes, and in a flash of insight he realized that she didn't. Not yet. Not fully. And that, he thought, was what was scaring the daylights out of her.

Holding her in his arms, with her sweet, elusive perfume tickling his nostrils, he thought about what he might do to help her along toward her own understanding. His fingers burned with the urge to stroke and to caress; his lips tingled with the impulse to blow those pale wisps of hair away from her temples and taste the diamond drops of moisture there.

What would it matter? What did he have to fear from a little mutual sexual attraction? He was only going to be around for a week or so. Long before the first snow fell in the Rockies, he'd be heading for the sunshine. Mauna Loa was erupting again; wasn't he scheduled to meet the team from Berkeley in Honolulu a week from next Friday?

So why not touch her in subtle, wooing ways, ways that would coax those tremors from her body and bring melting, clinging heat instead? Why not carry her bruised hand to his lips, and when she made her instinctive movement of withdrawal, instead of releasing, *claim* it, make love to it, watching her eyes for that smoky look that would tell him what he needed to know?

He didn't, but only because it wasn't the right time. Instead, he held her gently, swaying to the easy rhythms, softly humming the "Tennessee Waltz" and laughing at himself and at her for being fools enough to think they could resist the siren's song.

"Oh gosh," Sandy said, "I'm sorry." She didn't know what was the matter with her. It was the third time she'd stepped on Jason's foot—well, not *stepped* on, exactly; more like *bumped*—and she normally wasn't that big a klutz. In fact, she was a pretty good dancer.

"That's okay," Jason said. "It's probably my fault, anyway. I'm not the world's greatest dancer."

Sandy gave him a long look, then snorted with laughter. "Gallantry is not dead."

His laughter joined hers, easily...comfortably. Gazing at him from under her lashes, she wondered about the change in him and thought about Paul Bunyan. A subtle warming began inside her, as if the first rays of the sun were touching a frosty landscape.

The music ended. Jason's hand tightened briefly on her back, then fell away. He still held her hand, though, and for some reason Sandy found it hard to move away from him. She found herself wishing the music would start again right away so she could have an excuse to step back into the nice warm circle of his arms, and was surprised at how disappointed she was when they announced a short break instead.

"Well," Jason said, "would you like to go outside and get some fresh air?"

Sandy swallowed, shrugged and said, "Sure, why not?"

He let go of her hand, but she felt his fingers touching her back as they walked off the dance floor. The lightest of touches. Polite. No big deal. And yet she felt it like a brand on naked skin and was relieved when he put his hands in his pockets and moved up alongside her as they strolled together through the moonlit parking lot.

"Chilly," Jason remarked, hunching his shoulders.

"Yes," Sandy agreed, rubbing her arms.

They stopped beside the pickup truck. Jason lit a cigarette, then leaned against a fender, smoking. "Sorry I'm not a better dancer," he said after a while, smiling at her.

Sandy gave him a look and a soft snort, but didn't answer. She sort of eased back against the pickup, close to him but not touching him, and lifted her face to the night sky. "Quiet," she remarked.

"Yes," Jason agreed.

There were quite a few people standing around the entrance to the hall, smoking and talking, and drinking punch and coffee out of Styrofoam cups. Sandy nodded toward them. "Not very exciting night life, is it? Maybe you'd have been better off sticking with the Silver Horseshoe."

Jason looked at her, then took a drag on his cigarette and tossed it to the ground. "I'm having a good time."

"You are?"

"Sure, aren't you?"

"Oh, sure."

"Well, good."

I don't believe this, Sandy thought. I haven't been this tongue-tied since I was fourteen. How on earth, she wondered, am I going to stand being alone with this man for a week if we don't have anything to say to each other?

She turned her head and looked up at his craggy profile, dark against the sky. A thought came to her slowly, like a moon rising: *Or is it that there's too much to say?* Suddenly, standing there beside Jason in the Elks' Club parking lot listening to the sounds of laughter and music once again pouring from the lighted hall, Sandy felt herself turn cold.

Who are you, Jason Rivers? she wondered. What is this chill I feel when I look at you? What are you hiding behind the black-diamond glitter of your eyes? Do you harbor secrets that you shield from me, as I shield mine from you?

The outline of his profile blurred and disappeared. Sandy's heartbeat quickened as she realized he was looking down at her, studying her face as intently as she was studying his. And then he shifted slightly, straightened, slipped his hand under the coil of her hair and lowered his head, pausing a moment at her sharp intake of breath, then continuing when she didn't pull away. Just before his lips touched hers, he hesitated once more. She waited, her body rocking with the force of her heart's beating, not breathing, just . . . waiting.

Chapter 5

So gentle, she thought as he kissed her. Why was I afraid?

His touch was satiny, his mouth tobacco-scented and warm. His hand cradled her neck, while his lips found and memorized the shape of hers; when they parted, his tongue touched, then delicately probed, their soft inside. Their breaths merged like eddying currents, sending little rippling shock waves through them both.

And then he withdrew. His hand slipped from beneath her hair, rested briefly on her shoulder, then dropped. He put his head back and looked up at the sky, and Sandy heard the long, slow whisper of an exhaled breath.

She swallowed. "I thought you said I'm not your type."

His laughter was as intimate as a whisper. "I was just trying to make you feel better."

"About what? What you said last night? All that stuff about a working relationship?"

There was a little silence. Then Jason shifted uncomfortably and said, "I meant that."

"Then why...?"

"Why did I kiss you?" His voice rose a notch. "Hell, Sandy, I don't know. Why does any man kiss a woman? Because I wanted to. Because you're beautiful and you have a dynamite body—which I've just been holding intimately in my arms, remember—and we're standing here together in the dark, and you didn't give me an argument about it, I guess." He paused. "Look, if you're worried about it..."

"I'm not!"

His voice seemed very gentle. "Sandy, don't make more out of it than it was. I'm not about to attack you. It won't happen again unless you want it to."

"Oh," Sandy said. "Well, *fine.*" But she didn't feel fine; she was cold again, and this time she had no trouble identifying the chill as loneliness. Because, in some obscure way, she felt rejected.

Sandy, don't make more out of it than it was. Just a kiss, right? Hey, no big deal. She'd been kissed before, lots of times.

So why did she have this feeling inside, this hollow, shaky sense of having almost found something wonderful?

Jason lit another cigarette and smoked it in silence. After a while he said, "Cold?"

Sandy said, "A little bit, yeah."

"Want to go back inside?"

She shook her head. "Not really."

"Do you want to go home?"

Do you want to go home? She did and she didn't. She wanted to go somewhere, someplace where she felt warm and safe and cherished. The only trouble was, for the first time in a long time, she didn't know exactly where that place was.

She kept remembering the way she'd felt dancing in Jason's arms, slowly filling up with that sunlit warmth, feeling the intriguing, unexpected texture of his beard on her face. For those few moments she thought she might have caught a glimpse of what she was looking for, but if she had, it was gone now, like a mountain peak shrouded in clouds and snow.

Drawing in air, and along with it a healthy transfusion of pride and poise, Sandy said, "All right, sure, if you want to go, it's fine with me."

Taking the pickup's keys out of her pocket, she went around to the driver's side and climbed in. Jason hesitated, then got in beside her.

She drove one-handed, Jason noted; maybe even a little less than that, since she was also humming "Tennessee Waltz" and keeping time by tapping her fingers on the wheel. Corkscrews of tension wrapped themselves around his spine as the speedometer needle edged toward sixty, but though it took some effort, he kept his mouth shut.

As the pickup streaked on through the night, Jason wondered if she always drove this way, or if she was just nervous about being with him. Maybe more so than ever, now that he'd kissed her.

Her reaction to his kiss had surprised him, both during and after. He wasn't used to such... He searched for a word and came up with *honesty*. Not quite innocence. There had been awareness in the way her mouth had awaited his, so full and sweet, vibrant with the suspense of that first intimate touch. But there had been something, a certain lack of sophistication, that had made him feel acutely ashamed.

She'd responded to him, and she hadn't tried to hide it. Her response had confused her, but she hadn't tried to hide that either. Jason suspected there would never be any ploys or games with this woman. What she felt inside was what she would show on the outside—no more, no less. And Jason was quite certain that if she ever gave herself to a man, it would be for no other reason than that her feelings demanded it.

His own mental and emotional gymnastics where she was concerned seemed shabby by comparison.

Well, damn it, he hadn't expected it of her! He never knew *what* to expect of her. Where he'd expected a scrawny, bowlegged cowboy, instead he'd found a gorgeous, six-foot blonde, oozing raw sexuality from every pore, turning his libido to magma and knocking his emotional compass all out of whack. When he'd expected a little bit of feminine vulnerability, she'd decked a couple of drunken cowboys without batting an eye. And just when he thought he'd gotten her corralled and himself under control, she'd invaded his senses like a wind-borne fragrance, filled his dreams like a summer promise.

Confronted with his half-nude body, she'd blushed like a Victorian spinster, but in the setting of a Victorian parlor she'd looked as streamlined and up to the minute as the six o'clock news. How was he supposed to figure out a woman who looked as if she ought to be driving a Ferrari, then took him to a country dance in a pickup truck? A woman who appeared to be on pretty intimate terms with at least one forest ranger, yet reacted like a virgin to *his* touch?

Sandy Stewart confused the heck out of him, and he couldn't leave her alone. He had a feeling that she had depths he could never plumb in the short time he had available, but somehow he knew that wasn't going to keep him from trying.

"I'm going to go check on some livestock waterers tomorrow," Sandy said abruptly. "Want to come along?"

Trying to keep the surprise out of his voice, Jason said, "Sure, why not?"

They were sitting in front of Mrs. Clancy's. The motor was running; Sandy had pulled up and put the pickup in neutral, but she hadn't turned it off. She was looking not at him, but straight ahead through the windshield at the night-flying insects that whirled and danced in the head-light beams.

"There aren't any thermal activity sites where we'd be going. I just thought—" She glanced toward him, then quickly away. He saw her shrug. "If you think Saturdays are bad in this town...The bars close on Sundays, along with pretty much everything else, so unless you're into church, and fried chicken for Sunday dinner, you might as well forget it and stay in bed."

"Sounds like fun," Jason said. And then, because he didn't want her to think he meant that in response to her reference to staying in bed, he hurriedly added, "What time do you want to leave?"

"I'll stop by for you. Ten o'clock okay?"

"Fine. I'll be ready. Well, good night..." He put his hand on the door handle, then paused. "Sandy..."

She had turned toward him, but it was too dark to see her face; her eyes were just shadows, sooty reminders of the way they could smolder.

"Thanks for asking. I appreciate it."

"No problem," she said softly. "It's the least I could do, after..." She waved a hand, somehow encompassing the whole evening, the whole town.

"Sandy," Jason said, "I had a good time tonight. Really."

"Did you?" She sounded doubtful.

"Sure. It brought back lots of memories. I used to go to dances like that all the time, when I was in high school."

"Well, okay." She cleared her throat. "Good night, then. I guess I'll see you tomorrow morning."

"Right. See you then."

He got out of the pickup and stood watching it lurch and bounce up the street to her place. The sight left him with mixed feelings about tomorrow.

Sandy heard piano music coming from Mrs. Clancy's parlor as she opened the front gate Sunday morning. The song was "Tennessee Waltz." Since Mrs. Clancy was standing on the veranda pulling on her gloves, that left only one person who could be responsible for the music. And though it seemed unlikely, she knew it was true even before Mrs. Clancy told her, because of the way her heart had suddenly accelerated.

"Good morning, Sandy, dear," Mrs. Clancy called, coming out to meet her. "Isn't it a beautiful morning? These early autumn days are just *so* lovely, aren't they?" Sandy agreed that they were. Mrs. Clancy sidled up to her and nudged her with an elbow. "That's my new boarder," she said in a loud whisper. "He's the *nicest* young man—so *big*, but very polite. Doesn't he have a nice touch? He's never had a lesson, you know—plays entirely by ear." Mrs. Clancy beamed with proprietary pride, as if she were personally responsible. "I do believe he's quite talented. Well, I must be going or I'll be late for church. Goodbye, dear. Have a lovely time. Oh my, I almost forgot. I've packed a little something for you to take with you. It's on the kitchen table."

Sandy stammered her thanks. Mrs. Clancy beamed up at her, then abruptly drew back, placing a finger to her lips and adopting a thoughtful expression. "Sandy, you know, I do believe Mr. Rivers is taller than you are. Quite a bit taller, in fact." Her expression switched to one of bland innocence. "Well, I'm sure you've already noticed that. Not that those things matter, but still, it *is* nice to have a man you can look up to, isn't it?"

With no idea what in the world she'd replied to that, Sandy watched Mrs. Clancy bustle on down the walk. As the straight-backed, white-haired lady approached her front gate, Harvey Schmidt came around the corner of the house, hurrying to get to the gate before she did. As she passed through, Mrs. Clancy patted her dandelion fluff hair and gave Harvey a look of such sweetness it made Sandy's eyes water. She watched them go off down the street together, side by side, and then, utterly bemused, went on up the veranda steps and into the house.

Jason stopped playing the minute she walked into the parlor, turning on the stool like a kid caught swiping cookies. "Hi," he said. "Didn't know you were there."

"You told me you didn't play the piano," Sandy said accusingly, circling him the way she might a supposedly tame lion whose docility she had reason to doubt.

"Uh-uh." Jason shook his head, following her with his eyes. "I told you I'd never had lessons."

She gave a reproachful snort and looked away.

"What's wrong?"

"Nothing. I just feel a little stupid, that's all. You let me stand there plunking out my clumsy tunes last night, and all the time you..."

"All the time I what?" He shook his head and released a gust of exasperated laughter. "Sandy, what do you think I was thinking, anyway?"

He was watching her with narrow-eyed intensity. She didn't know why it embarrassed her that she'd revealed her lack of musical ability to him. It irritated her to find that she cared about what he thought of her, especially since she'd spent a good part of the night telling herself that she didn't. Trying to be cool about it, she shrugged and muttered, "Well . . . you're very talented."

"I can play a little." He turned on the stool to close the piano with a dismissive thump. With his back to her he paused; she saw his hands relax and briefly stroke the rich mahogany in what seemed almost like a caress. His voice was muffled. "My brother was the one with the real talent."

"Your brother?" Sandy prompted, not knowing why she was whispering.

Jason suddenly whirled on the stool and got to his feet, all in one fluid motion. Standing, he dwarfed the room and everything in it, including her. His eyes rested on her only briefly, but something inside her trembled from the impact.

She thought, With that look he could have ruled the Spanish Main.

"We'd better be on our way," he said, and strode from the room. His voice came rumbling back to her from the hallway. "Mrs. Clancy's packed us a picnic lunch, did she tell you?"

"She did mention she'd fixed 'a little something,'" Sandy said, catching up with him in the kitchen. She found him gazing with awe at an enormous basket on the table and went to join him. She felt out of breath, as if she'd just chased him half a block instead of down the hall.

She wanted to ask about his brother. She wanted to know what his name was, and where he was now, whether he was older or younger, and whether there were other brothers and sisters. In fact, she wanted to know all about Jason—where his home was and why he'd left it, and what he'd been doing in all the years since. Those and a hundred other questions roared through her mind like an avalanche, but she didn't ask any of them. She didn't ask because she was afraid they were all connected in some way to the one she most wanted the answer to. And how could she ask a man she'd known barely two days to tell her what had extinguished the light in his eyes?

"'A little something?'" Jason said, hefting the basket. "I hope to God she never fixes me a feast. You wouldn't believe what's in here. Fried chicken and apple pie, and that's just for starters. She must think I eat like a horse."

"Can't imagine why," Sandy murmured, planting her tongue in her cheek.

Jason looked pained. "I don't eat all that much, honest. Considering my size."

Which is why he looks so lean and moves like a cat, Sandy thought, remembering that he'd had fish and vegetables for dinner, while she'd polished off a cheeseburger and French fries. "Just as well," she said. "Because I do."

He regarded her with interest. "Oh, yeah?"

"Yeah. I eat like a horse."

His gaze lingered. Reminded all at once of what he'd said not so very long ago about her body, she felt it like a physical touch. Not a caress, exactly, more like the way a man runs his hands over a horse's flanks and legs, testing...judging...

"I wonder if there's anything in there to drink," she muttered, yanking open the refrigerator and peering into it. The air from inside felt blessedly cool on her cheeks.

"Oh yes, she took care of that, too. There's a bottle of wine—white, I believe."

"Oh."

"What's the matter?"

Boy, he's quick, Sandy thought. He sees so much with those empty eyes.

She shrugged. "Nothing. I just don't care for wine, that's all."

"No problem. We'll stop at the gas station and get a couple of cans of soda." He swung the basket off the table and waved her ahead of him. "That okay?"

She nodded. On the way out the front door she stopped as a much delayed thought struck her. "Mrs. Clancy put *wine* in a Sunday picnic basket?"

Jason chuckled. "Interesting, isn't it? Mrs. Clancy has a few unexpected qualities. She put cognac in my room."

"Really?" Sandy paused in the middle of the walk, intrigued. And then, remembering something else, she said, "You know something? I think Mrs. Clancy and Harvey are..." She hesitated, because the thought seemed so outrageous.

"Of course they are," Jason said placidly, holding the gate open for her.

She stopped to give him a scandalized look. "How do you know?"

"Have to be blind not to. Feelings like that are usually pretty hard to hide."

She was looking up at him, and he was looking down at her. His eyes were hooded and quiet. Sandy murmured a rather preoccupied "Hmm," because all of a sudden, all she could think of was what Mrs. Clancy had said about it being nice to have a man you could look up to.

They drove south again, into the Phantom Basin. Sandy explained that most of the lands the Bureau administered were in the lower, drier elevations—abandoned homesteads and such. Here and there old windmills still stood, monuments to failed dreams, offering meager shade to the cattle that grazed the land on BLM permits. It was in connection with these old wells that Sandy had established her livestock waterers. That they were working efficiently was attested to by the numbers of cattle lounging in the immediate vicinity.

"But you do patrol the high wilderness valleys?" Jason asked as they climbed into the pickup once more. "Even though that's not BLM territory?"

Sandy gave him a quick glance that struck him as being oddly evasive, then nodded. "Checking up on the wild horses. Late in the summer, when it gets dry like this and grass gets scarce, they like to move up to the high meadows. We like to keep track of them—making sure they don't interfere with the deer and elk, getting an accurate count, so we know what we're dealing with come roundup time."

"Roundup?" Jason prompted, though he knew already; he'd been briefed at BLM headquarters in Boise. He just liked hearing her talk this way, relaxed and self-confident as she explained how the mustang herds were culled every fall, and the healthy ones put up for adoption.

He glanced covertly at her as she drove, her strong hands steady on the wheel, her long golden arms streaked with dust and sweat, pale wisps of her hair blowing in the breeze from the open window. As always, she stirred sleeping desires in him, the way the dust devils raised chaff from the dry fields they passed.

His stomach rumbled loudly; it had been a hot, dusty morning, and he was getting hungry. As a matter of pride, he hadn't planned to mention it, but his stomach obviously had other ideas.

Sandy looked over at him and grinned. "Feel like you could eat that horse, yet?"

"Getting there," Jason said mildly.

"One more stop," Sandy said, letting her eyes rest on him in a way that brought a nice warmth to his hollow insides. "I know a good spot for that picnic lunch. This is right on the way."

Jason wasn't familiar with the Phantom Basin, but as Sandy drove he began to get the same sense of déjà vu that had hit him for those few moments in the helicopter coming in. They'd left the dry foothills behind; now the blacktopped road ran straight as an arrow through a narrow valley bordered on both sides by mountains darkly splotched with pines. On one side of the road were dry, yellow foothills dotted with grazing cattle. On the other, the creek meandered through lush meadows rank with wildflowers. At the foot of the distant mountains, aspen groves shimmered golden against the deep green of thick pine forest.

It reminded Jason so much of the Sawtooth Valley that when Sandy turned off into a dirt lane between two split rail and barbed wire fences, he half expected to see his own family's B-Heart brand burned into the gate's overhead crosspiece. For a moment he could see it so clearly, outlined against a brilliant blue September sky....

And his dad's old white Chevy pickup bouncing down the corduroy lane, trailed by its own thin plume of dust, Jared and the two border collies in the back....

"I just want to stop in here a minute," Sandy said as she turned off the motor and stomped on the emergency brake. "I want to see how some friends of mine are getting—" The smile she'd turned to Jason froze on her face. His eyes seared hers, eyes no longer empty, but red-rimmed and burning with unspeakable pain.

Her breath caught; she opened her mouth to ask him what was wrong. In the next instant, like one of those trick pictures that changes when you tilt it, the pain vanished from his eyes, leaving them opaque and unreadable. His face was no more fearsome and rugged than it usually was, and his voice, when he spoke, sounded perfectly normal.

"Fine with me," he said. "Let's go meet these friends of yours."

"This is Lucy. Isn't she pretty?" Sandy asked the question in a soft, crooning voice, then went on talking in baby-talk words and meaningless phrases while her hands smoothed the mare's rusty brown coat with long, firm strokes. Slowly, careful to use no sudden, unexpected movements, she lifted her eyes to where Jason lounged against the corral fence and smiled. "Lucy and Roughneck were just adopted this spring—weren't you, big girl? Yes...."

The mare lowered her head and snuffed loudly at Sandy's hip pocket. Sandy rubbed the velvety spot behind an ear. The mare jerked her head back up, looking affronted. Sandy chuckled. "You're doing a great job," she said to the dark-haired girl who had just walked over to her side. "She's gentling down very nicely. You giving her grain?"

"Oats," the girl said. "I have to watch out, though, or that Roughneck over there, he'll eat 'em all. He's a real pig."

"You know you can't let him have too much or he'll get sick, don't you?" The girl nodded soberly. Sandy went on in that soothing voice, asking about salt and pasture and plans for halterbreaking, and all the time her hands kept stroking the warm, soft hide.

As if, Jason thought, *she* were the one being soothed by it.

He lit a cigarette and watched her while he smoked it. He lounged against the fence, squinting against the smoke and dust, and he watched her hands and thought again how different they were from every woman's hands he'd ever seen—strong hands, work-worn and tough, but with long, aristocratic bones. He studied her profile—the nose too arrogant and the chin too strong for classic beauty—but that bee-stung mouth and golden skin and those sultry eyes made him think of sun-ripened peaches and warm, tropical nights. He noted the long, sleek lines of her body, and when she squatted to check the mare's feet, he saw the way the tip of her braid just brushed the dusty ground. Deep in the bottom of his belly, he felt the stirrings and tightenings of desire.

Lust. Pure lust, he thought, laughing at himself, and because it felt so good after the chill of his waking nightmare, he let the laughter come.

When the teenager went to see if she could get a lead rope on the skittish Roughneck, Jason straightened up and flicked his cigarette into the dust. The mare whuffed nervously and tossed her head at his approach, but stood still.

"You're good with them," he murmured, stopping close behind Sandy and reaching past her to touch the mare's neck.

"You sound surprised." Her voice was no more than a stirring of the warm air.

"I am, a little. You said you were from back east."

"They do have horses there, you know."

"Not like these."

"No."

"So your folks have horses?" Even in a barnyard, he could smell that sweet, ephemeral fragrance of hers. It reminded him of a meadow in spring. "Thoroughbreds?" he prodded, inhaling deeply, resisting the urge to touch her.

She nodded.

"Racehorses?"

"Hunters, mostly." As if the words were being forcibly pulled from her, she went on. "I had a hunter. A big black gelding named Rasputin."

"Oh, yeah?" He made his voice pleasant, coaxing. "Where was that?"

"Virginia."

Yes, he thought, he could see her in Virginia. Gracious manor house, white-painted stables, emerald-green paddocks bordered by white rail fences, like a glossy spread in some high-class magazine. He could see her in a black riding habit, mounted on a rangy black hunter, racing through an autumn wood....

"Virginia," he said, conversationally now. "I wouldn't have guessed that. You don't have an accent."

"I guess I've lost it. It was a long time ago." Her face was turned away from him; looking past her, he saw that her hand lay motionless on the mare's neck, her fingers curled into a white-knuckled fist.

"Oh, I don't know," he drawled. "I'm not sure time makes any difference. Some people keep their accents forever. I think it just depends on how badly a person wants to get rid of it."

As he spoke, he let his hand move slowly across the mare's sun-warmed hide, closing the gap between his hand and hers. When he covered her fist she flinched like a skittish colt, but didn't resist him. He picked it up, and with a gentle but inexorable pressure, inserted his thumb beneath the curled fingers. Her head turned; her eyes met his, smoky, angry, confused. Slowly he forced her fingers open one at a time. Her lips parted. Heat and tension hung heavy in the air.

And then her hand relaxed in his. Still holding her eyes, he drew his fingers lightly over her open palm, then replaced it on the mare's neck and let his own hand drop away.

"Let's go find that picnic spot," he said with grit in his voice. "I'm getting hungrier by the minute."

The rock-studded dirt road went on through the meadows for another bone-rattling half mile or so, then turned abruptly upward into the hills, becoming twin tracks in the rocky ground. They twisted and turned through thick groves of pines and had more forks than an elk's horns, but Sandy knew where she was going.

"There it is," she said suddenly, pointing ahead through the windshield. "Isn't it pretty? I don't even know if it has a name."

In her mind she'd always called it Treasure Lake, because of the way it sparkled through the trees like a cache of jewels, and because when she'd stumbled on it, she'd felt as if she'd discovered something hidden and precious. But she didn't tell Jason that.

When he didn't comment, she glanced over at him and saw that he was just staring straight ahead. His elbow was propped on the windowsill, and his hand covered his mouth in a casual, relaxed way, but Sandy knew he wasn't relaxed. His eyes were narrowed and intent, the way they'd been in the helicopter just before he'd told her about being born in Idaho. She knew better than to ask him if anything was wrong, so she didn't say anything at all. As soon as the pickup had rolled to a stop, he got out and headed straight for the water's edge without a word or a glance at her.

Now what? she wondered. She got out of the cab and slammed the door, but didn't follow Jason right away. Instead, she folded her arms and leaned against a fender, watching him, frowning.

He's so strange, she thought. One minute telling me it's all business between us, and the next minute kissing me like he means it. And then the *next* minute, saying *Hey, no big deal!*

Sometimes he laughs and smiles, but there's only emptiness in his eyes. And sometimes he looks at me as if he's seeing ghosts—or nightmares. Sometimes...

She hugged herself suddenly and rubbed at the goose bumps on her arms. Sometimes when he stood near her, so near that the heat and scent of him seemed to permeate her pores, she felt as if his body was exerting some sort of magnetic pull on her, so that she had to fight to keep from leaning just the little bit nearer it would take to close the gap.

She held up her hand, closed tightly into a fist, and slowly uncurled the fingers. Sometimes his hands were so strong, yet so gentle. Their touch made her feel protected and warm.

She snorted and abruptly turned her back on both Jason and the glittering water. And then sometimes—like now, for instance—he just seemed big and cold and forbidding. Like a mountain, she thought, laughing at herself. A mountain of a man. Had that expression ever been more apt? Some people, she supposed, would consider such a mountain a challenge. She wasn't one of them. She liked her life simple and uncomplicated; she conquered her mountains the easy way—with a helicopter.

Jason Rivers, with his ghosts and brooding silences, was a mystery someone else would have to solve. She wanted no part of his secrets. And as for that magnetic attraction, well, she'd just have to be sure to keep enough distance between them to avoid its pull.

She found Jason squatting on the narrow strip of grass between the lake and the trees, where the crystalline water lapped gently over a thin strip of white sand. When he heard her, he turned and squinted up at her, closing one eye against the sun's glare.

"Nice spot," he said, glancing at the picnic basket in her hands. He didn't comment about the fact that he'd left her to lug the thing down by herself.

Sandy figured that was just as well and decided not to say anything about it, either. He'd been entirely too attentive when it came to opening doors and gates for her as it was, considering the resolutions she'd just finished making. That sort of thing had a way of making her feel a little bit too conscious of her femininity—and of his masculinity. Starting tomorrow, they'd be going out every day in either the chopper or one of the BLM vehicles, and it was probably a good idea to get back on that solid business footing he'd talked about. Starting right now.

Which wasn't going to be easy, thanks to Mrs. Clancy and her picnic lunch. Mrs. Clancy and her matchmaking! *A man you can look up to....* Goodness knows what she'd been saying to Jason about *her*.

Though, to be honest, she knew that it wasn't all Mrs. Clancy's fault.

I shouldn't have had dinner with him that very first night, Sandy thought as she set the basket down on a flat rock. I shouldn't have let him walk me home.

As she sat cross-legged on the grass and began to take things out of the basket, she studied Jason's broad shoulders and the way his dark hair grew on the back of his neck. She felt a tiny squeezing sensation of panic in the pit of her stomach.

I shouldn't have asked him to that dumb dance. I shouldn't have danced with him. I shouldn't have kissed him!

From out on the water came a faint but distinct plop. Jason chuckled. "Sounds like there might be some good fishing on that lake."

Relieved at the distraction, Sandy said, "You like to fish?" It seemed like a safe subject.

"I used to, when I was a kid." He stood up, becoming a silhouette between her and that intense autumn sky. "As a matter of fact, my brother and I spent quite a bit of time fishing on a lake just like this one."

"Your brother," she said, knowing she shouldn't, knowing he was *not* a safe subject. "Where is he now?"

The world became still; insects hummed, breezes blew through pine trees, and out on the lake another fish broke the surface of the water.

Sandy thought he wasn't going to answer. With slow, unhurried movements, he took his cigarettes out of his shirt pocket, shook one out, put it between his lips and returned the pack to his pocket, then took out his lighter, flicked it on, held it to the tip of the cigarette and returned it to this pocket. And all the time Sandy watched him, her heart thumping painfully.

Jason's silhouette became a profile. The end of the cigarette crackled and glowed. Smoke drifted into the blue. Sandy watched the movement of his throat as he swallowed, and then at last the words came.

"He died."

His voice sounded as flat and final as a closing door.

Chapter 6

Well, she'd known it was going to be something like that; every instinct in her had told her to leave the subject alone. But she hadn't expected to feel so much pain. Jason's words, though softly spoken, had struck her like a physical blow. Her involuntary movement drew his gaze, and he watched her with hooded eyes, drawing deeply on his cigarette, while she mumbled an apology.

"It's all right," he said tonelessly. "It was a long time ago."

Then he squatted and, using the toe of his boot, painstakingly ground the glowing end of his cigarette into the ground. After examining the butt for sparks, he tucked it into his shirt pocket, so as not to spoil the beauty of the place with his litter.

Sandy remembered all that later, when she was trying to explain to herself how she'd come to fall in love with him; at that moment she felt only resentment. Damn it, she didn't *want* to be touched by him—not physically, and

definitely not emotionally. And she for sure didn't want to
have this urge to touch *him,* to smooth the harshness from
his face with her fingers, to ease the knots of tension from
his neck and shoulders, to put her arms around his big
body and hold him...just hold him close. *She didn't want
it!*

"I'm not sure time makes any difference," she said
harshly.

Jason paused in surprise, then glanced at her and gave
a short, dry laugh. "You're right—it doesn't."

"I'm sorry." Her face looked set, defensive. "Do you
want to talk about it?"

"No," Jason said, and then surprised himself by adding, "Not now." He'd never made that qualification before, even in his mind. Was it possible? he wondered. Did
he see himself at some point in the future telling Sandy
about Jared? And if so, *why?* Why did this particular
woman bring out that impulse in him, when he'd guarded
that part of himself so jealously and for so long?

It was the circumstances, he told himself, just the circumstances. The time, the place, his state of mind. He'd
get over it. If he could just hold the nightmares at bay until he got out of Idaho, he'd be fine. Just give him a beach
and a flat horizon, and a warm, firm, tanned, uncomplicated body....

Just then Sandy stood up, a 3-D Technicolor reminder
that her body was very warm and firm—tanned, too, at
least the part of it he'd seen. But not uncomplicated, he
thought, remembering her fist lying white-knuckled
against the mustang's neck. No sirree. He might have a few
ghosts and nightmares in his closet, but so, by all indica-
tions, did she. And he didn't need any more problems.

"Wine?" she said. "Or diet soda?"

Jason considered, then asked for soda. He would try to figure a way to shanghai that bottle of wine, though; it might come in handy when the nightmares got too bad.

He didn't resort to either wine or cognac that night; the bad dreams seemed distant, almost abstract, a mildly irritating background to his sleep, like elevator music. In some ways, his semiwaking sunshine dreams were more disturbing. He couldn't seem to make himself stick to white sand beaches, tropical sunsets and anonymous brown bodies. His imagination insisted on giving him a pair of long golden legs wrapped around the rippling black satin flanks of a thoroughbred stallion; strands of fine, silvery hair blowing in the wind, mingling with a coarse black mane; fragile hooves skipping through sun-dappled water, kicking up spray, spangling the horse's hide and pale gold skin alike with tiny diamonds.

He woke feeling tense and edgy, wishing to God he'd had the good sense to pass up this job. Wishing he'd at least had the good sense to hire his own pilot.

Sandy had always been an early riser; Jason, she discovered, was not. She had the chopper all checked out and ready to go by the time he finally showed up, just as the first rays of sunshine were peeking over the mountains. He was carrying the picnic basket.

Sandy smiled when she saw it. "Another of Mrs. Clancy's 'little somethings'?" Jason merely grunted as he hefted the thing into the chopper, then stalked off toward the main building.

"A little surly this morning, aren't we?" Sandy muttered to herself, watching him go, hunching her shoulders inside her sheepskin-lined jacket. It was just as well, she told herself. It was better like this. They had come too close for comfort to something that might have been very awkward. Better that they establish new terms, starting right now.

When Jason came back out to the chopper he looked a little bit more like the scientist he was—and which Sandy had forgotten about, for some reason. He was juggling an armload of charts and maps, a black leather case full of soil testing and core sampling equipment, and another case that held delicate and sophisticated-looking instruments Sandy didn't begin to know the purpose of. It was all part of the supplies he'd had shipped in advance of his arrival, and which Sandy had been skirting resentfully for the two weeks or so they'd been taking up space in her office.

Once everything had been stowed to his satisfaction, he unrolled a detailed topographical map overlaid with a meticulously hand-drawn grid. "This will give you a general idea of the areas I want to cover," he told her, using a red fine-point pen as a pointer. "We'll use the grid the same way search and rescue parties do in locating missing planes, so we're sure to cover everything. Understand?"

Sandy nodded, a heavy weight forming in her midsection. He was thorough, she had to say that for him.

"Actually, the areas of possibility are pretty limited. All this green is protected wilderness—this is the River of No Return Primitive Area right here, for example. Also, we'll stay out of the heavy timber areas, and any place where there's apt to be an abundance of deer and elk." When Sandy looked questioningly at him, he gave her a spare little smile without much amusement in it. "It's hunting season. I don't know about you, but I have no desire to walk into the sights of some overanxious hunter armed with a crossbow or a high-powered rifle. If necessary, I can always come back and check out any likely spots later on.

Any questions?'' Sandy shook her head. "All right then, let's go."

His manner was brisk, all business. All right, Sandy said to herself. That's good. I can handle this. It was the other Jason she couldn't deal with, the one with the gentle voice and gentler hands.

"Ready when you are, J.R.," she said with a bright, determined grin, putting on her aviator shades and tugging her hat lower on her forehead. Jason's eyes flicked over her impersonally. He didn't return the smile as he jerked a thumb toward the swishing rotors.

Okay, fine, Sandy thought. If that's the way you want it, that's the way you'll get it. She revved the engines until dust and chaff rose shimmering in the morning sunshine, them lifted them out of their own cloud in one stomach-dropping surge. She felt the look Jason gave her, but he didn't say anything as she headed the helicopter toward the northwest.

And, as always, when she got up there above it all, Sandy forgot her troubles and frustrations, forgot her worries about the changes Jason might bring to her wilderness. There was so much of it! A jumbled chaos of mountains, "new" ones like the Sawtooths and the White Clouds, so raw and ragged they looked as if they'd been freshly ripped from the earth's crust; older ranges, like the Bitterroots, whose summits had been rounded and softened by the scourings of wind and water over incomprehensible eons of time. There were watersheds that ran every way but up, glacier-carved valleys, volcanic moonscapes, boiling hot springs and shimmering ice caves. How could one man, or thousands, change all that?

Others had tried, though. They flew over an occasional trapper's cabin, mining claim or cattle ranch, but all were abandoned now. Men had come with the hope of con-

quering one of the wildest regions left on earth, and in the
end had gone away again, leaving it to the eagle and elk,
the cougar and mountain goat.

The wilderness had conquered all comers so far, and it
would win this battle, too. She was worrying for nothing;
she and Jason and their puny little helicopters were nothing—*nothing!*—in all this vastness. What did it matter?
She could take Jason wherever he wanted to go, let him do
all the testing and exploring he wanted to do, and in the
end the wilderness would win anyway.

That thought made her feel downright cheerful about
the whole thing. Jason gave her a funny look when she
suddenly started to sing at the top of her voice. He didn't
say anything, but he did seem to relax a little, and when he
turned back to the unrolling vista, Sandy could have sworn
his mouth was close to smiling.

What the hell, she thought. It was almost like a vaca-
tion; she'd just relax and enjoy the next couple of weeks,
and then get back to her own responsibilities when it was
over. And, she thought to herself, if she was smart and
careful, she could even exercise some control over what
Jason did—and did not—see.

Neither of them talked much; the rotors made too much
noise for conversation. They communicated with gestures
for the most part. When Jason pointed, Sandy nodded and
took the chopper down. Then, while Jason hiked around,
taking samples and readings and so forth, Sandy took a
nap in the shade, or, if there was a likely stream handy, got
out the fishing pole she always carried in the back of the
chopper, along with her spare sleeping bag and the first aid
and emergency supplies.

Sometimes she went along with Jason. At first she went
because watching him was more interesting than either
napping or fishing; eventually he got tired of her ques-

tions and started explaining what he was doing, even putting her to work helping him do it.

Time went by quickly. They ate lunch on a rocky moraine overlooking a sapphire lake, while Jason explained how a glacier had gouged out the valley beyond and then retreated, leaving behind the scrap pile they were sitting on. They flew back to Silverville with the setting sun at their backs. While Sandy put the chopper to bed, Jason went off to the main building to sort and catalog the data he'd collected. He was still at it when she was ready to go home, so she said "good-night" and walked up the hill alone.

That was the pattern of their days for the rest of that week.

On Friday afternoon Jason called it quits early. Back at BLM headquarters, he checked out a Bronco and offered Sandy a ride home in it. Later, when Sandy stopped by on her way down to the Mint Café for dinner to say "thank you" for the picnic lunches, Mrs. Clancy told her that Jason had gone to Idaho Falls for the weekend. Sandy told herself it was just as well; thank goodness she wouldn't have to worry about keeping him entertained. She told herself she was relieved.

On Saturday, following up a report from a rancher down in the Phantom Basin about a downed range fence, she spent an exhausting and frustrating morning struggling with barbed wire and a pair of pliers. More than once she found herself wishing for a pair of broad masculine shoulders and strong arms.

That afternoon Harvey Schmidt came over to fix her washing machine. After he left, she washed and dried her hair, a three-hour job. As she stood brushing and braiding it she looked out the window at the mountains and thought about what Jason was probably doing in Idaho Falls.

By evening she was feeling good and sorry for herself, so she went down to the Silver Horseshoe, even though she was a little afraid those two cowboys from the Rocking-W might show up again. She found herself a little sorry when they didn't.

On Sunday she went to the Methodist church with Mrs. Clancy and Harvey Schmidt. She came home depressed, and declined an invitation to stay for Sunday dinner. She read until she developed a headache, then went out for a walk and some fresh air, and for some reason wound up at the BLM. She puttered around there, doing odds and ends of paperwork, until nearly dark. When she passed by Mrs. Clancy's on the way home, she noticed that Jason's Bronco wasn't there, so he obviously wasn't back from Idaho Falls, yet. She fell asleep listening for him, but never did hear him come in.

When Sandy got to her office on Monday morning, Jason was there ahead of her. He had his map spread out on her desk and was leaning over it, making marks with his red pen, but when he saw her, he straightened and folded his arms on his chest.

"Okay, you want to tell me just what the hell you think you're trying to do?"

His voice was quiet, but had the ominous portent of distant cannon fire. It had been a long time since she'd thought of him in pirate's terms.

"I don't know what you mean," she said calmly, though her insides wanted to quail before that fierce, black glare.

"Come here."

She took her time about it, because she knew what he was going to show her. Red marks on the map forming an irregular doughnut. And somewhere in the hole in the middle of that doughnut would be Rogue's Valley.

Bravely, she said, "Hmm, looks like you missed a spot."

Her expression was all bland innocence. Jason wanted to throttle her.

"Not according to my grid." Damn her, she'd known his time was limited. She'd been against him from the first, he'd known that, but he hadn't expected outright sabotage. "According to my charts, I had you set us down within that circle at least three times."

"Oh well, we all make mistakes." She shrugged blithely and turned away.

For some reason, that got to him. He snaked an arm across the desk top and caught her by the wrist. "My only mistake," he said through clenched teeth, "was trusting you." He was angry, angrier than he'd been in a long time, angry out of proportion to the importance of what she'd done.

She tried to jerk her arm from his grasp. Tightening his grip, he felt the tiny tremor that vibrated through her. That, and the way her gaze battled his in mute defiance, reminded him suddenly of the last time he'd captured her wrist like this. There'd been trembling and defiance in her then, too, but it hadn't been because of him. The difference, he discovered, was a sick, hollow feeling in his stomach.

"Damn it, Sandy," he grated. "What's up there that you don't want me to see? What are you trying to hide from me?"

"I don't know what you're talking about."

"The hell you don't. You know that territory, you know how to fly a chopper, you can read a map, and there's nothing wrong with your hearing. You deliberately misled me, steered me away from that particular spot. What I want to know is *why*."

"How come you're so sure *you* didn't make a mistake? You said your grid—"

"Because when I checked all my data against the geological survey map, I realized that what I had couldn't possibly have come from the places I'd marked on my chart, that's why. Last night, after I got back—"

"Hah!" Sandy interrupted. "After your weekend, I'm surprised you could even read a map!"

She punctuated that with an angry jerk. Jason was so surprised he let go of her wrist. "What are you talking about? My *weekend?*"

"How could you do any work last night? You didn't even get home until God knows when this morning!"

She was so mad she was almost giving off sparks. Jason couldn't believe it. With an incredulous laugh he said, "How the hell would you know? What are you, my mother?"

"No, just your pilot and partner, remember? And about the last thing I need in my helicopter is somebody who's hung over, biting my head off, getting sick—"

"Hung over?" And then he just stared at her, too bemused to say anything at all. Because light had dawned, and though it seemed crazy and impossible to him, he thought he knew what was the matter with her. She was mad at him for leaving town! As ridiculous as it sounded, he could swear she was *jealous.*

"Now look here," he said, beginning to enjoy himself, "what I do with my spare time is none of your business as long as I show up here ready to go when you are, you got that?" Actually, what he'd done with his weekend was enjoy a steak dinner, take in a couple of movies and go shopping. His main purpose in going to Idaho Falls had been to buy himself some thermal underwear, warm gloves and a sheepskin jacket, because he'd been freezing his butt off in that helicopter all week. But he wasn't going to tell Sandy that. "And, I might add," he pointed out with relish, "I was here before you were this morning. If any-body's crabby, seems to me it's you. What's the matter, didn't your weekend go well?"

"That—" Sandy bit out her reply "—is none of your business."

"You're right," Jason said serenely, as if he couldn't care less. "So if you're through—"

"I had a *lovely* weekend!"

Jason raised his eyebrows. "Did you? Glad to hear it." He began to roll up his maps, resisting an urge to whistle. He wasn't angry anymore. In fact, he felt absurdly light-hearted. "In that case, I suggest you get your... fanny in gear. We have a long day ahead of us."

She looked ready to mutiny, but all she did was mutter, "Oh yeah, why?"

He stopped close beside her and looked down at her for a few seconds, saying nothing, deliberately using his height to his advantage, knowing someone as tall and proud as she was wouldn't be accustomed to being towered over and probably wouldn't like it much. Sure enough, he saw the anger in her eyes waver, saw them darken and become confused instead. He saw her mouth move—a nervous lit-tle tightening—and heard the soft sound of her throat being cleared. He felt a sudden and very strong desire to kiss her, but he resisted it. "I don't know whether we missed that spot because of my mistake or your design," he said softly, "and I don't really care. But I'll guarantee you we'll have covered every single square foot of it be-fore we come home tonight. You got that?"

"Loud and clear, sir," Sandy snapped sarcastically.

Sparring with her sure was fun. Jason grinned as he tucked the maps under his arm and strode out of the of-fice.

The valley was every bit as lovely as she remembered it. From high above it still looked like a jewel, though not an emerald; the thick grass on the valley floor had already turned to winter yellow. Everything seemed touched with gold. Yellowing fool's huckleberry and reddish thickets of wild rose crowded the shimmering aspens, and even the somber firs seemed to glow with the burnt orange of dead needles. The valley lay untouched in the midst of that jumble of towering granite crags, sparkling in the afternoon sun like a pirate's lost treasure.

Sandy felt the touch of Jason's eyes as she swept over the treetops and skimmed the wind-rippled grass, but ignored his unspoken questions. There was too much anger in her still, too much resentment, and a heaviness that was almost grief. As she settled onto a dry plateau at the foot of the jagged cliffs, she felt as if she were betraying a friend.

They sat without speaking, looking out across the valley through the chopper's bubble, while the rotors slowed and finally stopped. Without their noise the quiet seemed absolute. And then, from far away, came the high, thin cry of a hawk, breaking the spell of silence. Jason stirred and said, "Coming?"

Sandy shook her head. "No, I'll wait here." She'd brought him because she'd had no choice, but she didn't have to watch him while he picked and probed at her Eden.

Jason shrugged and stepped down from the chopper, then reached back for his cases. "Suit yourself."

Against her will, Sandy watched him walk back toward the edge of the mesa. Something in the set of his shoulders told her that he was angry, or at least annoyed. Good, she thought, sniffing, and was about to look away when she saw him gesture for her to join him. She ignored him, but he motioned again and called her name. Swearing resentfully, she jumped out of the helicopter, adjusted her hat and stalked over to him.

"Look," he said, pointing.

At this end, the mesa dropped off sharply into the mouth of a canyon. In the sandy soil of the canyon floor, plainly visible even from the rim of the mesa, were the imprints of horses' hooves. A sizable number of them from the looks of it.

Sandy nodded and said heavily, "I know. That's how I found this place."

Jason looked at her, then shaded his eyes and peered into the shadows of the canyon. "Looks like they came in this way. Must be a pass."

Sandy just nodded and went back to the helicopter. She took her hat off and sat down in the shade, then listened to the noise Jason made, slipping and sliding down the rocky slope. A pass. Perfect. That meant they could put in a road. Jason must be tickled pink.

As she sat irritably whacking her hat against her boots, she heard the scrabbling of falling rock off to her left somewhere, in the opposite direction from the one Jason had taken. A little curl of unease rolled down her spine. She hadn't noticed before how unstable those looming cliffs looked, but now she saw the scars and rubble left by previous slides. All a good distance from the chopper, though. The ground here was level and clear of rocks; it was still the safest landing spot in the valley. Sandy knew from hard experience that setting down in a meadow was chancy, at best; you never knew when you might find yourself up to your rotors in a bog. And she couldn't very well land in a stand of timber or on a slope. Besides, those cliffs had probably been intact for millenia. She was satisfied that they'd stay put for another couple of hours.

Nevertheless, she found that she couldn't sit still anymore. The quiet folded in around her like a suffocating blanket. She couldn't see or hear any sign of Jason; she might have been alone in that vastness. That had never bothered her before, but today she felt a strange, itchy unease. The world was just too quiet, too still.

She wondered whether Rogue and his band were still in the valley. She listened, straining to hear the clatter of hooves on rocky ground, a faint whicker or distant whinny. But if they were still here, they were keeping as quiet as everything else. Even the wind had died. It reminded her of the stillness before a thunderstorm, except there wasn't a cloud in the sky.

"This is ridiculous," Sandy said aloud, defying the silence. She decided she'd go do some exploring on her own, see if maybe she could find some sign of the mustangs. She was *not* going to go looking for Jason, though; she didn't care if she ever saw him again.

But when she'd made her way through the first thickets of fir and bracken and could see the meadow clearly, she stood for a long time, shading her eyes and scanning the sea of yellow grass. A lot longer than it took to determine that no band of mustangs, led by a big bay rogue of a stallion, grazed in the golden haze.

Good, she said to herself. Thank goodness Jason wasn't anywhere in sight. She told herself once more how glad she was that she didn't have to watch him tromping around in her valley, staking his claim on her special place.

A green ribbon snaked through the dry meadow. If she were to find mustang signs anywhere, it would be near water, Sandy thought, so she set off to look for a water hole, following the creek.

The high-altitude sun was fierce. Perspiration pooled beneath her hat brim, but when she took her hat off, there was no breeze to dry her skin. Her shirt stuck to her back; sweat trickled down between her breasts and into the waistband of her jeans. Gnats flew into her eyes and nose and whined in her ears. She was tempted to take a quick dip in the creek, but abandoned that idea when she stopped to wash her face in the crystal clear water. It was so cold it numbed her fingers.

She decided to abandon the idea of exploring the creek altogether and headed back uphill toward the beckoning shade of the forest. As she topped a little knoll that jutted out into the meadow, she caught a whiff of sulfur and knew that there must be a hot spring close by. That was what Jason would be looking for, of course; that was where he'd be.

Her impulse was to turn back to the chopper. For some reason, she found herself pushing on.

The odor of sulfur grew stronger. After skirting a stand of dense timber, Sandy found herself on the edge of a moonscape, a broad, gently sloping plane of mineral-crusted rock, lifeless and barren. Steam rose from hidden pools as if from a witch's cauldron, and sunlight caught in the drifting vapor cast a weird, brassy glow across the landscape. It looked, Sandy thought, like Dante's best vision of hell.

But it was empty; Jason wasn't here. Though he had been—Sandy spotted the flag that marked the seismic monitor he'd left behind.

Well, she thought with resignation, that's it, then. This was Jason's mother lode—water from the molten core of the earth. She knew that it took more than the presence of a natural hot spring to make a good geothermal drilling site, but she sensed with fatalistic certainty that this one was going to meet all the criteria. Her beautiful, un-spoiled valley was doomed.

But not yet. For now, for this moment, it was still hers. She was alone here. Jason had done his job and gone away; he was probably waiting for her right now back at the chopper. Well, she told herself, he could wait a while longer. Sandy had just decided she was going to do some-thing she'd never done before, something she'd always wanted to do but had never quite had the time, the oppor-tunity, or the courage for.

The spring itself was too hot for her purposes, of course, but down below, where the water ran over the rocks and collected in shallow depressions, it formed clean, quiet pools. Natural bathtubs. The temperature varied with the depth and size of the pool, but after a little searching she found one that was soothingly warm and deep enough for her to immerse herself completely.

Crouching beside the pool, she cast a quick, furtive look around her. She was truly alone; the silence was com-plete. Heart hammering with childlike anticipation, she stood and stripped off her clothes—all but her hat, which she jammed on tightly over her coiled braid to keep it from getting wet. A moment later, smiling and breathless, she was lowering herself into the water, leaving her clothing in an untidy heap on the rocks.

By the time he'd finished with everything, Jason was hot and itchy and more than ready for that dip in the hot spring he'd promised himself. He knew it was getting late—nearly sundown, in fact. Sandy would be antsy as hell, out of sorts and anxious to get home, but under the circumstances, he didn't feel guilty about making her wait a little longer. Not after that stunt she'd pulled, trying to hide this location from him. It was a good one, too, a definite possibility. He'd tried to be patient with her attitude; he understood how she felt. Like a lot of people, she just couldn't seem to grasp the broader picture, couldn't see that what he was trying to do was for the overall good of the area.

But, regardless of personal feelings, when she tried to keep him from doing his job, that was going too far. It wouldn't hurt her to stew a little.

He already had his shirt off when he stepped out of the woods that bordered the bathing pools. A moment later, for the second time since he'd known Sandy Stewart, Jason felt as if he'd walked into a wall.

There wasn't a darn thing he could do about it. When he came out of the trees, there she was, his sunshine vision in the flesh. Long legs bare, arms uplifted as she unbraided her hair, letting it tumble down past her buttocks, everything touched with the rosy glow of the setting sun....

She held that pose for only an instant, long enough to sear it forever in Jason's memory. Then she dropped into a half crouch; her arms came down across her body in the classic gesture of protective modesty, and her mouth opened in silent alarm. She looked, he thought, like a startled doe.

He probably should have stepped back into the trees; it would have been the gallant thing to do. But he didn't. Finding his voice, after a fashion, he managed to croak, "Sandy, I swear to God, I didn't know you were here. I thought you were back at the chopper."

He expected her to yell at him, to tell him to go away, but she didn't. She straightened slowly, still shielding her upper body with her arms, and he saw that she was wearing panties. The rest of her clothes, he realized, were lying on the rocks at his feet.

"That's funny," she said, her voice calm, though a touch husky. "That's where I thought *you* were. Would you mind handing me my shirt?"

He picked it up, shook it out and offered it to her. She just looked witheringly at him; reaching for it was going to deprive her of half her cover. Jason muttered something and was stepping across the pile of clothes when the ground rose up to meet his foot.

He heard Sandy utter a single shocked gasp, and then she pitched forward, hitting him in the chest, and knocking him backward. For a few precarious moments he gripped her arms and struggled for balance, but it was a losing battle; the ground beneath his feet was bucking like a wild bronc. When he went down, he went down hard, with Sandy on top of him.

She said, "Oh God—Jason!" Her eyes stared into his, wide and frightened. He felt the frantic knocking of her heart against his ribs.

"Earthquake," he rasped, fighting for breath. He hadn't heard the warning rumble, or felt the first mild tremors; his senses had already been on overload, fully occupied and reeling with impressions of Sandy. Now they both heard the sound—indescribable, and unlike anything else on earth. The ground rolled and pitched like a frail boat in a storm; over their heads trees lashed the sky, unleashing a stinging rain of dead needles. Acting on pure instinct, Jason wrapped his arms around Sandy and rolled her under him, protecting her with his body.

It seemed to go on forever, though it probably only lasted a few moments. When the rumbling and shaking stopped, they could still hear water splashing in the pools and the clatter of falling rock. Jason stayed where he was until the hail of pebbles and pine needles against his back had stopped, then lifted his head and croaked, "Sandy?"

She was lying very still, staring up at him. Her eyes were dark and slightly glazed. Her hands gripped his shoulders. He heard her make a tiny coughing sound, and glanced down at the place where their chests touched as they moved in and out with their frantic breathing. When he said her name again, it came from deep in his throat. "Sandy..."

Without a word, she put her arms around his neck and tangled her fingers in his hair. Before he claimed her mouth, he saw her eyes close and felt her body arch upward under his, and for one moment thought the earth had not finished quaking.

She gasped something—his name, he thought—but he smothered it, so that it became a sigh in his own mouth. She clung to him, pulling herself up into the kiss as if she couldn't get enough of it. Her hunger inflamed him; he threw away what little restraint he had left and bore her back down into the cradle of his arms, plundering her mouth until she pulled away, sobbing desperately for breath. Then he caught and held her hard against him, pressing her face into the hollow of his neck, while she fought to control the shudders that racked her.

When she seemed quieter, he whispered, "You all right now?" She nodded. "Your first quake?" Another nod. He relaxed his arms, and she lay back, her hair pooling like spilled milk on the ground. Her eyes searched his, not wide and frightened now, but heavy-lidded and slumberous.

"I think you're bleeding," she said huskily, drawing her fingers across his back.

"Scratches," he said. "Don't worry about it." He hadn't felt them, hardly felt them now. What he did feel was her lithe, slender body under his, the long silken caress of her legs. He shifted his weight experimentally to one side, and when she didn't try to sit up or move away, let his gaze travel downward. As if it had a mind of its own, his hand slipped from beneath her, rested for a moment on the curve of her waist, then moved up over the arch of her rib cage. He watched its progress, fascinated by the sight. Though he knew she was neither fragile nor small, his hand made her seem so; it looked big and dark and rough against the rose petal softness of her breast.

Under the weight of his hand, the rise and fall of her rib cage quickened. He said her name raggedly just as she gasped, "Jason..." He waited, searching her eyes, until she closed them and said it again, whispering this time. "Jason..."

Her mouth opened; his head descended. And then they both fell still, listening.

Sandy whispered, "What is that?"

Jason said, "Hush... listen."

"Oh God, it's not another—"

"No," Jason said in a voice that had gone hoarse with dread. "Landslide."

Chapter 7

*L*andslide.

The word galvanized them both. Swearing, Jason rolled away from Sandy and sat up, looking around for their clothes.

Sandy said, "Jason, the chopper—it's sitting beside—"

"I know." Grimly, he tossed her her shirt. He already had an arm through a sleeve of his; without bothering to button it, he stood and pulled her to her feet. *"Hurry."*

She looked at him and opened her mouth, but didn't say anything, and didn't waste time being modest. While she was buttoning her shirt, Jason shook the pine needles out of the rest of her clothes and handed them to her one at a time, socks first, then jeans. She put them on standing up, clutching his arm for balance. There was only one moment of embarrassment, and that was when he handed her her bra. She looked down at it, then back at him, and made a helpless little sound of frustration.

"Oh," Jason muttered, realizing she didn't really have a place to put it, and not knowing what else to do with it, thrust it into his pocket.

He didn't know why he felt such urgency; there wasn't much he could do to stop a landslide.

Damn. He had a bad feeling. Sound had a way of echoing and rebounding in a place like this, but he was pretty sure it had come from the far end of the valley where the chopper was parked. He'd noticed those cliffs, and the scree from earlier slides. He should have known better.

"Ready," Sandy said breathlessly, hopping on one foot as she struggled with her last boot. "You go ahead. I'll catch up with you." He hesitated only a moment, then nodded, handed her her hat and was off.

Damn, Sandy thought, watching Jason make his way across the slope, leaping from rock to rock with the lithe grace of a mountain cat. I should have known better.

She should have moved the chopper when she'd had the chance. But who could have foreseen an earthquake?

Praying hard, she twisted her hair into a coil on top of her head, jammed her hat over it and took off after Jason.

She found him at the foot of the mesa, standing near the bottom of the slide with his hands in his hip pockets, looking up toward the helicopter. A veil of dust drifted across the face of the mountain, purple-tinged with the last of the sunset glow. From a distance, in the waning light, the chopper looked untouched.

"How is it?" she gasped, coming up beside him, sure it would be all right because it *had* to be. Jason shook his head, not looking at her. She threw him a bitter glance and pushed past him, scrambling up the slope, unable to believe it, unwilling to accept it.

Jason joined her a few minutes later as she stood, numb with shock, beside the helicopter. "The tail rotor's gone," she said flatly. "The rear stabilizers and supports are damaged. I don't know what else."

"Well," he said grimly, "that's enough."

They stood there looking at each other, not saying anything. Darkness settled over the valley, and with it a cold, bitter chill that penetrated clothing and knifed through flesh. But a deadlier chill was settling around Sandy's heart. As the magnitude of the disaster penetrated the protective layers of shock, her teeth began to chatter.

"Sandy." She felt Jason's hands gripping her arms, felt him give her a little shake. "What about the radio?"

"What?" She frowned at him, struggling to make her mind work.

"A radio. You have one, don't you?"

Shaking her head, she mumbled, "Doesn't work. I was going to have Mike take a look at it next time he serviced the chopper. After the roundup...."

"Emergency beacon?"

Sandy lifted her shoulders. "Don't have one."

Jason swore.

"Jason," she whispered, frightened, "what are we going to do?"

"Do?" His laughter was harsh. "What do you think we're going to do? Survive, of course. Hell, Sandy, I'm a *survivor,* don't you know that?"

Why was there so much bitterness in his voice when he said that? Rather than giving her heart, for some reason his words made her feel worse.

"Well, I'm all for that. In fact, it's just fine and dandy," she said testily. "But I mean right *now.* What are we going to do tonight? It's cold. I think it's going to freeze."

"Yeah," Jason said. "I know." In the thickening darkness Sandy heard, rather than saw, him drag a hand through his hair, a gesture of indecision she'd never seen him make before. "Look, we don't have any real good options. It's too late to find shelter or build a fire. Our best bet would be to stay in the chopper tonight. Don't you have some emergency supplies? Blankets?"

"Sleeping bag."

"Right . . . right. The problem is the danger of another slide. There are bound to be aftershocks from that quake."

"Lovely," Sandy muttered, hugging herself. She didn't want to think about what she was going to do in the next minute, the next hour, the next day. She felt cold and sick and scared. She wanted to wake up and have the nightmare be over.

"Come here," Jason called from inside the helicopter, amidst grunts and scufflings. "If we move some of this stuff out of the way, I think there's plenty of room for both of us."

"To do what?" Her voice sounded high and felt perilously close to breaking. "Get buried in the next rock slide? I think I'd rather freeze to death than be crushed!"

"Here, put this on." Jason's bulk was a warm, solid presence beside her in the darkness; she wanted to reach for it, grasp it and cling to it, like a child to its mother's legs. Pride kept her rigid and silent as she shrugged into the jacket he gave her. "Better?"

"Yeah." The darkness became empty again. A moment later she heard an exclamation of satisfaction from inside the helicopter. A finger of light stabbed through the night.

"Found the flashlight." In its illumination, his grin looked more piratical than ever. "Come on. See, I've cleared a place here. Between our jackets and the sleeping bag we should be able to keep warm." When she just went on standing there, he came over to her and put a hand on her shoulder. Caught between their bodies, the flashlight's beam cast eerie shadows across his face, highlighting the crags and deepening the hollows, giving his eyes a feral glow. Suddenly remembering the way his face and eyes had looked, poised above her, slowly descending, Sandy felt as if she were experiencing an aftershock of her own.

"Look," Jason said softly as the tremor rippled through her, "it'll be all right. We'll take turns staying awake, keeping watch. At the first rumble of a quake, we're outa here, okay?" He waited for her nod. "All right, then—in you go."

And still she hesitated. The need to touch him was so overpowering that she couldn't resist it anymore; her hand found its own way to the front of his jacket, lay there for a moment, then moved upward to the sheepskin collar. "Where'd you get this?" she asked huskily, giving it a little pat. She'd chided him more than once on their cold mornings in the chopper for not having a warm jacket.

He gave a snort of laughter. "I just bought it in Idaho Falls. Talk about good timing. I'm just sorry I didn't wear my new thermal long johns. Without which I'm freezing my butt off, by the way, so if you'd get in the damn chopper, I'd appreciate it!"

She just wanted him to put his arms around her and hold her, that was all. She couldn't understand why he didn't; it seemed a natural thing to do under the circumstances, and surely not too much to ask. But she wouldn't ask. Because she remembered the way he'd withdrawn from her after the first time he'd kissed her, and she thought he must be doing the same thing now, after what had happened down at the hot spring. After what *almost* happened. Her stomach gave a painful lurch. What would have happened if it hadn't been for the slide?

They settled themselves behind the seats, with their backs against the chopper's Plexiglas bubble and their legs stretched out across the floor. Jason unzipped the sleeping bag and was about to spread it across their legs when Sandy said, "It would probably make more sense to get inside it."

Jason hesitated, then said, "You're right." So they wiggled and squirmed and managed to get the bottom half of the thing underneath them, the top half folded over, and the whole thing zipped up.

"There," Jason said, breathing hard. He leaned back against the wall and folded his arms on his chest. "I guess that's one way to get warm. I think I worked up a sweat."

"I feel like a Siamese twin," Sandy said. Her stomach responded with a loud growl.

Jason snapped his fingers and said, "I knew I forgot something. Can you reach the picnic basket?"

Sandy couldn't. They had to unzip the sleeping bag so she could get the basket from the pilot's seat. When they were all settled in and zipped up again, they attacked the remains of Mrs. Clancy's lunch with the breathless enthusiasm of children discovering a long-lost stash of candy. Mrs. Clancy was still packing enough food for an army, thank God; they had never managed to eat it all, and today had been no exception. The roast beef sandwiches had wilted a bit in the heat of the day, but the fresh peach cobbler looked and smelled like heaven. It took all Sandy's willpower to yield to Jason's suggestion that they save most of it for breakfast. The coffee in the Thermos was still fairly hot, though, and they drank it with the sandwiches, passing the bottle back and forth.

When it was gone and the basket was packed up and set aside, Jason lit a cigarette, a process that required some more wiggling and squirming. Sandy tried to get comfortable, but she was beginning to do some wiggling of her own.

"Um . . . Jason," she said after a while, unable to stand it any longer.

"Hmm?"

"I hate to tell you this, but I have to go to the bathroom."

"Don't you think you should have thought of that *before* you got into bed?" Jason said plaintively. He gave a put-upon sigh and reached for the zipper. As she was crawling over his feet he said with mock severity, "Sandy, I do hope you're not going to be up and down like this all night."

The low rumble of his laughter followed her into the darkness, making her smile in spite of everything.

By the time she came back the moon was rising, thinning the darkness to charcoal gray. She was shivering with cold, and Jason wasn't much warmer, having taken advantage of her absence to see to his own needs.

He was about to zip them back into the sleeping bag when he remembered the wine.

Mrs. Clancy's bottle of Chablis. He'd carried it around in his instrument case all week, forgetting to take it home with him until this morning, when he'd decided he didn't want to cart the extra weight. On their first stop he'd taken it out and stashed it under the seat. And there it still was, a little bruised, no doubt, but nicely chilled.

Jason pulled it out of its hiding place and held it up so he could peer at it in the darkness. Sandy stopped shivering long enough to stammer, "What's that?"

"Mrs. Clancy's bottle of wine. From the picnic, remember?"

"You still have it? What are you going to do with it?"

"I was planning on drinking it. I was thinking it would probably help warm us up."

"It would most likely put us to sleep," Sandy said dubiously.

"Maybe. But we did drink the coffee, too." He didn't tell her there was no way in hell, after this day's events, that he was going to shut his eyes. No way. He unstoppered the bottle, started to take a drink, then remembered his manners and offered it to her instead.

She shook her head, then hesitated. "Would it really help warm me up? I don't think I'll ever be warm again."

"Cognac would be better," Jason said, a little wistfully, "but this'll do in a pinch. Here—try it." He jerked the bottle back. "Unless you have a real problem with alcohol."

She shook her head. "I just don't like it. Makes me feel lightheaded."

"It's supposed to."

"Well, I don't like it." But she took the bottle, and then a tentative sip. "Hmm," she said judiciously, tipping the bottle and taking a good hefty swig. "You know, it does feel nice and warm in your tummy."

"Your tummy, huh?" Jason took the bottle from her and tested her observation for himself. "You're right," he said. "It does." He took another drink.

"Don't hog it," she said, stretching out her hand.

"Take it easy. I'm not sure how much of this a confirmed teetotaler can handle."

"Hah! I'll have you know I was practically raised on the stuff."

"Oh yeah? Down in ol' Virginny?"

"Nope, in Washington, D.C."

Jason found that very interesting. Thinking it would be even more interesting to see what else she might let slip, he decided to stop trying to ration her alcohol. Besides, he told himself, there were a lot of reasons why it would be a good idea if she went to sleep tonight. For one thing, he didn't know how much longer he was going to be able to share this single sleeping bag with her and keep his hands off her. The layers of clothing separating them now weren't doing a darn thing to dim recent memories of that long body, naked in his arms.

By the time they'd finished two-thirds of the bottle, Sandy was loudly singing cowboy songs.

When she paused for breath, Jason asked, "What I want to know is, how the hell did a thoroughbred like you ever grow up to be a cowboy?"

"I'm not a cowboy." She sounded miffed.

"Wrangler, then."

She shook her head. "I am what is known as—" she coughed and intoned "—a range technician. Sounds impressive, huh?"

Jason shook his head. "All I know is, I thought I was supposed to meet some gnarled, beat-up old cowpoke."

"Why in the world would you think that?"

"S. J. Stewart, Chief Wrangler for the Salmon River District. What would *you* think?"

Sandy raised herself up to stare at him. "No kidding, you didn't know I was a woman?" When she settled back down again, for some reason she wound up nestled in the curve of his arm. "Jeez," she murmured, "no wonder."

He didn't ask her what she meant by that. After a while he said, "So what does the J stand for?"

She just said, "Hmm?" and snuggled closer to him, so he repeated it.

"Your middle name—what does the J stand for?"

"None of your business," she said sleepily.

"Okay, let me guess. Sandra Jane. Sandra . . . Joy. Sandra Jeanette?"

She sighed. "Jaimison. It stands for Jaimison."

"*James?* What kind of middle name is that for a girl?"

"Not James. *Jaimison.*"

There was a long silence, while Jason played that over in his mind. Sandra Jaimison Stewart. He tried it out loud, and it sounded the same. "Sandra Jaimison Stewart. . . ." He stared down at the silvery head snuggled just below his chin. So that's the ghost in her closet, he thought. And one hell of a ghost it was, too.

He took another swallow of wine and said carefully, "So. You're *that* Sandra Jaimison Stewart?"

She nodded and sighed. "'Fraid so."

Jason swore and set the bottle down with a thump. Sandy pushed herself up off his chest and peered into his face. "That intimidates you, doesn't it?"

"Hell no!"

"It does too. It always intimidates people. Guys especially."

"Well," Jason muttered, "I hate to disappoint you, but you don't intimidate me."

"Oh yeah?" He felt the tempo of her breathing change, as if she were angry, or close to tears. "I'll bet I do. I'll bet you it makes a difference. I'll bet you a dollar you wouldn't have kissed me if you'd known who I was!"

"Lady, you're on," Jason growled, and caught a handful of her hair. "I know who you are *now*." He brought her mouth to his, knowing by the sharp whisper of her indrawn breath that she was going to be open and ready for him.

She tasted of the wine, cool and sweet and as heady as a tropical night. It would be easy to lose himself in the kiss, to just go on and on, exploring the soft insides of her mouth, letting things grow and blossom in a natural way.

She leaned her weight against him and, laying her hand along his jaw, began a tentative exploration of the unfamiliar textures of his beard. When her hand slipped around to the back of his neck, he knew he had to put a stop to things now, or else he never would.

Pulling away from her, he said, "Lady, you owe me a buck." When he heard the beginnings of a protest, he kissed her again, hard and quickly, and tucked her head back under his chin. Then he swallowed a couple of times and concentrated on breathing deeply and slowly, while he held her and stroked her hair with the same easy rhythm. He held her like that, staring up into the darkness, until her own breathing grew heavy and even, telling him that the wine had had its way with her.

Lord, he thought. Sandra Jaimison Stewart. No wonder she'd looked a little bit familiar to him. He wasn't intimidated by that, but he sure as hell was impressed. And confused. He had more questions now than he'd had before he knew who she was, and he knew that he wasn't going to be able to leave the subject alone until he'd figured out all the answers. Starting with the answer to the biggest question of all.

What in the world was a former president's niece, the daughter of a U.S. senator, doing working wild mustangs in the wilds of central Idaho? What was a president's niece doing lying in his arms in a wrecked helicopter, stranded a hundred miles from civilization?

Jason knew that there wasn't the slightest danger of his falling asleep tonight, not if he drank a whole vat of wine.

Sandy came awake instantly, the echoes of the sound that had wakened her still hanging in the air. It was daylight; the air smelled of early morning. She was alone in the helicopter, lying on her side with her head pillowed on her arm.

She lay still, staring fuzzily at the underside of the pilot's seat, trying to stave off reality for a while longer, but it tumbled in on her anyway, with the crushing weight of a landslide. *Stranded*. She and Jason were stranded here in this valley, in the middle of one of the last great wilderness areas left in the country, probably the biggest outside Alaska. This was true wilderness, untouched and untraveled. Even Lewis and Clark had passed far to the north of here. There were no roads or hiking trails, no towns or trappers' cabins. They were absolutely alone.

A shrill scream slashed through the morning. Before the last echoes had died, Sandy was sitting up, every muscle and nerve in her body twanging. The horses! That was the sound that had wakened her from wine-deep sleep. With her heart in full gallop, she kicked off the sleeping bag and scrambled out of the helicopter.

Jason was standing at the edge of the mesa, looking down. As Sandy ran toward him, he heard the scrape of her boots on the dry ground and turned. His hair was wild this morning, as if he'd tried to tame it with his fingers and failed.

"Morning," he grunted, glancing at her.

"Morning." She felt breathless—from running, she told herself—and her heart was thundering, probably from the excitement of hearing the mustang's call. She was light-headed, too, but that was because of the wine she'd drunk last night, and from jumping up too quickly this morning.

She couldn't as easily explain the fact that the urge to touch him was as strong in the morning sunlight as it had been in the cold, lonely darkness. She couldn't explain or deny the impulse she'd had to run headlong into his arms.

"Friends of yours?" Jason said, jerking his head toward the rim of the mesa, then bringing his gaze to rest on the disordered tumble of her hair. Made self-conscious by the look in his eyes, she dragged it back from her face with one hand and began to twist it into its wrist-thick rope again.

"I wondered if they were still here," she said, walking over until she could see down into the canyon. Dust and the dull drumming of hoofbeats rose to meet her. Another shrill whinny rang out, then hung in the air, never quite dying away. There they were, the big bay rogue and his band. Seven mares and four colts, three of them spring foals, sturdy and well grown. The fourth... "Well, hello there, you little red rascal you," Sandy whispered to the colt trotting so earnestly at his mother's flank.

"I think the slide must have blocked the pass," Jason said. "They're trapped, just like we are."

Sandy threw him a hard, fierce glare of denial, then looked quickly back at the mustangs. As the sound of human voices reached the stallion's ears, he threw up his head, reared and wheeled, bugling a warning. In an instant the band had stopped its confused milling about at the base of the slide and was in full stampede, making for the meadow's wide open spaces. With her heart's thundering drowning out their hoofbeats, Sandy was barely aware that Jason had come to stand behind her until he spoke.

"That's something I've never seen before," he said softly, watching the horses race through the frost-burned grass, a cloud of sun-shot dust rising like golden vapor around them until they almost disappeared in it, like creatures of myth or fantasy.

"I'll never forget the first time I saw horses running wild and free," Sandy said slowly. She hesitated, pressing against the lump that always rose in her throat at that sight, then went on. "It was so exciting, I was so thrilled, and yet..." How could she explain the terrible *yearning?* "And yet I felt this awful sadness, too. I wanted to go with them, to be as free as they were. I felt...as though my soul were in prison, watching them through the bars."

She surrendered the rope of her hair to Jason's gentle tugging, letting him pull it behind her shoulder, where it unwound itself and tumbled unfettered down her back.

"I used to feel that way," he said, "watching dolphins play." She turned to stare at him and saw the look in his eyes her friend Bert had called sad. It came to her as a small shock that his eyes looked the way she felt. "I envied them," he went on, looking out over her head. "Only it was more than envy. It was...a kind of yearning."

"Yes," Sandy whispered, overcome by the fact that he had felt the same feelings, and more, that he had chosen the word to describe them. And isn't it funny, she thought, that people in their isolation, when they do discover a kindred spirit, view it as a genuine miracle?

"We can't have it, you know," Jason said flatly. She felt his hand rest for a moment on the back of her neck, warm and heavy, and then drop away. She looked quickly up at him and caught the bitter twist of his lips. "What we're yearning for is something we can't have—complete freedom. Freedom from responsibility, consequences, commitment—everything. I tried. God knows I tried. I chased those damn dolphins for years." He gave a sharp, bitter laugh, so cold and hard it made Sandy shudder. "And eventually I found out I couldn't be a dolphin. No matter how hard I tried, I still had the brain, the heart, the *memories* of Jason Rivers. So let me tell you something, lady.

If you're chasing those wild horses, you better give it up, because in *here*—'' he brushed her temple with the backs of his fingers ''—in here, you're always going to be Sandy Jaimison Stewart. You can't run away from that—ever.''

He turned abruptly and walked away from her, back toward the chopper. There was something defensive in the way he walked, with his hands jammed into his back pockets and his shoulders sort of hunched, that made Sandy wonder if he'd embarrassed himself, talking that way. It did seem like a strange conversation to be having, this first morning after being stranded in a hostile wilderness, when their thoughts should have been on more practical things, like food, shelter and survival. And then she thought that maybe it wasn't so strange after all, that maybe it was natural for people facing the possibility of death to search for meanings and answers.

In any case, she didn't want to put the subject aside. She felt as if she'd been left hanging, as if something were unfinished. Stalking off after Jason, she found him kneeling inside the helicopter, searching through her meager store of emergency supplies.

''Is that what you think I'm doing?'' she demanded of his back. ''Chasing wild horses?''

Without turning, he said evenly, ''I don't know. Are you?''

''No!'' And then, less certainly, ''I don't think I am.''

''Well,'' Jason grunted, ''I don't know if you're chasing something or running away, but you're sure as hell doing *some* kind of running.''

''Why do you say that?''

''What else would Sandy Jaimison Stewart be doing out here in this godforsaken wilderness?''

Say **Yes** to
romance

AND YOU'LL GET:

---

4 FREE BOOKS
A FREE CLOCK/
CALENDAR
A FREE SURPRISE GIFT

NO RISK • NO OBLIGATION
NO STRINGS • NO KIDDING

Say YES to free gifts worth over $20.00

Say YES to a rendezvous with romance, and you'll get 4 classic love stories—FREE! You'll get an attractive digital quartz clock/calendar—FREE! And you'll get a delightful surprise—FREE! These gifts carry a value of over $20.00—but you can have them without spending even a penny!

FREE HOME DELIVERY

Say YES to Silhouette and you'll enjoy the convenience of previewing 4 brand-new books delivered right to your home every month before they appear in stores. Each book is yours for only $2.49—26¢ less than retail, and there is no extra charge for postage and handling.

SPECIAL EXTRAS—FREE!

You'll get our monthly newsletter, packed with news of your favorite authors and upcoming books—FREE! You'll also get additional free gifts from time to time as a token of our appreciation for being a home subscriber.

Say YES to a Silhouette love affair. Complete, detach and mail your Free Offer Card today!

FREE—COMBINATION CLOCK/CALENDAR.

You'll love your new LCD digital quartz clock, which also shows the current month and date. This lovely lucite piece includes a handy month-at-a-glance calendar, or you can display your favorite photo in the calendar area. This is our special gift to you!

SILHOUETTE BOOKS®

FREE OFFER CARD

4 FREE BOOKS

FREE HOME DELIVERY

Place YES sticker here

FREE CLOCK/ CALENDAR

FREE SURPRISE BONUS

Please send me 4 Silhouette Intimate Moments® novels, free, along with my free combination clock/calendar and surprise gift as explained on the opposite page.

240 CIL YACU

Name _____
(PLEASE PRINT)

Address _____ Apt. _____

City _____

State _____ Zip _____

RUSH! FREE
GIFTS DEPT.

BUSINESS REPLY CARD

First Class   Permit No. 717   Buffalo, NY

Postage will be paid by addressee

Silhouette Books®
901 Fuhrmann Blvd.
P.O. Box 1867
Buffalo, New York 14240-9952

NO POSTAGE
NECESSARY
IF MAILED
IN THE
UNITED STATES

Sandy swore and sat down in the doorway, turning her back to him. "I wish I hadn't told you that. Now you see why I don't like to drink!"

"Wouldn't have made any difference," Jason said blandly. "I didn't know exactly who you were, but I had you pegged right from the start."

"Pegged?" Tremors of anger rippled through her chest.

"I knew you had to be running away from something."

"Oh?" she said softly. "And how did you know that?"

"I don't know. You just didn't fit."

"Didn't *fit?*" She shifted around to face him. "What, you mean the way I look? The way I talk? *What?* I swear, you men are all alike. All you see are externals. You don't know anything, you know that? You don't know a damn thing!"

And suddenly, without warning, she was crying.

Chapter 8

Jason turned toward her, still crouching, and balanced there, not touching or comforting her in any way, just watching her with a stony face and brooding eyes. After a few minutes, during which her natural pride jousted with an unfamiliar desire to be held and comforted, Sandy turned her back on him and swiped angrily at her cheeks with both hands.

"The only place I didn't fit," she said, feeling tight and precarious, "was *there*. At home, with my family." She drew in a breath, then let it out with great care. "I was always a misfit. A black sheep."

When Jason didn't respond to that she stole a glance at him and was surprised to see that while she'd been indulging in self-pity, he'd been making himself comfortable on the sleeping bag.

"Breakfast?" he said calmly, waving a plastic bowl full of peach cobbler at her. His gaze was cool and direct, like a dash of cold water. It made her angry, but more at herself than at him, angry for wanting warmth and comfort from someone who obviously wasn't capable of either.

Control restored, she took the cobbler and muttered a grudging, "Thanks."

"Spoon?"

"Sure." After a while, around a bite of cobbler, she mumbled, "I don't know why I did that. I mean, I don't usually."

"Of course not," Jason said with gentle bluntness. "Cowboys don't cry. Everybody knows that."

She flicked a glance at him, then looked quickly away, offering no more rebuttal than a mild snort. Although a smile was threatening, so was a new torrent of tears. All at once she knew with absolute certainty that she'd been wrong about Jason Rivers. Cold and uncaring? Oh no, far from it. She could feel the tenderness and compassion in him. But she could feel the fear in him, too, and knew that it was that fear, and not indifference, that made him distant.

She didn't know how she could feel it, because such insights were new to her, and she hadn't yet come to acknowledge their source. For now, she just hugged them to her and tucked them away in her heart for safekeeping.

"Oh . . . God," she said after a while, putting aside her empty dish and leaning her head back against the door frame with a deep sigh. "Jason, what are we going to do?"

"That," he said dryly, gathering up his bowl and hers, "is something we need to discuss."

"You know what I just realized? I don't even have a *brush*."

He laughed, but wondered if she were even aware of the absurdity of worrying about a hairbrush when they were faced with starvation. Fear burned cold in his belly as his fingers closed around the last morsel of food in the picnic basket—the smooth, waxy skin of an apple.

"Hey, listen," she insisted, "for someone with hair like mine, that's a real disaster, you know. At least you don't have to worry about a razor."

This time he heard the edge in her voice and knew that she was only trying, as he was, to hold fear at bay. "That's true," he said absently, curling his fingers around the apple, hefting its meager weight. He took it out of the basket and laid it on the sleeping bag between them. Her gaze unwillingly followed it, and he saw the slight movement of her throat as she swallowed.

"Well," she said, turning her back to him again, dangling her legs out the door of the chopper, "I guess I'd better at least try to get it braided again. I don't want to start looking like the queen of the jungle." Her laugh was breathless.

As she gathered her hair into her hands and pulled it over her shoulder, something in the way she moved made him wonder if she was crying again. He hoped not; her tears had made him feel achy and stiff, as if he were locked inside a tight, airless box. He had wanted to go to her, touch her, say comforting words, but for some reason he'd been unable to move or speak.

Right now, sitting in silence, studying the bowed nape of her neck, Jason knew that if he lifted his hand he could reach out and touch her hair. If he closed his eyes he could see it the way it had looked yesterday, rippling down over her body like a fall of silver water. He could smell the sun-warmed fragrance of it, feel the silky weight of it in his hands. He could braid it for her now, comb it with his fingers, smooth the wisps on her face and neck, then pull her back against him and wrap his arms around her and let physical closeness comfort them both.

He wanted to. He ached with that wanting. But he didn't touch her.

"I don't know what in the world I'm going to tie the end with," Sandy said, looking back over the thick rope of her hair to give him a rueful smile. "I'd give a lot for a rubber band or a shoelace right now. You don't happen to have anything I could use, do you?"

"Hmm," Jason muttered, reaching into his pocket. His fingers encountered something foreign, something he'd forgotten all about. Bemused, he drew out the scrap of lace-edged nylon and handed it to her.

She gave a small cough, half amused, half embarrassed. "Um, I don't think this is going to do the job, Jason."

"Here." He grunted as he unfolded himself and slipped past her, pausing to drop his pocketknife into her lap. "Cut it up. You don't really need it anyway."

Sandy watched him stalk across the plateau and drop out of sight beyond the rim. Well, she thought, I guess he *might* have meant that as a compliment.

She picked up the knife and stared at it, a small, compact weight, still warm from Jason's body. After a moment she opened it and began methodically to cut the straps off her bra.

By the time Jason came back, her braid, sporting a white bow, was once again hanging neatly down her back. She'd been busy in other ways, too. She'd dragged everything movable out of the helicopter and spread it out on the ground so they could take stock of what was there.

There was precious little: two sheepskin-lined jackets; the sleeping bag; the flashlight; some roadside flares; and the picnic basket, holding nothing edible now except for that one lonely apple. There was also the first aid kit, which she'd forgotten about when she was looking for something to tie up her braid. She could have used adhesive tape or a length of gauze bandage and saved herself the sacrifice of a perfectly good bra. Rope, a box of staples, a hammer and pliers, heavy leather work gloves. Small odds and ends—Jason's knife, the empty wine bottle, a tube of lip protector, her sunglasses and hat, a package of sugarless gum. The fishing pole.

"That's it?" Jason said, coming up behind her as she sat cross-legged, surveying the collection.

"That's it."

"No gun?"

"No." She threw him a shocked look. "I hate guns."

"I'm not crazy about 'em either, having seen firsthand what they're capable of," he said absently, squatting beside her and picking up the fishing pole. He gave it a couple of experimental casts, then tested the tension in the reel. "You might wish you had one, though. If there are fish in that creek we won't starve, but I think we're going to be damn tired of fish by the time we're rescued."

"Will we be?" Sandy asked in a brittle voice.

"Rescued?" Jason threw her a quick look. "It's at least a possibility. They're bound to miss us and start a search sooner or later."

"Later rather than sooner," Sandy mumbled.

"Why's that?"

She took a deep breath. "Because I've been known to stay away for more than a day or two at a time. That's why I keep the sleeping bag in here. With you here..." She stopped, coughed and looked away. "They'll probably just think we decided to, um, stay overnight someplace."

There was a little silence. She felt his eyes on her, but she didn't turn, and after a moment he stood up and dusted off his hands. "Okay, so it's later. But they will search. The question is,'' he muttered, more to himself than to her, "will they find us...?"

He walked slowly toward the helicopter, studying it. Sandy saw it now as he did—small, battered, dusty gray. It would be hard to spot from the air.

"We could build a fire," she said.

Jason's laugh was a hard, empty sound, like falling rock. "Sandy, it's hunting season. Even if somebody did spot smoke, they'd just think it was another hunter's fire."

"So," she said flatly, "it's apt to be a while. And meantime..." She took a deep breath and got stiffly to her feet. "It's September. At this elevation, the first snowstorms could come any day. The way I see it, we've got two choices. We can build a shelter and stay here until somebody finds us, or we can try to walk out ourselves."

He didn't answer. With her hands in her pockets and her shoulders hunched, Sandy stared fixedly at Jason's back and willed him to turn around, to make some sort of contact with her. She'd never felt so isolated in the company of another human being. She had the feeling that if she touched him now she would find that those broad shoulders and sculpted muscles weren't flesh at all, but something hard and unyielding, like granite. Chilled, she counted heartbeats until she saw his shoulders lift slightly with his indrawn breath.

"I have no particular desire to wait around for the snow." His voice sounded odd, almost metallic, and when he finally turned around to look at her, she wished he hadn't. His eyes were like black, empty holes.

Shaken without knowing why, she said, "Well, I guess we walk, then. Any ideas about which way?"

"I dunno, let's look at a map." And just like that, his manner became brisk, businesslike; the ghosts had been temporarily banished.

Jason's maps had been left with the rest of his equipment beside the hot spring, so they got Sandy's map out of the chopper and spread it on the ground.

"That's north," he muttered, getting a reckoning from the morning sun, "and that—" he jerked a thumb toward the slide-blocked canyon, "—is southeast. By far the best way out. Damn."

"Surely not the only way," Sandy declared, straightening to stare at the encircling mountains. "There must be another way out of here. We just have to find it."

Jason shook his head. "That pass would have taken us down to the lower elevations. Look at this—in any other direction, all we do is run into more mountains. Higher mountains. It would take us weeks to walk out that way, and if winter comes . . ." He let his voice trail off.

Sandy took a deep breath and released it slowly.

From out of the meadow came the drumming of hooves. She walked to the edge of the mesa to watch the band of mustangs come racing down the valley, then circle to come to a milling halt in a cloud of dust.

"They're looking for a way out, too," she said softly when Jason joined her. "Look at him. Isn't he marvelous?"

The stallion had veered away from the herd and was approaching at a full gallop, head high, mane and tail streaming. As he drew near to where they stood watching from the heights, he shook his head and then dropped it, making strange, serpentine movements along the ground. Right below them, he stopped dead, lifted his muzzle toward them and stood poised, nostrils flared, flanks quivering. Then, with a long, earsplitting scream, he whirled and raced back to the band.

Beside him, Jason felt Sandy sigh, as if she'd been holding her breath. "Magnificent," she whispered.

"Doesn't seem pleased," Jason commented.

Sandy chuckled. "He's angry. And frustrated. His escape route is blocked. And I swear, I think he knows I'm here, too."

"You sound like you know him."

"Oh yeah, I know that big red rogue." She smiled up at him. A stray breeze stirred the wisps of hair around her face. "I've been trying for years to cull his band, but he always manages to get away somehow. He's smart, and he's not afraid of anything—except being corralled. I'll never forget one time. I'd managed to drive him and his band into a blind, and we were struggling to get the barricade in place. Next thing I knew, that stallion was coming at me like a juggernaut—knocked me flat on my back. There I lay with the wind knocked out of me, half under the logs, while the whole band went sailing right over the top of me, one by one. I wasn't stepped on or kicked, but I've never been so scared in my life. That's the only time in my life I really thought I was going to die."

Incredibly, there were no shadows in her face now; it was sunny with laughter. And why not? Jason thought. It was hard to believe in the possibility of mortality on a morning like this, with blue skies overhead, and the air soft and warm and smelling of pine and sun-baked earth. Hard to believe how quickly the air could turn cold, and those same skies bring horror, darkness, death....

"Shucks," he said with a snap of his fingers. "There goes my idea of riding out of here in style."

"Riding? You mean, on one of those mustangs?" He'd expected her to laugh, but she didn't. She looked at him, then back at the horses. "You know..."

"Come on, Sandy, I was kidding. You just said that stallion almost killed you."

"Oh, we'd never be able to catch him—and if we did, nobody'd ever ride him. But I was just thinking that there are a couple of his mares that have to be getting pretty old. That buckskin, for instance, the one with the little colt. I think maybe that's why she had such a late foal this year." She turned a somber look on him, the smoky kind that made his belly throb. "I was going to try to pick them up in the roundup this year," she said in a low voice. "That colt probably won't survive the winter. None of them will, Jason, if they can't find a way out of here. There won't be any food when the snow falls."

"Hey," Jason said fiercely, catching her by the arms and giving her a quick, hard shake. He hated seeing that dark, scared look in her eyes. "They'll find a way out—and so will we. You got that?"

She pressed her lips tightly together and nodded. "Yeah. You're right. We'll probably find another pass without any trouble at all. Besides," she said brightly, "they've probably figured out that we're missing by this time. Maybe we'll be picked up before we even have a chance to look."

"Sure," Jason said. And maybe, he thought grimly as he watched the mustangs race across the meadow, we'll fly out of here on the back of Pegasus.

The first thing they had to do was move everything they could out of the slide area. Jason knew there was still a real possibility of an aftershock from that quake. For want of a better idea, and because he'd left the rest of his gear there, they agreed on the hot spring for their new campsite, but though it was the logical thing to do, he had some misgivings about it.

"Not the greatest smell in the world," he muttered as they approached, voicing the only fear he dared mention.

Sandy glanced at him, but all she said was, "Yeah." She sounded out of breath, though her load wasn't that heavy, and they hadn't set a particularly demanding pace.

Ahead, through the trees, Jason could see steam twisting and curling like ghosts above an eerie, almost surreal landscape, like a Hollywood set decorator's idea of hell. Even now, in the clear light of morning, the place seemed haunted to him; a natural collecting ground for erotic fantasies and forbidden passions, the permanent setting for his own waking dreams.

Jason swore silently, cursing himself for having allowed those dreams to become reality, even for a little while. Stealing a glance at Sandy, he saw that her tan had a moist, rosy sheen and knew that the ghosts were haunting her, too. *Damn!* He knew he never should have allowed himself to hold her the way he had yesterday. He knew he should have turned around the minute he saw her standing there with her hair hanging down her back and her arms raised to the sun, and headed straight back to the chopper.

But, as he knew all too well, the road to hell was strewn with should-have-dones.

What was done was done; it was what he did from now on that mattered. And now, more than ever, he dared not let himself get too close. For his own sake. He didn't think he could survive if he let himself get too close to this woman and then lost her.

They found Jason's gear right where he'd left it, at the edge of the trees.

"I guess we can leave everything here while we look for some kind of shelter," Jason said as they unloaded the things they'd brought from the helicopter. "I don't think anybody's going to steal it, do you?"

Sandy was looking fixedly at the meager pile. In a curiously expressionless voice she said, "I don't know about you, but I'm hungry."

Neither of them said it, but both of them were thinking that hunger was something they might have to get used to.

"There's the apple," Jason reminded her and, bending over, searched through the picnic basket until he found it. He held it for a moment, weighing it in his hand, then polished it on his sleeve and held it out to Sandy. She took it from him, held it for a moment, then handed it back.

"You eat it," she said, swallowing.

Jason smiled. "We'll share. You first."

Smudgy gray eyes clung to his. He watched her lift the apple to her mouth, watched her lips part, baring her even white teeth. Her eyes closed; her teeth pierced the flesh of the apple with a loud crunching sound, and juice spangled her lips. Saliva pooled in Jason's mouth, and he swallowed.

Without a word, she passed the apple to him. As he bit into it, he watched her chew and swallow, then lick the juice from her lips. The apple might have been ambrosia, but he didn't taste it. He felt its coolness in his throat, but when he licked his lips, he tasted *her* there.

They ate the apple slowly, passing it back and forth, each savoring the other's portion as well as his own. They ate it all, including the core, and when it was gone, they stood gazing at each other and smiling the same little half smile. Jason felt as though his half of the apple had gotten caught in his esophagus, making a lump in the general vicinity of his heart.

"Hey," he said gruffly, "what do you say we go fishin'?"

"I hope you're better at this than I am," Sandy said, giving the bedraggled fly on the end of her line a doubtful look. "I've always considered fishing more or less an excuse for napping in the middle of the day."

"Give me that," Jason said, looking alarmed. "Go dig some worms or something."

Laughter bubbled up in Sandy and spilled over, blending with the creek's chuckle. As she lay back on her elbows on the grassy bank, feeling the high-altitude sun burn through her shirt and jeans, smelling the rich hay smell of dry grass, listening to the low whine of insects and the soothing chatter of the creek, it was hard to remember that they were caught up in a life and death struggle for survival.

"Okay, Mr. Expert," she said lazily, "be my guest. You can call me when dinner's ready."

Jason's answering chuckle nearly covered the whickering sound. Sandy sat up straight, all thoughts of a nap in the sunshine banished for good. "Did you hear that?"

"Yeah, I did. Look, there they are."

Sandy stood beside him, shading her eyes with her hand. Rogue and his band were there in the meadow with them, grazing in the open near a clump of aspens on the other side of the creek. The stallion kept a watchful eye on the two intruders, always placing himself between them and his band, lifting his head to gaze at them while he chewed.

"You know what this means?" Sandy asked in a hushed voice. "They've accepted us. We're a part of their world now."

Leaving Jason to his fishing, she began to walk slowly along the creek, moving closer to the mustangs, pausing whenever the stallion's head turned her way. The herd continued to ignore her presence and graze placidly, except for the little russet foal, who frisked and scampered about the fringes of the group, racing with his own shadow. When he strayed too far, his mother called him back with the gentle whickerings that had first alerted Sandy to the herd's presence.

And then, suddenly, the stallion's cry echoed through the air, and the band exploded into flight. They didn't go far—just a dozen yards or so—before they once again settled down to graze.

"So, that's as close as you'll let me come, is it?" Sandy said aloud, chuckling as the stallion's head swung toward her for a long, measuring look. "Well, okay then—for now."

She dropped cross-legged into the grass and began to poke idly through the loamy soil with her fingers. Jason *had* mentioned digging for worms. Grasping a small clump of coarse meadow grass, she pulled it up by the roots and peered into the hole it had left. Then, with a sharp exclamation, she began to dig in earnest, first with her hands, then with a stick.

So engrossed was she in what she was doing that she forgot everything else, even the mustangs, until a flicker of something reddish caught the corner of her eye. She looked up, and her heart nearly jumped into her mouth. There, on the other side of the creek, not ten feet away, stood the little bay colt, neck outstretched, nostrils flaring, every muscle in his body quivering with curiosity.

Not moving, barely breathing, Sandy whispered, "Well, hello there, you little rascal." The colt's ears twitched; he pulled his head back, but he didn't bolt. Encouraged, Sandy began to talk in a low, soothing murmur, saying anything that came to mind, saying nothing in particular, just making sounds. The colt took one step closer.

The air was suddenly filled with sounds: pounding hooves; the mare's low whinny; the stallion's scream.

Paralyzed, Sandy watched the stallion bear down on her and the foal, ears flattened, head snaking low. With a frightened whinny, the colt eluded his sire's slashing teeth and raced for the safety of his mother's side. A moment later, with the stallion's warning still hanging in the air, the entire band disappeared into the trees.

"Sandy? What the hell?" It was Jason, but it didn't sound like him.

Whirling on him, the incredible thrill of the encounter with the colt still quivering through her, she cried, "Jason, did you see that? Did you see it? He came right up to me! I nearly died!"

She'd never seen a man as awesome in anger as Jason was at that moment. Her throat dried up, choking off words. He was like a mythical god, with lightning in his eyes and thunder in his voice.

"Yeah, you did—you might have! What in bloody hell were you trying to do, huh? Get yourself *killed?*"

Chastened, Sandy sat open-mouthed while Jason hurled the thing he'd been carrying—a piece of wood as long and thick as his arm—into the grass. She'd never heard him shout before. She'd never even seen him really angry. It scared her a lot more than the stallion's charge.

"Jason," she said, reaching toward him, but afraid to move closer, afraid to touch him, "I'm sorry. I..." She finished in a lame whisper. "I'm sorry."

For a few minutes he stood with his back to her, breathing hard. When he turned, his face still looked dark and strained, but the savage light in his eyes had dimmed.

"Don't...ever do that." His voice sounded raw, and it cracked on the last word. After that, he just stood there, looking at her. Looking back at him, unable to move, impaled by those terrible eyes, Sandy felt a perilous urge to cry.

"Look," she said at last, in a high, desperate voice, pointing to the ground near her feet. "Look what I found!"

Jason stared at the pile of small, brown, onion-looking things and muttered, "What are they?"

"Camas bulbs! I've been digging them up. Jason, they're edible!"

"Camas?" He looked and sounded skeptical. "Never heard of them. Are you sure they're not poisonous?"

Sandy snorted, relieved that he seemed to have forgotten his anger, relieved to hear him sounding like himself again. "Oh, ye of little faith! The Nez Percé ate them. Lewis and Clark ate them. I guess we can, too. They'll go nicely with the fish you've caught—assuming you *have* caught any fish?"

"Oh, ye of little faith," Jason said smugly, lifting the lid of the picnic basket to reveal at least a dozen small, silvery trout.

"A veritable feast," Sandy said with a sigh, dislodging the last of the camas bulbs from the coals and rolling it onto the rocks to cool. They'd tried them raw and they'd tried them roasted; the best that could be said for them was that they were edible.

The fish, however, were delicious. The last of them were still sizzling over the fire, skewered like hot dogs on green willow sticks. Sandy picked up one of the sticks and blew on the fish to cool it, then offered it to Jason.

"No thanks." His voice sounded lazy. "I believe I've had enough."

Sandy knew just how he felt. With blue skies overhead, the smell of pine smoke in the air, and the fish dripping aromatically in the glowing coals, this seemed like a picnic, a relaxing little camp-out. She felt like stretching out in the warm sunshine and taking a nap.

At the moment, sitting with his back against a boulder, his legs extended in front of him, arms folded on his chest, Jason looked as if he might do just that. His eyes were closed, giving Sandy an opportunity to study him unawares. And, as always when she thought about Jason, most of her thoughts were questions.

Some were simple, like noticing the shadows under his eyes and wondering whether he'd slept at all last night. Some were complex. Why did he withdraw from her? And some disquieting. Why had he been so angry this morning in the meadow? Some were dangerous. What would have happened yesterday if there hadn't been a landslide? What would it be like to make love with him?

Dangerous. Jason's eyes were open now, looking straight into hers, and she felt as if he could read her thoughts. His gaze was veiled but steady; it held her mesmerized, so she couldn't look away. She opened her mouth to say something, then couldn't think of anything to say. Her cheeks grew warm and her body heavy.

Still holding her gaze, Jason reached into his shirt pocket and drew out his cigarettes. Sandy's eyes fell to his lips as he put the cigarette between them, and unconsciously she licked hers, tasting him there. . . .

Jason flicked the lighter and touched its flame to the end of his cigarette, watching Sandy's image waver in the heat. Then a chill wafted through him, scattering erotic daydreams.

"Here," he said roughly, tossing the lighter into Sandy's lap. "You'd better keep it. I don't know how many flicks there are left in this thing."

When the lighter landed in her lap, Sandy gave a little gasp, as if he'd startled her out of a daydream, then nodded and pocketed it without a word.

Jason drew his knees up and, resting his forearms on them, smoked in silence while he stared flinty-eyed at the mountains that surrounded them. Not his last cigarette—he had a few left in the pack. He'd just have to light them with a brand from the fire from now on.

He needed to be thinking about things like that, things like food and shelter and getting out of here before the snow fell. Basic elements of survival. He had no business letting his mind wander off into some erotic fantasy. He couldn't afford the luxury of thinking about sex right now.

But, something deep within him insisted on pointing out, sex is a basic element of survival, too.

Chapter 9

The silence lengthened. Neither of them seemed to know what to do with it until Sandy coughed and said, "I don't think there are enough fish for both tonight and tomorrow morning. Do you think we ought to go catch some more?"

"We?" Relieved to be dealing once more with the concrete, Jason lifted a sardonic eyebrow. "Go catch some more, huh? Just like that?"

"Sure," she said with a little half smile. "I figure you've got the magic touch."

Jason snorted. "Nothing magic about it."

"Couldn't prove it by me."

"All it takes is knowin' how," he said, getting up and bestowing a smile of masculine superiority on her. "Nothin' to it. Come on, I'll teach you."

"Are you sure you can? I've drowned an awful lot of worms."

"Don't know why not," Jason drawled. "I taught my kid brother, so I guess I can teach you." He turned as he bent to pick up the fishing pole, hiding his face from her view.

On the way down to the creek, Sandy screwed up her courage and said, "Jason?"

"Hmm?"

"You said it was a long time ago. I was wondering—how did your brother die?"

Silence. And then, "It was an accident. Skiing."

"Was he ... very young?"

"He was fourteen. Just."

They tramped a little way in silence, and then Sandy said, "Jason?"

"Hmm?"

"Were you there when it happened?"

Another silence. "Yes. I was."

"Oh..." Sandy said, her voice breaking. She finished in a whisper. " ... God."

By the time they'd restocked their larder with trout and camas bulbs, there wasn't time to do much besides find temporary shelter and lay in enough firewood to last the night. The days, Jason observed grimly, were growing short.

In a rocky outcropping near the bathing pools they found a V-shaped crevice, wide enough at the entrance to accommodate the sleeping bag, with room for the rest of their gear farther back. It was crude, and wouldn't be any shelter at all if it rained, but Sandy seemed pleased with it.

"Look at this, hot and cold running water *and* a view. Do you know what a place like this would cost you in Washington?"

Jason, who was down on his hands and knees gouging out a basin for a fire with the claw end of the hammer, looked up at her and grunted, "Without a roof?"

"Minor detail," she said with an airy wave of her hand. And then, thoughtfully gazing at the site, "Hmm. You know, with a roof, this place wouldn't be bad. A few logs laid across the top, some pine boughs..."

"Isn't it a little small?" Jason asked, catching a droplet of perspiration with the back of his hand.

"All right, look—we add a little lean-to out here. It would be easy, see, just put the logs here and here—"

"Jeez," Jason said, laughing, "you sound like a Girl Scout!"

Sandy gave him an affronted glare. "I'll have you know I *was* a Girl Scout—and a darn good one, too. I had more badges than anybody in my troop."

"You mean to tell me," Jason drawled, mocking her gently, "that the Stewart kids got to be Scouts and everything, just like regular kids?"

"Jason," she said reflectively, gazing out across the valley, "we got to do *everything*. I had the most wonderful childhood, everything any little girl could possibly wish for." Her expression was dreamy, and a little sad. Catching herself, she laughed and squatted beside him, hugging her knees. "And I don't mean just the things money can buy, either. I had parents who loved me, brothers and sisters, aunts and uncles, cousins to play with. I had dogs and cats, skinned knees and snowball fights, birthday cakes with candles, visits from the tooth fairy...." Her voice trailed off. She looked away, but not before he saw her press her lips tightly together. To stop a threatening tremor? he wondered.

"So," he said softly, knowing every word she spoke was sinking him deeper, pulling him closer, but somehow unable to stop himself from asking the question. "Why did you leave?"

"I grew up," she replied in a flat voice, sitting down hard on the ground.

"What's that supposed to mean?"

Her smile was wry. "When I was little, you see, I didn't know that we were *the* Stewarts." She looked at him, waiting for him to comment. When he didn't, she gave a short, dry laugh and leaned back on her hands. "I guess I just didn't notice that there were always photographers, reporters and bodyguards around. They were just a bunch of people who were nice to me, who pampered me and gave me chewing gum—which I wasn't supposed to have, because it was bad for my teeth." She grimaced, showing him her perfect, healthy white smile. He laughed softly in appreciation, and she shrugged and went on.

"By the time I realized what it all meant, I was supposed to be an active part of it. It was expected of all of us, and everybody else loved doing it—the public appearances, charity obligations and so on. I never did. I always hated it. I felt like such a misfit. I used to fantasize, the way kids do, that I was really adopted, or there'd been a mix-up in the hospital or something. I used to run away to the stables to avoid reporters, or to get out of some public appearance or other. It was the only place where I could relax and just be myself, I guess. The only thing I ever wanted was to just . . . be myself."

"So eventually, instead of running away to the family stables, you ran away from home, is that it?" His tone was ironic.

She turned her head to look at him. He didn't know whether it was a trick of the waning light, but her eyes seemed to darken as he watched. For some reason, the look in them made him feel ashamed.

"What did you do in high school, Jason?" she asked evenly. "Play football? Basketball? Go out with the guys for burgers and fries? Take girls to dances or the movies? Make out in the back of your dad's pickup truck? Do you know how I went to my senior prom? There were four of us, me, my date—and I had to ask *him,* by the way—and two secret service guys."

With controlled anger in her movements, she stood up and brushed off the seat of her pants. "I'm going to take a bath," she announced in disgust, and stalked off toward the bathing pools.

Poor little rich girl, Jason said disdainfully to himself, staring after her. It was the only way he could shield himself from the bombardment of mental images of a shy, coltish teenager with long silver hair and smoky eyes, trying desperately to cope with a life of notoriety she hadn't asked for.

It was full dusk and growing nippy when Sandy got back to the campsite. Jason was sitting cross-legged on the sleeping bag before a nicely laid—and unlit—fire.

"You have the lighter," he reminded her when she complained through chattering teeth. "What's the matter? I thought you just got out of a nice warm tub."

"I did, but since the maid forgot the towels, I had to dress *wet.* I'm f-freezing."

Jason "Tsk'd" gently and said, "Come here." He stood up and shook out the sleeping bag, then draped it over her shoulders. "Bundle up," he murmured in her ear as his arms folded her close. "Don't catch cold."

The embrace was brief and brotherly. "Better?" Jason asked gruffly, and when she nodded, he let go of her and stepped back. "Ahem . . . the lighter?"

"Oh," Sandy muttered, still shivering. She dug it out of her pocket and gave it to him. He dropped to one knee and touched its flame to tinder. The fire flared and crackled, but for Sandy, the cold had returned the moment he'd released her.

"Have a seat," Jason said cheerfully as he reached for a willow stick and neatly skewered a fish. "Dinner will be ready in a minute."

Muttering a grudging, "Thanks," Sandy hitched closer to the fire, but she kept her face turned away, toward the shadows. He doesn't understand, she thought bleakly. No one ever does.

"So," Jason asked conversationally, "how did you manage to escape?"

She turned slowly to stare at him. "Escape?"

"Yeah; from your family."

For a few minutes she struggled with the memories in silence, the long habit of reticence fighting the faint hope that he might, after all, understand. "That's funny," she murmured at last. "That's exactly how I thought of it—escape." She went on slowly, tentatively, not quite trusting him, but wanting so badly to make him understand. "I thought, when I went away to college, that that was what I was doing. What I found out instead was that there was no escape. Uncle Jack might only be in the White House for eight years, but we were always going to be *the* Stewarts. No matter where I went, for the rest of my life I was going to be Sandra . . . Jaimison . . . Stewart."

She drew the words out, like a judge pronouncing sentence.

"But," Jason pointed out, "you *did* escape."

"What I did," Sandy said heavily, "was more like get a divorce."

Jason asked, "How can you divorce your whole family?" But there was a hollowness inside him, because he knew the answer. Separations, by divorce, or by death...they both came with their own kind of anguish.

"It was the summer after my second year at college," she told him as they ate flaky-tender fish right off the willow sticks, burning their mouths and fingers. "I had this friend—she was from Colorado. Her folks had this guest ranch, and she worked there in the summertime. She invited me to come and work, too. Jason, it was wonderful. Out there everything was so big and wide and open. No one knew me. No one cared. I was just plain Sandy Stewart, and all that mattered was how well I could ride a horse or muck out a stall. And then, of course..." She shrugged matter-of-factly, as if that said it all. "I saw the wild horses. I made up my mind right then that I was never going back. And I didn't."

"And your family?" Jason frowned at her, his eyes picking up the flickering firelight. "How did they take it?"

She shrugged and looked down at her hands. "I don't know."

"Do you mean to tell me, they don't know where you are?"

She shook her head; he saw her swallow and wince, as if something had caught in her throat. "I'm sure they do. They have the resources to find me no matter what I do, so I just asked them not to try to contact me, and they haven't."

"And you haven't contacted them?"

She shook her head and looked down again, hiding her face from him. Her voice sounded muffled. "I had to do it that way. With a family like mine, it's all or nothing, don't you see?"

"Yeah, I do," Jason said softly. "What I don't understand is why they let you get away with it."

She shrugged and said simply, "They love me."

"A great deal, it seems to me. And you—"

"They loved me too much!" She whirled on him with harsh, angry words. "Damn it, they were smothering me, killing me. They held me so tightly they were crushing the life out of me. Only, when I told them what they were doing, they loved me enough—"

She stopped with a choked sound, and Jason finished for her. "To let you go...."

"Yes!" And then she was crying, covering her face with both hands and crying with great, shuddering sobs. "Oh God, Jason, I've been sitting here thinking. And I realized that this time even they don't know where I am. If we die out here, they'll never know what happened to me!"

Jason watched her for several moments in stony silence, feeling as if he were being torn apart. When he couldn't stand it any longer, he carefully laid aside his half-eaten trout and got to his feet.

"Guess I'll go take a bath," he muttered hoarsely. As he passed her, he was unable to help himself; he laid his hand on her head, then let it slip down to her shoulder. Giving it a hard squeeze, he rasped, "I'll be back...." and left her there, still crying.

The moon was rising. A brilliant, three-quarter autumn moon that cast eerie shadows across a ghostly landscape. As Jason lifted his face to its cold light and drew in painful lungfuls of frosty air, he felt awfully close to panic. He felt like a man hanging by his fingernails from a precipice.

I'm falling, he thought. And I don't know how to stop myself.

The sound came without warning, as shocking as a cry of terror, rending the night. Fear crawled across Sandy's skin like the touch of a cold, dead hand. Frozen in a half crouch, shaking from head to foot, she managed a hoarse whisper. *"Jason?"*

At the first crunch of his shoe on gravel, before he'd even reached the firelight, she launched herself headlong into his arms, sobbing with relief.

"Oh God, Jason! I thought—what *was* that?"

"Mountain lion," he grunted matter-of-factly, staggering a little from the impact of her body. "I think." After what seemed an eternity, his arms came around her.

Sandy relaxed, sighing, and rested her forehead against his jaw. "Mountain lion. Oh boy." His beard was soft and slightly moist, unlike his voice, which sounded like windblown sand.

"Never heard one before?"

"Never in my life. It sounded like someone dying. I thought . . . I don't know what I thought."

A tremor passed through his body, and his arms tightened around her, then eased. "All right now?" Unwillingly, she nodded. His arms fell away from her as he took a step back, then turned stiffly toward the fire.

"Jason, I . . ."

He looked back. "What is it?"

Please hold me. She ached with longing. "Nothing," she mumbled, jamming her hands into the pockets of her jacket and staring fixedly at the toes of her boots. "Never mind."

There was a waiting silence, and then she heard the scrape of his shoes and the rustle of his clothing as he settled himself on the ground by the fire.

What could she say to him? She had too much pride to ask the questions that had been eating away at her ever since yesterday, when he'd kissed her and held her in a passionate embrace, almost on this very spot. To her, that kiss had been a taste of something wonderful, a promise unfulfilled. But to him?

Jason, she cried silently, I don't understand you. Why did you kiss me like that and then act as if you didn't even want to touch me?

Oh sure, she thought in bitter self-derision, I know. I hurled myself practically stark naked into your arms. Automatic male responses took over. It was just a kind of temporary lust-induced madness.

Only she didn't believe it. She didn't know why, but she knew in the depths of her woman's soul that Jason wasn't indifferent to her. She knew it with the same instincts that had told her this morning that he wasn't indifferent to her tears. And as they had then, her instincts gave her an answer to her question.

Jason was afraid. Afraid of her. Afraid of getting too close, of getting involved with her, of letting himself care. He might want her every bit as much as she wanted him—in fact, she was almost sure he did—but he'd go on denying them both that closeness, because his fear was greater than his desire.

Who needs this? Sandy thought in loneliness, frustration and anger. So the guy's got problems. Who needs it?

But as she gazed at Jason's broad shoulders, at the damp feathers of hair on the back of his neck, she had an almost overwhelming longing to go to him and slip her arms around his neck, to lean forward against him and lay her cheek next to his. What would he do, she wondered, her pulse quickening with the thought, if I slipped my hands inside his shirt? If I touched my lips to his ear?

And what would I do, she thought sardonically, if he turned me down cold? She didn't really think she could carry it off, anyway. She wasn't exactly experienced at seduction.

Silently, she went about spreading out the sleeping bag in the mouth of the shelter. Though it was only a few feet from the fire, and from Jason, he didn't look at her, or comment.

"Well," she said finally, "I guess I'll turn in."

"Okay." He reached for another piece of wood to add to the fire. "Good night."

"Good night. Jason?"

"Yeah?"

"Are you going to sit up all night?"

"For a while longer." His eyes crinkled with his smile. "That sleeping bag's a little small for two."

After a moment Sandy said, "Want to take turns?"

"Don't worry, if I get sleepy, I'll roust you out or tell you to move over. You go ahead and get some sleep."

Sandy lay awake listening to night sounds: the rush of wind and the gurgle of water; a bird's soft cry—an owl, probably. She could hear the horses down in the meadow. They were restless tonight, probably because of the lion, but wherever he was, the big cat didn't scream again. She heard Jason get up and add more wood to the fire, but he never did come share her sleeping bag.

When Sandy awoke, the sunlight was just reaching across the crags of the eastern mountains, touching the frosty meadow like Midas's fingers, turning it to spun gold.

Jason wasn't anywhere in sight, but by the time she had stretched herself awake, had crawled out of the warm sleeping bag and was hobbling stiffly to the fire, she could see him coming up the slope with an armload of wood.

When he saw her he called out a cheerful, "Good morning."

"Morning," Sandy said huskily, extending her arms high above her head, then dropping forward from the waist until her palms touched the ground. Straightening, she groaned loudly and rubbed the small of her back.

"Sleep well?" Jason inquired facetiously.

"Yeah . . . except somebody put rocks in my bed."

"I'll speak to the maid." His chuckle sounded relaxed, but the dark hollows under his eyes made her wonder if he'd closed them at all last night. After dropping the wood beside the fire, he dusted his hands and stood smiling down at her. Sandy's breath caught, then resumed, more shallow than before. "I'd offer you a cup of coffee, but . . ." His shrug was eloquent.

"I'd *kill* for a cup of coffee," Sandy sighed, then brightened. "Hey, I saw trapper's tea down in the meadow. How 'bout—"

"Nothing to boil water in," Jason pointed out regretfully.

"Rats, that's true." Again, inspiration struck. "There's boiling water in the spring!"

"I wouldn't drink that if I were you," he warned, turning serious. "I don't know what's in it."

"You could test it," Sandy suggested. "You have the equipment."

"Yeah, I do." He gave her an intent, measuring look. "But I don't think we're going to be here long enough for it to matter one way or the other, do you?"

"No, I guess not," Sandy agreed quickly. And then, "You still think we ought to try to hike out of here?"

Jason drew a deep breath and looked up at the sky. Nothing moved across its vastness but a hawk, balancing on an air current high above the meadow. "Yeah, I do. If anybody's looking, they're not looking in the right place, and we could have a storm any day. Be realistic, Sandy. How long do you really think we can survive here?"

After a cold little silence, Sandy said, "Okay, but we can't just take off walking, either. At least here we know we've got food, water, shelter. Out there, who knows what we'll find—and it could still snow any day!"

They faced each other, seeing grim awareness mirrored in each other's eyes. Finally Jason took a deep breath and let it out through his mouth, puffing his cheeks like a runner preparing for a race. "All right, why don't we do some exploring today? See what we can find? And at the same time we can look for something to build a roof on that shelter, and maybe something to eat besides fish and those damn roots."

"Okay," Sandy murmured, agreeing because she was fully aware that the alternatives weren't any better.

It was early afternoon when they came across the avalanche scar. It wasn't far from their camp—they'd almost completed a circle of the valley and had come upon it from the opposite direction—but it was on a south-facing slope, so it wasn't visible from down in the valley.

Sandy thought at first it was a burn.

"No," Jason said flatly. "Avalanche." He went on to point out in a curiously toneless voice how the fallen trees were all pointing the same way—downhill. It was an old one, he told her, several years, at least. The wood was decaying, the new vegetation well grown.

But Sandy had already discovered that for herself and was moving out into the vast, open area rampant with red grouseberry and dotted with young evergreens.

"Oh, Jason, look! It's like a supermarket!" She whirled, arms spread wide to encompass it all: thickets of wild rose, heavy with orange rose hips; tangles of currant and gooseberry bushes, some with a few overlooked berries still clinging to low-hanging branches. A bird flew up, flushed from cover by her intrusion. A grouse of some kind, or perhaps a partridge, Sandy thought, her mouth watering. If only they could find a way to kill it.

"This is great!" she called to Jason, bending over to pick up a tapering log no bigger around than her arm. "There's plenty of wood here for the fire *and* a shelter." When there was no answer she looked up and saw that he was still standing where she'd left him, hip deep in brush, staring up at the scarred mountainside. There was something about the way he was just standing there, as if, Sandy thought, he'd turned to stone—or wood. He looked like one of the broken stumps.

She went over to him and put a hand on his arm. "Jason?"

"Yeah?" His eyes burned at her from shadowed sockets. "Sorry. I was just thinking."

"What about?" For some reason she was whispering.

He waved a hand. "Nothing. Just . . . about the kind of force it takes to cause destruction like this, I guess." After a moment he went on briskly. "Well, I guess we've got our work cut out for us, if we're going to sleep indoors tonight."

His mouth stretched in a grin, but Sandy felt no urge at all to smile in return.

On the way back to the scar after leaving their first load of wood at the campsite, Sandy listened to the steady swish-swish of brush against their pant legs and felt her heartbeat grow loud in the silence that yawned between them. Tension rolled in her stomach.

At last, screwing up all the courage she had, she said, "Jason?"

"Hmm?"

"The accident—the one that killed your brother—it was an avalanche, wasn't it?"

He walked steadily on for a dozen paces, then said simply, "Yes."

That was all, but no more was necessary. For Sandy, all the pieces fell neatly into place; all the questions were answered.

Jason's brother had died in an avalanche. Jason had been there; most probably the avalanche had caught him, too. But his brother, just fourteen, had died. And Jason had survived.

"I'm a survivor, don't you know that?"

He blames himself, Sandy thought. She felt cold and sick, sharing the ache of a wound that had never healed.

She thought she knew now why Jason was afraid. He was afraid of loving...and then losing the one he loved.

The horses seemed restless tonight. In the red glow of dusk Jason could see them milling about down in the meadow, could hear their squeals and the sporadic drumming of their hooves. He leaned against the granite walls of the shelter, smoking, watching them and thinking that the restlessness must be contagious.

He was tired. His body was, anyway, and his mind should have been, after two nights without sleep. Instead, it seemed to be working in a kind of fever. Something was happening to him here in this place, some sort of crisis. No big surprise, he supposed; he was probably long overdue for one. Though he'd never believed in such things, he was beginning to wonder if he was on a collision course with destiny.

Fifteen years ago Jared had died in a place a lot like this, while *he* had lived. Jason had spent the last fifteen years of his life running away from that. He'd come back finally, just to do a job, thinking he could skirt the thing and go away again without having to face it. Fate, it seemed, had had other ideas.

Fate had hauled him up by the scruff of the neck, given him a good shake, then set him down in this valley and said, "Here now, Jason Rivers. You are going to meet this thing head-on, once and for all! You're either going to lick it, or it'll lick you."

Well, he thought, he'd met it head-on, all right. But the battle was still raging, and the victory, as far as he could see, was still pretty much up in the air.

He just wondered how much longer he was going to be able to postpone sleep.

He pushed himself away from the rocks and walked around to the mouth of the shelter, tossing his cigarette into the fire on the way. He gave the roof of logs and pine boughs an experimental shake, testing its stability, and made a little noise of satisfaction. Not a half-bad job, actually. They'd even gotten a lean-to over the entrance. Sandy had called it cozy.

Stooping to look inside, he noticed that the sleeping bag was gone; she must have taken it with her to the bathing pools. He noticed that she'd spread a thick mat of pine needles to make a spongy mattress on the hard dirt floor. He thought it might even be comfortable.

He backed out of the shelter, pausing to add several logs to the fire before moving past it to stand at the perimeter of the light. The horses were still down there. Though it had grown too dark to see them, he could hear their squeals and grunts, their fitful stirrings and thumpings.

He felt an itchiness, though there was nothing he could find to scratch.

Jason felt, rather than heard, Sandy come back to the campfire. She didn't make a sound, but somehow he knew that when he turned around she would be standing there, watching him with those smoky eyes of hers.

She had the sleeping bag wrapped around her like an Indian blanket, covering her from head to ankles. Only her face, one hand and a single strand of her long hair showed pale in the waning light. Her feet were bare.

Jason's heartbeat settled into a slow, heavy rhythm. "You'll catch cold," he said.

"I washed my clothes." Her voice had a certain note in it, a huskiness. "My shirt and socks and underwear. I couldn't stand them any longer."

"What if they don't dry by tomorrow morning?" Odd; his own voice had the same huskiness.

She shrugged. "I'll put them on wet, I guess."

"Spread them out near the fire," he said gruffly.

"I will." But she went on standing there, looking at him.

And he looked at her. Firelight played across her features and danced in her eyes.

"Are you going to sleep in the shelter tonight?" As she lifted her hand to wipe moisture from her throat, the wrap fell away from her head. She caught and adjusted it around herself, just below her shoulders. A stray puff of wind caught the wings of hair beside her face and lifted them.

He couldn't answer her. And he couldn't stop looking at her. She looked like a pagan priestess standing there in the leaping firelight, painted in colors of wine and honey and molten gold.

At last, afraid he was falling under some sort of spell, he tore his eyes away from her and turned his face toward the darkness, gulping the air like a man deprived of oxygen.

"The horses are noisy tonight," he said, still with that rasp in his voice.

"Yes," she said. "I know. The mares are in heat. They're mating."

It was strange, Jason thought. He'd been all over the world, lived in a lot of tight quarters; he was used to the sounds of human coupling and had never found them particularly disturbing. This was different. There was something so...elemental about this, something both primitive and powerful.

Wildfire ran unchecked through his blood; he felt the vague and edgy disquiet in him blossom into a fierce, unquenchable hunger. Erotic images played in his mind with a savage grace.

She came toward him, moving silently on bare feet. A short distance away from him, she stopped, and he saw her eyes slide past him to stare out into the darkness. "They aren't gentle about it," she said.

"I know," he said. "I've seen it."

Her chin lifted; he saw her throat move with a dry swallow. "I've always found it...rather beautiful."

"Sandy." Her eyes jerked back to his. He stared down at her mouth, at her soft lower lip and the delicate upper one, until he saw them escape her tenuous control and part of their own accord. Then, in a voice so quiet it wasn't really sound, he said, "Come here."

Chapter 10

She didn't know whether he reached for her, or whether she moved to him in obedience to his quiet command. The firelight burned in his eyes, giving them a feral glow, but she felt no fear. Echoes of the stallion's scream of triumph and mastery hung in the air and shimmered through her body like the aftereffects of champagne, bringing liquid heat and a fine, tingling effervescence.

His arm came roughly around her neck; his other hand covered hers where it clutched the edges of the sleeping bag and rested there, vibrating with the tension inside him. Craggy and fierce, his face hung above hers while the battle raged inside him, a battle she felt in his fevered body and knotted muscles. Fear...and desire. Which would triumph? Any second now he would take full possession—or cast her away.

But Sandy didn't wait for the outcome. She didn't wait for Jason's choice. She had had enough of waiting. The hunger in her was stronger than her habits of shyness and reserve, stronger than pride, stronger even than fear. Her need had gone beyond the desire to hold and be held, to comfort and be comforted. They had very little to do with sensual pleasure. She was female; he was male. The forces that had set the tides in motion and started the earth spinning on its axis had ordained that the two should be joined together. For her, at that moment, it was as simple as that.

Opening her arms wide, and the edges of the sleeping bag with them, she stepped forward. The barriers came crashing down; with a ragged groan, Jason claimed what she offered. His arms gathered her in, the one across the back of her neck supporting her head, the other hooking around her waist inside the enveloping cocoon to drag her hard against him. His mouth came down on hers and found it open and eager; his tongue plunged quickly and deeply, sealing the possession. Teeth clashed, and he shifted, seeking softer, yielding flesh and hotter, sweeter depths.

The stallion's scream came again, and again Sandy felt that silvery champagne fire coursing through her. In her mind random, shifting patterns came together to make images so erotic they seemed surreal, a swirling montage of arching necks and rippling muscles, flashing hooves and wind-whipped manes.

In a way she didn't understand, and that would have embarrassed her to admit or explain, she felt an intense kinship with the horses, almost a merging of spirits. She'd felt it before, the first time she'd ever seen wild horses running free, and only a few times since: that lifting of spirits, that invitation to come join with them and be free. And always, knowing the limitations of her humanness, she'd declined with yearning and regret.

Tonight, when the wild horses called to her, she joyfully went with them.

Coltish. Jason had thought of her that way so often, saying "coltish grace" in his mind when what he really meant was a kind of endearing awkwardness. But there was a kind of grace in the way she moved against him, her body slender but taut, a solid weight in his arms. She felt good, so good, there.

Her mouth moved under his, not frantically, but with a slow, seductive rhythm that seemed to meld with his own body rhythms, pulling him into a dizzying spiral, immersing him deeper and deeper in her.

He surfaced by slow, reluctant degrees and, grasping a handful of her hair, turned her head from side to side while his tongue teased and tasted and then withdrew, leaving her glazed and gasping. The firelight painted the moisture on her lips, spattering them with orange and scarlet. Tiny droplets on her closed eyelids became flecks of gold and bronze. Lowering his head once more, he took each tiny colored particle onto his tongue, savoring the varied flavors and textures of her until she began to breathe in ragged little bursts and pull against the discipline of his hand.

"Sandy." He said it softly, but she heard, and opened her eyes. Jason felt as if he were drowning in liquid smoke.

Sandy. Just her name, spoken in a tone of quiet but unmistakable command. Hearing it, she sighed. Yielding now to the firm guidance of his hand, she tilted her head to offer him the sensitive column of her neck.

For a moment, poised there above her, he seemed so fierce, dominant, almost frighteningly masculine. *They aren't gentle....*

But then she felt the silky brush of his beard against her skin, the hot, drawing pressure of his mouth on her nape and on her throat; she felt his teeth score the taut tendons of her neck, but lightly, only evoking and simulating more savage acts. And she knew that he *was* gentle.

Fear fled; joy and love came pouring in like morning sunlight. This was Jason! *Jason.* With the sunlight came the revelation that she *knew* him, knew his heart and soul and mind almost as well as she knew her own. She trusted him. She loved him.

Desire made a hot, aching pool down deep in the center of her body. Rising higher, it ran in a stinging flood through the rest of her, creating in her a hundred vague but frantic hungers. Forgetting that her hands were occupied, she opened her fingers and buried them in his hair. Already breathing in sharp, desperate gasps, she hardly flinched when the heavy wrap fell away, leaving her naked in the cold.

Jason swore softly. He was becoming impatient with inconvenience. His clothing and the blasted sleeping bag. The cold. He wanted Sandy on a soft bed under a tropical moon, where he could look at her and unlock all her body's secrets, one by one, for sweet, unhurried hours. He wanted her nipples erect in response to his touch, not the cold, her only shivers to be of ecstasy. But reality was a mid-September Idaho night, redolent of sulfur and wood smoke, and sharp with the promise of winter.

She uttered a whimpering noise of protest when he bent to pick up the sleeping bag, then made a convulsive movement, as if to cover herself.

"You're cold," he said gruffly, pulling the sleeping bag back around her. "Here, come closer to the fire."

"Jason..." Shudders wracked her body.

"Shh." Pulling on the edges of the fabric, he guided her to the warmth. "Better?" When she nodded, lifting her face blindly to him, he touched his lips to hers and felt her smile.

"I thought—I was afraid—"

"Hey, don't be afraid."

"I'm not. Just...that you were going to pull away from me again."

A tiny pain stabbed him. Resting his forehead on hers, he closed his eyes and let his breath out in a sigh. The horses were quiet now; there were just the two of them, alone in the vast, moonlit night.

"I'm not going to pull away from you," he said in a low growl. "Not this time."

Now Sandy felt the sleeping bag pull taut across her back, bringing her into the warmth of his body. Though it was what she wanted, she resisted momentarily, laying her palms on his chest, inside the front of his jacket. She could feel the heat soaking through his shirt, seeping into her fingers, feel the heavy pounding of his heart. Swaying forward, she pressed her open mouth to the hollow at the base of his throat.

"Yeah," he groaned when her fingers found his shirt buttons, touching his lips to her forehead. "Good move...."

To his relief, she dealt quickly with the buttons, and with the fastenings of his pants, too. There was urgency in her movements as she tugged his shirt free, urgency that was echoed in the tight tremors corkscrewing through his muscles, vestiges, he supposed, of his self-control.

And now, when he pulled, she came to him, gasping with shock and then sighing with pleasure as his naked chest met hers. While his hands were employed with the sleeping bag she was free to do as she pleased—and she did please, inordinately. Her breasts nested softly in the hair on his chest, and her belly moved in and out against his; with an instinctive and sinuous grace she moved against him, caressing him with her body. When he groaned and shifted restively, seeking relief for the fire in his loins, she chuckled low in her throat. Her hands slipped around to his back, gently kneading, then dived beneath his waist-band. Her fine, strong hands flattened against his lower back.

A fireball of desire rolled through him. When she arched her back and lifted her face to his, he was ready to take back control. And she surrendered it willingly, joyfully. Her mouth opened hungrily, blossoming under his as he bore her back and down into the sling made by the sleeping bag.

"The shelter," she gasped when he laid her down beside the fire.

"Not yet," he said thickly. "I want to see you first."

She sighed and closed her eyes, too steeped in passion to be self-conscious, even when he raised her hands above her head and, with excruciating slowness, drew his fingers down the center of her body from the base of her throat to the cleft of her thighs.

"Hey, my lady... open your eyes. Look at me."

Again it was a quiet command. And again she obeyed it, though her eyelids were heavy and her vision misted.

"Yes...." Jason growled softly. Sultry eyes....

The look in his eyes would have frightened her not so long ago. It seemed impossible to her now that she'd ever thought of him as a brigand, and she wanted him to know. Touching the deeply shadowed hollows of his face with her fingertips, in a hushed and hazy voice she murmured, "I used to think... that you looked like a pirate. I was a little bit afraid of you."

"Afraid? Of me?" His voice was ragged. "Why?"

"Oh..." Inexplicably, she wanted to cry. "The look in your eyes... this nose, the beard." Touching each part of him in turn, she brought her fingers to his mouth. "Your mouth, though..." Her voice broke, and she finished in a whisper. "Your mouth is so gentle. I love your mouth.

Oh.'' With tears of overpowering emotion springing from her eyes, she lifted herself blindly to him.

Shaken, he caught her shuddering body and filled her hungry, questing mouth. In just a moment or two, though, she tore away from him, breathing in sobs.

"Easy," he whispered, tenderly stroking her forehead, touching his lips to the damp wisps of hair there. There was more he wanted to do; there were so many ways he wanted to touch her, ways no man had ever touched her before. He could have gone on looking at her, touching her, loving her with his mouth and hands, until he reached the absolute limits of his control. But he understood that, for her, it had gone on too long already.

She was far beyond impatience, sunk deep in sensual lethargy, too weak and heavy to offer more than breathless protest when he left her for a few necessary moments. She was on fire, aching and burning in places she hadn't even been aware of before. When Jason came to her she reached for him, forgetting that she'd ever suggested moving to the softer floor of the shelter, wanting only one thing, regardless of the consequences.

But Jason hadn't forgotten. Conscious of the fact that he was so much bigger than she was, he gently but firmly took her hands and placed them above her head, then adjusted his body and hers so she wouldn't have to bear so much of his weight.

And when he was sheathed in her at last, when her body had adjusted to him and her ragged respirations had become sobs of relief and joy, he turned them both and gave the reins back to her.

There had been a moment when, poised on the threshold of her body, he'd had a vague, disquieting sense of barriers being crossed, of things being altered forever. Now, though, lost in a fog of passion, all he could think about was the feel of her body around him, and her hair, pouring down like a waterfall over them both.

Later, with passions spent and Sandy lying limp and somnolent on his chest, their legs haphazardly entwined, her soft breath sighing gently against his throat, Jason stared up at the stars and felt a loosening inside him, as if something that had been stretched to the limit had very gently given way. As he enfolded her in his arms and tenderly kissed the top of her head...he let go of the precipice. With fatalistic acceptance, and with full awareness of the consequences, he fell irretrievably in love.

Sandy woke up in the shelter, curled spoon-fashion against Jason. He was wearing his jacket, because the sleeping bag wasn't long enough to cover his top half, and Sandy's rolled-up jacket was providing him with a pillow. Sandy hadn't needed either pillow or cover, except for the sleeping bag. Naked, she had been as warm as toast in Jason's embrace.

Jason still slept, the sleep of pure exhaustion. His breathing was heavy and deep, and though his arm lay possessively across Sandy's waist, he didn't stir when she unzipped the sleeping bag and eased herself quietly away from him. Huddled, shivering, in a crouch, she paused a moment to look at his face, feeling her heart swell with never-before-felt feelings, wondering how she could ever have thought this man frightening. But it was too cold to spend much time that way, so she tenderly touched his forehead with her lips, then went out to find her clothes.

The sun was already up and the frost in the meadow ablaze; the campfire had burned down to a few dying coals. Jason's clothes lay where they'd been discarded last night; hers were where she'd left them spread out to dry. She dressed quickly, teeth chattering, and for a little added warmth put on Jason's shirt over her own. Her socks were still damp, but she reasoned that they'd probably warm up eventually inside her leather boots, and in the meantime, they were still better than nothing.

By the time she'd managed to get the fire going again with a handful of pine needles and a fresh supply of wood, she was beginning to feel almost warm. She ate two of the fish they'd caught and cooked yesterday, and drank a few swallows of cold water from the Thermos, while she day-dreamed about cheeseburgers with everything, and French fries smothered in ketchup. And pizza. Pepperoni pizza with mushrooms and green peppers. And extra chèese.

And then she sat for a while, staring out across the valley, listening to the quiet sounds of a wilderness morning: birds' songs and hawks' cries, and the constant background noises of wind and water. Her mind followed random pathways through her memories, like a child picking wildflowers in a meadow.

She wondered where the horses were this morning; she thought of last night and lingered there a while, hugging those brand-new memories to herself in wonder and awe. She thought about Jason. She thought about the short time she'd known him, and of all she knew about him, and felt apprehensive but resigned. Since when had human beings ever fallen in love sensibly?

She thought about other people she loved, people whose faces she hadn't looked on in years, but which appeared in her mind's eye as sharply and clearly as if she'd spoken to them yesterday. People she now realized she might never see again. Funny, when it had been her choice not to see them, she'd felt only an occasional pang of loneliness and regret; the idea that the option might be taken from her made her want to curl herself into a ball and cry like a child.

The world was entirely too empty and quiet! Sandy wondered how Jason had endured those long night hours sitting up alone while she slept. She thought he must be a man accustomed to solitude, and to loneliness, too.

Since there was no telling how long Jason might sleep, she decided to go back to the avalanche scar to see if she could find something new and exciting to eat. And since the chances of that happening were slim, she took along the hammer so she could dig some more camas bulbs on the way back. It would be so nice, she thought wistfully as she hefted the picnic basket and tucked the hammer into the waistband of her jeans; if she could find a nice fat partridge with a broken wing....

The first thing Jason thought about when he woke up was that he hadn't had the nightmare. For the first time since he'd agreed to the Idaho job, he'd slept through the night soundly and peacefully.

The second thought was that he wanted a cigarette. The third was of Sandy, though she'd actually been there in his mind concurrently with the other things, and had been since before he'd even opened his eyes. He felt a little nervous about facing her, because he still couldn't quite believe what had happened. He couldn't believe he'd allowed it to happen. Last night had been one hell of a night; he just wasn't sure how it was going to look to him in the cold light of day.

He couldn't hear any sounds from outside except for the crackling of the fire, so he threw off the sleeping bag and jacket and emerged from the shelter naked—like a caveman, he thought, rubbing ruefully at his beard and raking his fingers through his hair. That reminded him of what Sandy had said to him last night, about looking like a pirate. Did he really look that bad? he wondered.

When he couldn't find his shirt, he realized right away that Sandy must have borrowed it, since he'd been sleeping on top of her coat. He didn't mind, except that his cigarettes were in his shirt pocket. Oh well, he thought, what the hell, she'll be back soon. Any minute, probably. He would go take a dip in the bathing pool while she was gone. He needed a bath more than he needed a cigarette, anyway.

When he was bathed and dressed in his trousers and shoes and she still wasn't back, he figured she'd probably gone foraging for food. The sun was warming things up nicely, and he didn't mind going shirtless, but he really did want those cigarettes. Besides, he was beginning to feel a needling sense of loneliness without Sandy around. Since the only places they knew of with anything edible in them were the meadow and the avalanche scar, he decided to take a chance and go look for her.

The horses were grazing quietly in the meadow just below the scar. Sandy gave them a wide berth and was pleased to note that, though they lifted their heads and followed her progress with pricked ears and watchful eyes, they stayed where they were.

Except for the little russet colt, of course, who was racing up and down along the lower edge of the brushy area, pushing the limits of his independence. He sure was a spunky little rascal, she thought, pausing to watch him for a moment. If he survived his first year, he'd probably end up leading a band of his own, someday—maybe even this one. His sire had enjoyed a long reign, but as powerful as the old rogue was, he couldn't hold off the young pretenders forever.

As Sandy approached the scar, she startled a small band of deer that had been grazing farther up the slope, and they bounded into the timber on the far side. She watched them go, kicking herself again for her stupid prejudice against firearms. All right, maybe it wasn't stupid, but the fact remained that if she'd only had a gun in the chopper, they'd be enjoying a whole lot more varied and satisfying foods right now. How frustrating it was to stand there in the brush listening to those silly grouse, or whatever they were, calling to each other, knowing there wasn't any way in the world she could catch one. Unless she threw rocks at them and just happened, by sheer luck, to hit one on the head.

Inspiration struck. Why not try it? If she walked through the brush she'd probably flush the dumb things from cover; wasn't that was hunters did? If they were close enough, she might even hit one. She'd had a pretty fair arm in her younger days; her family's softball games were legendary. Further inspired, it occurred to her that the hammer might make a more effective missile than a rock; she could throw it with more leverage, and its spinning flight...

Lord, she thought, laughing at herself, get hold of yourself, Sandy! Hunger was making her crazy. She could just see herself, charging through the brush like a mad-woman, chasing a bunch of quail with a hammer! It was ludicrous. And besides, if she did throw the hammer, it would get lost in the brush and she'd never find it again.

She was still giggling about that when a movement in the corner of her eye drew her attention. The colt had ventured into the chest-high brush, proceeding cautiously, pausing to nibble a leaf here, sniff a blossom there, and then, legs straddled, lower his muzzle to blow at something suspicious on the ground. And for once his parents seemed oblivious to his whereabouts.

Knowing she shouldn't—she'd promised Jason she wouldn't—Sandy eased the picnic basket to the ground, settled herself on a log and, holding herself absolutely still, waited to see how close the colt would be willing to come to her in order to satisfy his rampant curiosity. Knowing that a direct gaze might be threatening to him, she shifted hers to one side, so she could still watch him with her peripheral vision. When she did, once again something—the slightest movements—flickered at the corner of her eye.

There. The movement came again, from the top of a rocky knoll only a few yards uphill from the colt. This time Sandy identified it. It was the twitch of a tawny, serpentine tail.

The lion had undoubtedly been stalking the deer, or maybe even grouse. Sandy's intrusion had spoiled his chance at his original quarry, but the colt, alone and unprotected for once, made a fine and unexpected alternative.

Except for a single, soft gasp, Sandy froze. Her mouth dropped open, but no sound came out. Her muscles locked; all she could do, it seemed, was watch helplessly while the big cat, in graceful slow motion, gathered himself for his spring. Below the rocks, the little russet colt gamboled unsuspectingly.

A massive bolt of adrenaline shot through Sandy's muscles, propelling her out of her temporary paralysis. Gripping the hammer, she screamed *"No!"* at the top of her lungs and sprang off the log.

The startled colt sat back on his haunches, then whirled and bolted. Already in midspring, the lion hit the ground and came up empty. With an angry squall, he bounded after the frantic colt. Sobbing, Sandy ran after them both, knowing she wasn't going to be able to prevent what was about to happen. In another second the lion would be on top of the little colt. In the grip of those deadly jaws and powerful feline muscles, the colt's neck would snap, and that would be that.

She couldn't let it happen—she couldn't! At the last desperate second, Sandy raised the hammer, took aim and let it fly.

It struck the mountain lion a glancing blow on the haunches, just as his front legs were reaching for the colt's hindquarters. One outstretched claw raked the frightened baby's rump, and then the cat whirled, ears flat and teeth bared, and with another squall, which sounded almost comically like *"Ow!"* he bounded away.

With a terrified whinny, the colt raced off in the other direction, as fast as he could go. By this time, alerted by the commotion, the stallion and the colt's mother were both charging to the rescue at full gallop. Meeting her baby and finding him safe and sound, the buckskin mare halted, touched noses and then, reassured, escorted him back to the herd. The stallion's charge carried him on a dozen or so yards more, before he pounded to a stop, stamping, shaking his head and bugling furiously. And then he, too, wheeled and raced back to his band.

When Jason tore out of the trees a few minutes later, Sandy was down on her hands and knees, sobbing and crawling frantically through the brush.

For a minute or two he couldn't see her, and icy terror clawed at his insides. And then he heard her, and that was almost worse. All he could think about was that she was hurt, injured, and he had no way of helping her, and she would... And then he realized that between sobs she was swearing, and that what wasn't swearing went something like, "I knew it. I *knew* it! Now I can't find it! Damn it, I *knew* it."

That angry litany guided him to her. Bemused and weak in the knees, he squatted on his heels beside her and, laughing uncertainly, said, "Sandy? Honey? What are you looking for?"

She ignored him at first. She just went right on scratching through the weeds and dead leaves with her hands, cussing like a sailor. Then she paused and threw him a look that nearly stopped his heart. Her face was tear-streaked and dusty, but her eyes smoldered with fury; her hair was loose and streaming, full of leaves and grass and bits of brush. She looked like some strange, wild creature, not quite real.

And then she said, "I can't find the damn *hammer!*"

She sounded so furious that he didn't dare laugh. "Uh, Sandy? What happened? I heard you scream."

"I knew I'd lose it if I threw it. I knew it!"

"Sandy," Jason said in his gentlest voice, "why did you throw the hammer?"

She caught impatiently at her hair and dragged it back from her face, then covered her mouth with her hand. Over it, he saw her eyes lose their light and become dark pools.

"Oh ... God," she said in a high, thin voice he'd never heard before. "Jason ..."

He sat down on the ground and gathered her into his arms, and for a while he just held her and stroked her hair, trying to be patient while she shook and sniffled against his naked chest. Presently, though, he coughed in a warning way, picked a bit of debris out of her hair, patted her on the back and said gruffly, "Hey, you want to tell me what happened now? You scared the hell out of me!"

She pushed herself away from him, and he let her go. Touching the back of her hand to her lips, she cleared her throat and said, "The lion was after the colt." He waited, and then she went on. "I hit him with the hammer."

Smothering a snort of incredulous laughter with his hand, Jason said, "You *what?*"

She gave a liquid gurgle. "I threw the hammer at him. I actually hit him. I can't believe I hit him."

"You drove off a mountain lion with a *hammer?*"

Still pressing her hand against her lips, she solemnly nodded. Then laughter exploded through her fingers. Jason gathered her back into his arms, and they held on to each other, rocking and gasping.

Jason gave himself up to the laughter because it was a safe enough release for the turbulence inside him. If he'd awakened with doubts this morning, they were gone now, gone forever. Life took some crazy twists and turns sometimes, and he was probably equally crazy to go along for the ride, but it was too late now to turn back. The feelings rumbling around inside him—tender, protective, fierce, possessive—were things he hadn't allowed himself to feel for fifteen years. It had been so long, and yet it felt so right, loving someone. Like coming back to a much loved place after a long absence and feeling as if he'd never left.

Sandy drew away from him finally, brushing at her cheeks.

"You're crazy, you know that?" Jason said huskily.

"Yeah, I know." Her eyes had a kind of glow. They made his insides feel as if he'd just swallowed a tumbler of brandy.

Suddenly awkward, but needing to touch her, Jason brushed at a smudge on her cheek with this thumb. "Hey, listen, forget about the hammer. We don't need it."

"No!" She shook her head. "Jason, we have to find that hammer. It's the only weapon, the only tool we've got."

She was so adamant about it that he gave in. "Okay," he groaned, joining her on his hands and knees. "Let's find it, then. It's got to be around here somewhere."

By the time Jason found the hammer they were both hot and itchy and covered with dirt and scratches. "Got it!" he announced, waving it triumphantly over his head. And then, plaintively, "Hey, I'm hungry. Can we go home now?"

Home. He was laughing as he pulled Sandy to her feet, picked a twig from her hair and kissed her, dust and all. But that word hung there in the back of his mind, as poignant and wistful as a childhood memory.

Chapter 11

Hmm," Sandy murmured, licking her lips. "You taste dusty."

Jason laughed softly. "So do you."

She drew back a little, brushing her fingers across the smooth bronze curve of his shoulder. "And you're all scratched up."

"Hey, don't worry about it. I think some of them are probably from the other day. Remember? The earthquake?"

"Oh yeah...." She remembered. Oh, how she remembered. She remembered the way he'd touched her and then withdrawn from her afterward, and knew that without realizing it she'd been half afraid of how he would be with her this morning. Afraid he would put their night of passion down to a bad case of moon madness and try to pretend it had never happened.

But there was nothing withdrawn about Jason this morning. There hadn't been a trace of reserve in the way he'd pulled her into his arms; she hadn't even noticed it right then, because it had seemed to come as naturally to him as breathing. And right now, this minute, she was standing in the circle of his arms, and his hands were caressing her back and shoulders as if he couldn't get enough of touching her.

"Hmm," Sandy said again, feeling groggy. All of a sudden the air had turned sultry. She was about to yield to a strong desire to press her mouth to the hot, moist hollow at the base of his throat when she suddenly stopped. "Jason," she observed in surprise, focusing on the pattern her splayed fingers made in the hair on his chest, "you're not wearing a shirt." And then, closing her eyes in chagrin, "*I'm* wearing your shirt. I completely forgot. Here, want it back?"

"Not unless you especially want me to put it on. I wouldn't want to scare you."

"*Scare* me?"

"Last night you said I did. You said I looked like a pirate. And that was with a shirt on." He was smiling, but a question hovered in his eyes. He looked perplexed and rueful, and in spite of his bare chest and wild hair, nothing at all like a pirate.

"Hmm," she whispered as her breathing became tremulous. "Am I about to be ravished?"

"Yes," he said, considering. "But not until I clean you up a little."

"Oh." Laughing, she gave his chest a shove, pushing him backward just as he caught her to him, so that they swayed precariously into a kiss. Suspended there, off balance, her feet not touching the ground, she knew a moment of giddy buoyancy, like a child on a swing. She felt the same swift upsurge of spirit, that breathless certainty, if only for an instant, that the world was beautiful and all things possible.

Am I crazy? she asked herself. Yes, she thought. Completely. What a crazy, ridiculous, impossible time to fall in love.

But, she reminded herself, falling in love was her problem, not his. She wasn't so naive as to think that just because he'd allowed himself to become physically intimate with her it meant all his protective barricades had come tumbling down. There were probably a lot of good, logical reasons why last night had happened—loneliness and stress, physical proximity, combined with a certain amount of natural chemistry and a moonlit night—and not one of them had anything to do with love.

Jason Rivers, she reminded herself, was a man with problems, a man afraid to love. And it was going to take a lot more than one night of passion to change that.

"Jason, you're crazy," she gasped, laughing as he suddenly lifted her into his arms. "Put me down! I'm not exactly your basic dainty Southern belle type, you know."

"I noticed that," he said in mock distress, and added fervently, "Thank God."

"Jason, come on now. This is silly. I haven't been carried since I was six years old!"

"Hush, woman! How can I ravish you properly if I don't carry you off to my lair?"

"Oh. Well then, shouldn't I at least be kicking and screaming?"

He considered that. "Screaming, okay. If you kick I might drop you."

"Jason . . ."

"What now?" He was beginning to pant a little, she noticed with some satisfaction.

"We left the picnic basket back there."

He uttered a sibilant expletive. "We'll get it later. I'm sure not going back for it now!"

In her best Southern accent she said sweetly, "My, my, aren't we in a hurry?" blowing the words softly against the shell of his ear.

"Damn right I'm in a hurry," Jason growled, bending over her and leering fiercely. "I want a cigarette!"

By the time they got back to camp, though, he'd pretty much forgotten about the cigarettes. To Sandy's relief, he'd given up carrying her about halfway. She thought it was so much nicer to be walking side by side, arms around each other's waists, matching strides and sharing laughter and outrageous nonsense. In fact, it was more than nice. It was pure, unadulterated fun. She couldn't remember a time in her life, not even as a child, when she'd felt so unreservedly playful.

Again she asked herself, Am I crazy? Here she was, stranded in a wilderness and in real danger of dying there, and yet she felt ridiculously happy. Happier than she'd ever been in her life.

It's Jason, she thought, gazing in awe at the laughing, black-bearded giant beside her. Who could have guessed that he could be like this? Pirate...Paul Bunyan...and now lover, playmate and friend.

When they were standing face-to-face on the edge of the bathing pools, however, the mood seemed to change. Something about the air in that place, Sandy thought, something hot and humid that sapped the strength and fogged the mind.

"Well," she said huskily as Jason reached for her shirt buttons, touching his hands with hers, "I guess this is where..." Her voice trailed off as she swallowed and looked up at him, suddenly shy, feeling as if last night had been a dream, as if he'd never made love to her before, never seen or touched her naked body.

Incredibly, he seemed to understand. Eyes smiling, mouth solemn, instead of undoing her buttons he slipped his hands under her arms and, lightly massaging the sides of her breasts through her shirt, drew her to him.

He touched her lips with his, then just her lower lip, teasing it, tracing its outline with his tongue. It began to feel swollen, tingly, feverish. Holding herself still, she parted her lips and took a single soft sip of air when his tongue fluttered delicately along their sensitive insides.

Tender and wondering, she smiled and felt his lips curve with hers, felt the warm puffs of his breath when he chuckled. His hands moved, slowly rotating, dragging cloth across the sensitive tips of her breasts so that when he cradled them at last in his palms, she gasped once at the shock, and again at the pleasure.

She willed her hands, which had been gripping his forearms like life preservers, to relax and savor the textures of coarse hair and satin skin and firm, rounded muscle. Starting them on a slow, wondering journey upward, she found herself remembering that very first night outside the Silver Horseshoe, and the way his forearms had felt then, so strong and smooth, like blocks of polished wood beneath her palms. Holding his face in her hands, she tunneled her fingers through his beard and remembered how surprised she'd been that night to learn of its softness.

"I love—" she whispered, and paused to draw a meager ration of air "—the way you feel." She wanted her shirt off now, wanted only *his* textures against her skin.

"I love the way you feel, too, believe me." The words were a muffled groan that expired in her mouth as the tongue-teasing deepened. Exquisitely aroused, she made small hungry sounds and leaned into his hands.

"Then touch me," she whispered between gasps, pleading. "Touch... *me*..

"I will," he whispered back. "All over...."

"Now!" she cried. "Now, please."

His soft chuckle of pleasure feathered over her skin. "Patience, my lady... patience."

He undid her buttons slowly, watching her eyes. Holding on to his gaze, as if to a lifeline, she unfastened his belt. As his hands glided warmly over her breasts, pushing fabric aside, hers slipped inside the waistband of his trousers and found the shallow indentations at the sides of his buttocks. With his hands pressed flat against her shoulder blades, he brought her slowly to him. With their bodies touching lightly, exquisitely, he lowered his head and kissed her long and deeply, until her knees weakened and she swayed against him, weak as a kitten.

"Enough of this," he growled, and the rest of their undressing became a matter of expediency.

When they were both naked, he guided her to the water. She sat beside him in the shallow basin carved by who knows what forces from solid granite, sliding her feet over smooth, slippery rock, feeling that odorous, healing water caress her body. And feeling as shy as a teenager. His body was still a little strange to her, still a little overwhelming.

Making a cup of his hand, Jason brought the water to her shoulder. It ran like quicksilver over her sun-heated skin and made opaline droplets in the hollows below her throat and above her collarbones. His big hands followed its path, smoothing the drops across her skin like fragrant oils while he watched with hungry, heavy-lidded eyes. Watching him watch her, she saw him in new ways, the transparent fragility of an eyelid, the fine sheen of moisture on dusky skin, the varying textures of hair, including a silver strand or two. Love caught and swelled inside her, tangling with her breathing, making her ache.

More water sluiced over her breasts, as warm as syrup. His hands ran down her body, up and over turgid crests and into shivering hollows, circling, stroking, massaging, caressing. Her breath came in sharp, shallow bursts that lifted her breasts against the weight of his palm. Lowering his head, he filled his mouth with the tip of one breast, while his hair and beard tickled her skin like feathers made of silk. The muscles in her neck melted, her head fell back, and the world revolved slowly in a dizzy, wondering spiral.

Shifting his legs, Jason brought her between his thighs and eased them both deeper into the pool. "Here," he murmured gruffly. "Lie back on me." Half reclining, he felt her weight settle against him. The water carried her hair away on undulating currents, laying it out on the surface like filaments of spun silver, then brought it back to bathe his skin with a touch as subtle as moonlight. Bringing his hand up under a floating strand of it, he lifted it from the water and felt its weight and texture change and cling.

"I love your hair," he murmured, carrying the strand to his lips. Thinking of that elusive, wind-borne fragrance he'd noticed so often, he whispered, "I love the way it smells."

"I think it's called Eau de Sulfur," she said in a husky, sleepy voice, making him laugh.

Hitching himself higher, he cradled her head against his belly and began to comb through her hair with his fingers, sifting out bits of brush, unraveling tangles, letting the water fan it around him in billowing ripples, like seaweed. He massaged her scalp, marveling at the elegant shape of her head, the fine, strong bones of her face. He noticed that her lashes were long, but pale at the tips; uncolored, they lay like flecks of golden chaff against the sunblushed velvet of her cheeks.

She sighed and stirred like a sleepy child, rolling her head on the firm, water-cushioned pillow of his stomach, turning her body in his legs' embrace, blindly seeking him with her mouth. Her hair got in her way, sticking to him like wet cloth, slicking down in a weighted curtain across her cheek when she tried to raise her head.

"Darn hair," she muttered, vexed. Laughing softly, Jason gathered it into his hands and lifted it over her shoulder.

And then, pressing lightly against her shoulder blades, he gave himself over to the sweet, sensuous explorations of her mouth and tongue. Her hands touched, then stroked and fondled, making exquisite patterns of fire and water on his skin, while her body moved with sinuous grace in the fork of his legs, until his body became fevered and the heated water a cooling caress. His limits of endurance reached, he locked his legs around her and rolled her over, sinking into deeper water so that she had to surface, gasping and blinking water from her eyes.

Laughing in joyful, ecstatic gulps, breathing in stolen fragments, they tumbled and frolicked, sliding their water-slippery bodies together like porpoises cavorting in tropical shallows. They kissed randomly and deeply, under the water and out of it, not caring, not even seeming to know the difference. Warm water and sunshine—each seemed to give the same sweet velvety caress.

He caught her to him at last, and she went gladly, their joining as easy and natural as laughter.

"We weren't very gentle with each other," Sandy said ruefully, dabbing antiseptic cream on a fresh scrape on Jason's back.

"Ouch! You're right. And you're not being very gentle right now, either. What *is* that stuff?"

"Hush. Don't be a baby. This doesn't sting."

"The hell it doesn't! Can't you just kiss it and make it better?"

"If I did that," Sandy said, a trifle smugly, "we'd probably only wind up with a new batch."

He turned to give her a look of incredulity. "Woman, what do you think I am? Superhuman?" She just looked at him, smiling demurely. He made a sound halfway between a laugh and a groan. "Don't do that to me."

"Do what?"

"Look at me like that. Your eyes are..."

"What?" Her smile wavered a little, because he looked so fierce.

"Sexy," he breathed, reaching for her. "Don't you know you have the sexiest eyes I've ever seen in my life? Sultry as a summer night in Georgia."

"Jason, stop that," Sandy said weakly. "I have to finish putting stuff on your scratches."

"My scratches are fine. Hand over that tube. It's my turn."

They were sitting on the broad expanse of gently sloping rock near the bathing pool, sunning and lazily sparring, like seals. Jason was wearing his pants, but was still shirtless; Sandy had on underpants and her shirt, but had left it unbuttoned. When he drew the edges of it aside she made a little fluttering gesture across her front with her hand, slight, automatic, quickly controlled. But slight though it was, Jason noticed it and paused.

"What is it?"

"Nothing," she responded hurriedly, then closed her eyes and gave a little laugh of chagrin. "In a manner of speaking."

He gave her a hard look, then shook his head in amazement. "What? Do you think you're too *small?*" he asked bluntly. "Whatever gave you that idea?"

"Oh, well, I don't know," she joked, trying to ignore the shaky little pain in her chest, knowing she was being silly and ridiculous. "Maybe the fact that in high school my friends used to mistake my bras for slingshots."

Unsmiling, Jason slowly pushed the shirt over her shoulders, gazing unrelenting at her. Resigned, she watched his face, feeling her skin turn hot. Finally he said simply, quietly, "You're beautiful." .

She stared at him, overcome. *You're beautiful.* He'd never said that to her before. She didn't think anyone ever had. Oh, yes, "You look nice," or "You look very pretty, Sandy," or even, "You look gorgeous tonight, Sandy." But except in romantic books and movies, men just didn't go around saying things like that, not with that kind of quiet sincerity. "You're beautiful...." Saying it in such a way that, for the first time, deep down in her soul, she really did believe it.

"Well," she said with a small, liquid-sounded laugh. "No scratches there."

"Shucks," he murmured with a disappointed snap of his fingers. "Oh well, can't blame a guy for trying. Here, let me see your legs. I know I saw some scrapes on your legs."

Muttering, "Some people never give up," Sandy gave him a look of mock disgust, but she did stretch out her long, tanned legs for his inspection. There were several scrapes on her knees and thighs, and a number of angry-looking scratches on her hands and arms from the bush.

"Ouch," she said when he touched her tender abraded skin with the cream. "That does smart a little, doesn't it?"

"It's good for you," Jason said placidly. "Builds character."

"You know," she said, looking thoughtfully at a reddening scratch, "there's yarrow growing all over this valley. Tons of it. Horses won't eat it. If we just had a cooking pot of some kind, I could make salve from it. I bet it would feel a lot better than this stuff."

"Yarrow?" he said, laughing. "Where do you get all this information?"

"Hey, yarrow's been used for healing since ancient times, don't you know that? The Indians used to chew its leaves to cure toothache."

"Camas, trapper's tea, and now yarrow. I swear, if I didn't know you were one of *the* Stewarts," Jason teased, tweaking her braid, "I'd think *you* were an Indian! Albino, of course."

"Oh, but I *am* part Indian." Smiling, she watched her feet and waited for his reaction.

"Sure," he said softly, drawing a finger slowly down her arm, just brushing the silky, spun-gold hair that grew there, "and I'm the tooth fairy."

"No, it's true, I swear. One of my grandmothers—I don't know how many greats—it was in Daniel Boone's time, when the Kentucky wilderness was being settled. Anyway, this ancestor of mine married an Indian woman—well, I don't suppose he actually *married* her, given the way most people felt about Indians at the time, but anyway, there's no doubt about it, because it's all there in the old Stewart family Bible. Honest Injun."

"Maybe you're a throwback," Jason said, smiling, transferring his thoughtfully exploratory finger to the top of her thigh.

"Believe me, I've thought about it," Sandy said, not smiling, pulling her knee up as shivers spangled her skin with goose bumps. "When I was young, and feeling so out of place, I used to wonder about things like... reincarnation and things like that. Do you believe in reincarnation?"

"You mean, do I believe we've all lived any number of times before, and that when innocent people suffer, that it's for sins committed in a past life? No," he said harshly, "I don't." He put the cap back on the tube of antiseptic and gave it to her, then got to his feet. With his back to her, looking off across the valley, he stretched, arching his back, flexing his muscles, swiveling at the waist. Turning to look down at her, he said, "It's getting late. If we're going to have anything for dinner, we'd better go fishing."

His voice was gentle, but for the first time in nearly twenty-four hours there was a distance between them, and that old bleak emptiness was back in his eyes.

They'd waited too long to go fishing. Though they roamed quite a way looking for new spots to try, it was no use; the fish just weren't biting. Eventually they had to give up and try to appease their hunger with raw camas. Jason told himself he didn't really mind, he'd been hungry before, and besides, it wouldn't hurt him to drop a few pounds. He was getting worried about Sandy, though. If he wasn't mistaken, her jeans were already starting to hang loosely on her slender hips, and she didn't have any pounds to spare.

Not for the first time, Jason found himself thinking about last night and everything that had happened since, and about the fact that neither he nor Sandy seemed to be giving a thought to possible consequences. *Conse-*

quences. A big word for a tiny speck of matter that could already be well on its way to becoming a new life. That such a life might even now be growing in Sandy was, he knew, more than a possibility. It had occurred to him that there might have been a biological reason for the way she'd come to him last night, so ripe and ready, with that honesty he'd come to expect of her, and something more. There had been a kind of intensity about her, a single-mindedness, as if she were governed by forces too strong to be denied.

But, he thought, watching Sandy's slender form striding ahead of him through the dry meadow grass, walking with that particular awkwardness he found so appealing, if biology accounted for her behavior, it didn't explain his. Granted, neither he nor Sandy had any means of protection available to them here, but still, he hadn't made even the most minimal effort. That wasn't like him; he'd never been careless about such things before.

And even less like him was the fact that he felt no sense of apprehension, thinking about the possibility of having conceived a child. It wasn't something he'd ever wanted to do before, but this was different. Instead of the cold chill of morning-after panic, he felt both humble and proud, possessive and protective. Maybe it was the wilderness getting to him, but he found himself thinking of Sandy as his woman, his *mate,* and of what had happened between them as mating in the truest sense.

He had to laugh a little at himself, knowing what Sandy would have to say if she knew what direction his thoughts had been taking. He had an idea women didn't think in quite those terms these days, especially women like Sandy, who were so big on freedom and independence. It didn't change anything, though. He didn't know why he felt the way he did—he thought the circumstances might have something to do with it, instincts for survival and so forth—but he felt responsible for Sandy, fiercely protective toward her and the tiny part of him she might be carrying. He vowed to get her out of this, somehow. He'd get her out, or die trying.

They spotted the horses just before dusk, at the farthest end of the valley, near the water hole.

"I don't see Rascal," Sandy said with fear in her heart. "You don't suppose—?"

"Rascal?" Jason interrupted, frowning.

"The colt. I don't see him anywhere." She moved closer to the horses, until Jason said, "Sandy," in quiet, warning tones. Then she stopped, but went on looking, shading her eyes against the sunset's glare.

She almost missed him, because for once he wasn't racing around, chasing butterflies, real and imagined. Instead he was standing quietly at his mother's side, only occasionally switching his tail, or lowering his head to nibble something on the ground.

"Find him?" Jason asked softly, coming behind her to put his hands on her shoulders.

She nodded and leaned back against the comforting bulk of his chest. She had to swallow twice before she could say, "He's hurt. I was afraid of that. The cougar got him on the rump, I think, or the flank." She was silent for a while, feeling heavy, aching inside, but determined not to give in to tears. There were too many things to cry about, if she let herself think about them, if she let herself break down. And she didn't want to do that. She *wouldn't* do that.

"If I could only catch him and doctor him," she said in a kind of low, constricted voice that was balanced precariously on the edge of a sob.

"What would you doctor him with?" Jason's voice was gentle. "Sandy, these things happen."

"I know.... If only I had a pot to cook in, I could make a poultice out of yarrow, or something. As it is, all we've got is the tube of antiseptic. It's better than nothing, though." She broke out of his arms and turned, angry not at him, but at fate and nature, both cruel and unopposable forces. "Damn it, Jason, he's going to die if I don't do something. Even if he doesn't get an infection from that cat's claws, he can't run. He won't be able to run fast enough to get away next time."

"It's the law of the wilderness," Jason said with a sad half smile, gently touching her chin. "You should know that. The strong survive, the weak don't. You can't change that."

"Yeah? Well, we're human beings, and we don't have to obey that law! We defy it all the time. Every time I bring a mustang or a wild burro in off the range, I'm defying the law of survival of the fittest. Jason, I *can* do something. If I can just catch that little guy and take care of him . . .' "

"And then what? Take care of him until he gets well? That's what you'd have to do. What would you feed him?"

"Oh," Sandy said. "Well, of course, I'd have to catch his mother, too."

"His mother." Jason turned away with an exasperated sigh. After a moment he faced her again, his eyes grave. "Sandy, you're forgetting one thing. We have to get out of here, or *we* won't survive. We can't stay here while you nurse one scrawny mustang colt back to health. We don't have any food. It's going to start snowing any day." He took her arms in a grip that hurt. "Do you want to die here? Are you willing to sacrifice yourself for that colt?"

"No," she whispered. "Of course not." Looking at Jason's face made her ache and feel ashamed. There was something almost Lincolnesque about him, with that bleak, gentle look in his eyes, his face craggier than ever, the cheekbones more prominent, the eye sockets shadowed. He was losing weight, too much weight, while she'd been playing happy camper and worrying about horses. "You're right," she said heavily. "I'm sorry. Tomorrow we get busy and find a way out of this place, okay?"

But she didn't give up on the idea of saving Rascal—not quite. On the way back to camp, with Jason's arm a companionable weight across her shoulders, hers around his waist, she ventured, "Jason?"

"Hmm?"

"If I *could* catch him and just put some antiseptic on that gash, at least it would change the odds a little bit in his favor."

"Yeah," Jason murmured warily, "I imagine it would." He laughed suddenly and tweaked her braid. "Sandy, tell me something. How do you think you're going to catch a wild mustang on foot, anyway?"

"Hey!" She leaned back to give him an affronted glare. "You're forgetting—I'm a professional wrangler, you know. And a darn good one. Listen, how about a deal? If I can come up with a plan that will work, and that won't affect our own survival, will you help me? Please?"

He paused to look down at her, a long dark look that made her heart beat faster, but also made her wonder uneasily what he was thinking. Then he pulled her hard against his side and began walking again. "Okay," he said gruffly. "*If* you come up with a workable plan." He muttered something under his breath and added, "I don't know what I'm worried about."

"Oh, ye of little faith," Sandy said happily, and began to sing.

Chapter 12

They'd done such a good job on the shelter roof that dawn came inside only in slender streaks, reaching like bony fingers through cracks in the lean-to. Sandy lay still, staring at the light, feeling as if those fingers had just crawled across her flesh. Something had awakened her so suddenly that she still felt jangled—a cry, she thought, or a moan.

The sound came again, desolate...heartbreaking. With a sense of shock, she realized that it had come from inside the shelter. From the man asleep beside her.

Shaken, cold inside, she touched Jason's face. Her fingers came away wet. Prickling with icy shards of panic, she began to touch him frantically, his face, his neck, his chest, his arms and shoulders, patting, stroking, kissing.

"Jason! Jason, wake up...oh, please wake up!"

He muttered something she couldn't understand and threw out an arm. When his hand encountered her shoulder, he hesitated, then gripped her hard, so hard she couldn't prevent a small cry.

"Sandy?" His voice sounded strangled. And then, suddenly relaxing, he groaned, "Oh...God," and dragged his hand over his face. A moment later he said in a voice that sounded almost normal, "I'm sorry. I thought I was over that."

She whispered, "Was it a nightmare?" Under her open palm his heart was still beating a sharp tattoo. When he nodded, she ducked her head and touched her mouth to his chest in silent sympathy. She felt him sigh, felt his hand come to cradle the back of her head, turn it and hold it pressed against him.

"Don't worry about it," he said gently, but with gravel in his voice.

She didn't trust her own voice beyond a whisper. "You've had them before?"

She felt him hesitate, then nod. "Yeah, I used to have them all the time, a long time ago. Lately they've started up again."

That was why he hadn't slept those first two nights, Sandy thought, aching for him. He'd been afraid to. And the next night, exhaustion had made his sleep too deep for dreams.

"Hey, come on, let's get up," Jason said suddenly, briskly. "Got lots to do today, remember? Today's the day we split this place." He turned her face up and kissed her hard and briefly, then gave her bottom a swat through the sleeping bag's thick padding. "Up, lady, and put on the coffee!"

Sandy groaned. "What I wouldn't give to be able to."

They'd slept fully clothed that night, but even so, it was hard to leave the cocoon of warmth and run shivering to the meager consolation of the banked fire. The weather was noticeably colder; outside the shelter their breath made feathery plumes, the sky had a pearly luminescence, and there was a different smell in the air. The smell of winter.

While Jason breathed life into the fire, Sandy sat beside him on the cold ground to put on her boots. Once he glanced at the boots, then went back to puffing at the glowing coals.

"What's the matter?" Sandy asked, noting the worried crease between his eyes.

"Nothing." He shrugged and added another handful of twigs to the infant flames. "I was just thinking that those aren't exactly hiking boots you're wearing. Oops—*damn.*" He laughed suddenly as his stomach emitted a loud growl, then leaned over, hugging his middle. "I don't know about you, but I'm starting to dream about things to eat."

"Me too. Like a great big platter of bacon and eggs."

Jason smacked his lips. "Amen. With Mrs. Clancy's blueberry muffins."

"Mrs. Clancy's fried chicken," Sandy said with a sigh, closing her eyes. "Hot apple pie à la mode."

"Spaghetti with meatballs and hot garlic bread!"

"Pizza with everything!"

"A great big juicy slab of prime rib, medium rare, and a baked potato, steaming hot, smothered in sour cream and sprinkled with chives and melted cheese."

"You win," Sandy said with a laughing groan, holding her own empty stomach. "And when we get out of here, I swear to God I'm never going to eat another fish as long as I live!"

Rueful laughter expired into silence. They sat staring at the flames, spreading their fingers wide to warm them. After a while Sandy said, "Jason?"

"Hmm?"

"Those nightmares of yours—what are they about?"

When he didn't answer, she glanced at him and saw the crease between his eyes again. She wasn't sure whether he was thoughtful or annoyed, but though her heart beat faster, she felt a kind of quiet determination. He wasn't going to close himself off from her, not this time. And if she had anything to say about it, not ever again. "Are they always the same?" she prodded. "Or are they different?"

Picking up a slender branch, Jason began to poke needlessly at the fire. "They start differently," he said, clearing his throat. "Usually. But they always end up the same."

"And that is . . . ?"

He cleared his throat again. "With the avalanche. With Jared's death." He looked up at the sky and gave a hollow laugh. "I guess I've relived those moments a thousand times."

Though the words rasped painfully in her throat, Sandy said, "Jason, tell me about him—about Jared. Please."

For a few moments she thought he wouldn't. But then he shifted abruptly and, resting his arms on his drawn-up knees, brought his dark, pain-filled eyes to her face. His lips twisted, his shoulders lifted and fell, and then he coughed and said with heartbreaking simplicity, "I don't know if I can."

Unyielding, she whispered, "Try."

He gave a harsh little laugh and looked away, into the fire. "Where shall I start? He was my baby brother. I was eight years old when he was born. I'd been an only child, and I didn't like it—everybody else I knew had brothers and sisters by the handful—so I was tickled to death. From the very beginning, he was *mine*." The last word had a guttural, almost angry sound. After a moment, he went carefully on.

"When he learned to walk, it was so he could come to me. I put him on his first horse. I taught him to swim and to fish. I even taught him to play the piano, only he turned out to be better than I was. Jared could play just about any

usical instrument, and sing, too. He was always sing-
ng—you remind me a little bit of him, that way you have
f just breaking into a song. He was so ...exuberant. Did
verything full tilt, you know what I mean?"

Unable to speak, Sandy just nodded.

When he began again, Jason's voice had a jagged edge.
"For Jared's fourteenth birthday, I'd promised to take him
skiing. I was going to the University of Washington then,
ut it was a short hop home. He was a pretty fair skier. I'd
aught him a couple of years before, and he'd gotten good
t it—as good as he was at everything else. So I figured
ve'd do something special, you know? The resorts were
ooking pretty tame to us—crowded lifts, graded runs—so
 suggested we get away from the crush and ski the back
ountry. See some pretty, unspoiled sights, do some *real*
kiing."

Fire scorched the backs of Sandy's hands, but inside her
lenched fists, her palms were wet and clammy. Uncon-
ciously she tightened her body, as if she were expecting a
low.

"It was March," Jason said tonelessly. "We talked
bout the danger of an avalanche, but it hadn't been a bad
ear, and I knew what to look out for, so we went ahead.
t was so beautiful, I remember. So beautiful.

"We were traversing a slope when it happened. There
vasn't a mark on it, just the tracks of our skis behind us
nd this immaculate blanket of white spread out in front
f us, like a blank sheet of paper waiting for someone—for
s—to write on it. And then there was this...sound. Like
n explosion. It seemed so far away, these white plumes
eaching out into the blue sky, like something that couldn't
possibly harm us. Only I knew. I *knew*.

"We couldn't possibly outrun it—the only hope was to
et to the shelter of some boulders on the far side of the
lope. I was the stronger skier, so I was in the lead. I made

it to the rocks and turned to look back. Jared
just...disappeared in this wall of white. I thought I heard
him call out to me, but I don't see how I could have—the
noise was...indescribable. A split second later the thing
hit me. I was buried, but in a little pocket formed by the
boulders, so I had some air, and I wasn't hurt, just banged
up a little. After I dug myself out, I looked for Jared. It
was a miracle I found him at all, I suppose." He shrugged.
"But it didn't make any difference."

He didn't say any more, and Sandy was glad. She sat silently crying, imagining the unimaginable, thinking that in
tragedies of such magnitude, sometimes the dead are the
lucky ones.

There was ice along the edges of the creek this morning, but what worried Jason more than the falling temperature was the lowering sky. Not only did the overcast
clouds carry the threat of snow, if anybody was out there
looking for them, they'd never be able to see them.

At least the fish were biting, so he'd keep fishing, even
though the cold wind was seeping into his bones, making
his jaws ache and his fingers cramp. He'd like to get back
to the fire and eat a few of the damn things, but he hated
to quit while he was still pulling them in. No telling when
he'd have this kind of luck again, and they were going to
need as much food as they could carry if they were going
to try to walk out of here.

Walk. He looked over to where Sandy was poking
around in the dirt, looking for camas bulbs. Those cowboy boots of hers. How on earth was she going to hike over
those mountains wearing cowboy boots?

Self-doubt coiled and twisted in his belly like an angry
snake. Could he get them out of this godforsaken place
alive? The odds certainly did seem to keep piling up against
it.

Self-discipline drove out the snake, and resolve settled in its place, like a lump of cold steel. He *would* get them out, even if he had to carry Sandy over the mountains on his back!

Thoughtfully, his gaze wandered to where the horses grazed against a shimmering backdrop of aspen. For the first time and for just a moment he allowed himself to wonder seriously whether it might be possible to corral and capture a couple of those mustangs. Sandy seemed to think it was, and she certainly ought to know. But then he dismissed the idea as a crazy pipe dream. Even if they could get a rope on one, those mustangs were completely wild. It would take weeks to break them to ride, even with bridles and saddles. Impossible, he told himself. Forget it. And they still had to find a pass over the mountains.

It was around noon when he heard the plane. He thought at first it was his imagination, because he'd been thinking about it earlier, and besides, the creek was making quite a bit of noise. But Sandy was out in the meadow, away from the sound of running water, and she'd obviously heard something, too. She called to him breathlessly, "Jason?" and stood up slowly, shading her eyes and staring up into the pearly overcast.

As if at a prearranged signal, the horses suddenly thundered away toward the trees, leaving the stallion's scream shivering behind them in the thin, cold air.

"Old Rogue!" Sandy said, laughing, cheeks glowing with excitement. "Did you see that? He hears it, too! Jason—"

"I know, I know...." He held himself tense, hoping.

She came up beside him, and he put his arm around her and drew her against him, and together they stood looking into the sky, listening with every nerve in their bodies. But the low droning sound stayed far in the distance, and after a while they couldn't hear it at all anymore.

"Close," Jason said, letting his breath out, "but no ci
gar."

"At least they're looking," Sandy said. Her tone wa
listless.

Jason looked at her and said gently, "We don't know
that it was a search plane."

She gave a quavery snort of laughter. "Rogue knows
Did you see how he took off? I swear he can tell a BLM
chopper from a Forest Service—"

"Shh," Jason said, folding her into his arms.

"I know," she muttered after a moment. And then, with
a furious swipe at her cheeks, "I'm sorry. I hadn't eve
thought about it—about getting rescued. I didn't think w
would be. I guess hearing it sort of..." She let her voic
trail off and leaned against him, holding him tightl
around the waist. The rest of what she said was muffled
"I guess I didn't realize how scared I am."

"I know," he said gruffly. "Me too."

She squeezed him hard and after a moment whispered
"You're getting skinny. I can feel your ribs."

"So are you." He let his hands slide downward
"You've got no bottom at all!" Laughing, she delivered
smart slap to his.

After an unrepentant "Ouch!" he said, "Hey, I thin
I'd better go cook some of these fishes in a hurry. If yo
get any bonier, you'll keep me awake nights."

"I already do," she replied smugly. "Listen, mister
you'd better eat a bunch yourself, just to keep up you
strength."

They laughed, kissed each other breathless, then gath
ered the fishing gear and walked back to camp with thei
arms around each other's waists, each one stealing glance
at the sky and hoping the other wouldn't notice, but foo
ing no one.

Sandy had lost the tie off the end of her braid. She 'asn't sure how—whether it had just come loose and allen off, or gotten snagged on a branch—or where she'd st it, and there wasn't much point in looking. After ooking the fish, eating their fill and storing the rest in the ack of the shelter, they had split up to do some more exloring. Sandy had elected to go back to the slide on the ff chance they might have missed a possible exit in that irection, and to see if there was anything useful left in the hopper, but the answer had been no on both counts.

But she did come up with an idea for corralling the orses, at least long enough to catch the colt and doctor aose wounds. She was so anxious to find Jason and tell im about it that she went back to the camp by way of the valanche scar, hoping she might meet him on the way, but ll she did was flush the covey of grouse again. The silly irds frustrated her beyond bearing. It was intolerable to ave all that lovely food so near, while Jason grew more aunt and haggard every day. If only, she thought, she ould figure out a way to bring them down....

Anyway, by the time she got back to camp her braid had ome all unraveled, so the first thing she did was sit down y the fire and redo it, while trying to remember what ne'd done with the other strap she'd cut off her bra. She aought she remembered seeing it in the first aid kit, and, ure enough, there it was, along with the rest of the bra— bsolutely useless now, of course. She thought about using a piece of gauze bandage instead, but decided against ; who knew when she might need that gauze for someaing more urgent?

With the end of her braid once again secured by a neat 'hite bow, Sandy picked up what was left of her bra and an the bit of white nylon thoughtfully through her hands. ason had been right; she really didn't have any reason to 'ear one. She was getting so used to going without it that

she thought she might go right on doing so once she go
back home.

It sure wasn't much of a thing, she thought ruefully, a
she put it back in the box. *Slingshot.* For some reason, tha
teasing barb from her girlhood kept hanging in the back o
her mind. As if, she thought, it should mean some
thing....

And, quite suddenly, it did.

In the flush of her brainstorm, Sandy snatched up th
bra and ran over to the open sweep of rock near the bath
ing pools, pausing on the way to pick up a handful o
pebbles of assorted shapes and sizes. Biting her lip an
trying not to feel like a complete idiot, she selected a roc
about the size of a lemon and inserted it into one of the bra
cups. Then, trying to remember whether she'd ever seer
this done before, she straightened, gripped the ends of th
bra in her fingers, swung it back and forth a couple o
times to get it started, then whirled it around her head an
let it fly. Which it did—straight into one of the shallowe
pools, bra and rock and all.

Undaunted, Sandy fished the bra out. This time she wa
careful to grip the ends separately, so she could release on
while holding on to the other. Once again, she went int
her windup. This time the rock rolled out on the back
swing and hit her in the head. It felt as big as a cannon
ball.

She decided to try a smaller rock. The pebble looked s
lost in the "pocket" that she added a couple more to kee
it company. This time, to her great delight, the pebble
went flying while the sling stayed in her hand. She wasn'
sure *where* they went, but she could hear the faint plin
plink plink of their landing, some distance away.

Encouraged, she gathered a good supply of pebbles an
set to work, practicing in earnest. On about the twentiet
try she actually got the pebbles to go in the direction sh

was aiming. She got so excited at her success that she forgot all about the time—and Jason. When she heard his voice, she jumped as if he'd shot her.

"Sandy, what in the name of heaven are you doing?"

"Oh!" she breathed, dizzy with adrenaline. "You scared the life out of me!"

"Sandy?"

She felt him come up behind her as she frantically tried to stuff the evidence of her foolishness into the pocket of her jeans. She didn't know whether it was out of embarrassment or some faint hope of eventually surprising him with success, but she didn't want Jason to know about her "slingshot." So she said, "Huh?" about as innocently as a kid up to her elbows in the cookie jar.

Jason couldn't possibly have told her how it affected him, coming out of the trees to find her poised there, looking like some magnificent, primitive goddess of the hunt. It was even worse than the last time he'd surprised her, here in this same spot. Not like a swinging door this time; more like getting kicked in the solar plexus by a mule.

Laughing, he wrapped his arms across the front of her and brought her against him. "Come on," he cajoled, blowing the words past the tip of her ear. "What are you hiding?"

"Nothing," she insisted, sounding as convincing as a three-dollar bill. "I was...practicing." She brightened. "I was practicing roping. Jason, I think I have an idea."

"Without a rope?".

"Well, there's nothing to rope," she said witheringly, turning in his arms. "I was just, you know, going through the motions." She demonstrated on a small scale, twirling one finger in the air. "See?"

"I see," Jason said gravely, keeping a straight face with difficulty. "Practicing for what, if I may ask?"

"Well, for catching the colt, of course. Jason, I think I have an idea that will work. Want to hear it?"

"Hmm. I'm more interested in hearing whether you found us a way out of here. Any luck?"

"No." She pulled back to look at him. "That slide looks as impregnable as it ever did. I think a few more rocks have come down, too. The helicopter looks sort of lopsided, you know? Like a great big crippled insect. How about you?"

He shook his head grimly. He'd elected to follow the creek downstream to the west, figuring they might be able to follow its path through the mountains. But while the creek was fascinating from a geological point of view, it wasn't going to be much use to them as an escape route. Just beyond the water hole it simply vanished into the rocks, following some prehistoric streambed to emerge God-knew-where, probably as an underground spring. He'd love to explore it some day, but for now...

"No," he said flatly. "West is out. So is north."

"And east," Sandy put in.

"Right. Tomorrow we'll pack up and head south. It seems to be our best bet." And the last, although he didn't say that out loud. He didn't dare let himself think about what they'd do if they couldn't find a way out to the south, either.

"Okay," Sandy agreed, setting her mouth in stubborn lines. "But first I want to take a shot at catching that colt. I have a plan, Jason. It'll work. I'll bet a steak dinner on it. And you promised you'd help."

"Sandy..."

"It will only take a couple of hours. Come on, what difference can a couple of hours make?"

Maybe the difference between life and death, he thought bleakly, looking up at the sky. But he could feel the tension in her spine.

"Please," she whispered.

It meant a lot to her, he knew. More than a lot. This thing she had about the horses seemed almost spiritual, a strange kind of kinship. But maybe, he thought, it wasn't strange at all; didn't the Indians believe themselves to be brothers to all living things?

"All right," he said gruffly, knowing he was crazy, but unable to resist the silent appeal in her eyes. "But you know—" He stopped himself before he voiced the thing they both knew was true: *You know they'll all die here anyway, when the snow covers the grass and there's no more food.* Instead he said gruffly, "All right, show me this plan of yours—and it better be good!"

It wasn't a bad plan, he had to admit. Not foolproof, but not completely farfetched, either. And, like all good plans, its beauty was in its simplicity. With growing admiration, he watched her sketch it out for him with a stick in the hard dirt near the fire.

"I thought of it when I was up there at the slide, looking at the chopper. Now, the chopper sits on that little mesa at the mouth of the canyon, right? But the canyon continues on in kind of a curve, like *this,* for another fifty yards or so before the slide blocks it off. Now, if we can drive the herd into that canyon—"

"How are you going to manage that?" Jason broke in. "On foot?" He lit a cigarette—the second-to-last one— and squatted beside her, fascinated against his better judgment.

"Okay, look, every morning the horses graze in the meadow, right? And they keep their distance from us. So if we keep crowding them, they'll just keep moving farther and farther up toward the slide end. Once we get them close, we split up. I circle around to the chopper. You wait until I get there, then set a small grass fire, right about here. The wind always blows toward that end of the valley, so the smoke smell ought to spook them pretty good."

She paused to grin at him. "And if it doesn't, you can jump up and down and yell."

Jason snorted.

She went on anyway. "Now, the way I figure it, if they're in a panic and down close to their old exit, they may try to get out that way, even though they know it's blocked. They run into the canyon. As soon as they're all in, I fire up the chopper's engines. Rogue hates the sound of a helicopter, and I swear he knows mine. All his instincts will tell him to stay away. I don't think he'll try to get past it, Jason. I think he'll stay in the canyon."

"He'll probably go berserk," he said dryly. "I've seen that animal in action. When he finds out he can't get past it any other way, I wouldn't even put it past him to attack the chopper."

"Oh sure, eventually he'd made a break for it. But all I need is a few minutes, just to get down there and get into position to get a rope on that colt. He's slower than the rest of the herd because of his injury, so when they make a break for it, I can get him while he's lagging behind."

"Get down there?" Jason said, frowning. "That's dangerous."

"No it isn't," Sandy insisted. "I wouldn't be in the open, I'd be behind some kind of cover, and besides, by that time you'd be there to help me. Between the two of us we ought to be able to cut the colt off from the rest of the herd, so I can get a rope on him."

"You keep saying that, as if it's the easiest thing in the world. How good are you with a rope, anyway?"

"Pretty darn good," Sandy said, grinning immodestly.

"You sure?"

"Bet a steak dinner on it."

"A steak dinner..."

"With all the trimmings. If I get a rope on that colt, you buy. If I don't, I buy. Deal?"

"Deal," Jason growled. They sealed it with a handshake. "One more thing..." He tossed his cigarette into the fire and reached for her. Hooking a hand around her neck, he gave it a little shake and said roughly, "What happens if you break your neck, huh? Who pays up then?"

Her mouth curved in a smile, and her eyes took on that smoky look. "Nothing's going to happen to me, I promise. You'll get your chance to pay up, don't worry."

"Yeah, well you'd better be damn sure of that, you hear me? I don't want anything happening—"

"Jason..." She gripped his wrists and squeezed hard. "I promise, nothing's going to happen to me. *Nothing.*" Her eyes sharpened their focus and for a long moment held his with all the force of her will behind them. Fear eased its fierce and painful grip on his insides, and he began to breathe again.

Tight-lipped, exhaling slowly through his nose, he nodded and brought her mouth to his. Just as their lips touched, he felt the slightest of tremors flutter through hers. Wondering what emotion caused it, he pressed into it, stifling it with the heated urgency of his kiss.

His hand moved to her throat, rested there for a moment, then unfastened her shirt and slipped inside. Cradling the small and tender weight of her breast, he drew back to whisper once more, brokenly, "I just don't want anything to happen to you, lady, understand?"

Leaning into him, licking lips already glazed with his essence, she nodded. His hand slipped lower and found the fastening of her jeans. After opening them quickly, he reached inside, splaying his fingers across her belly, gently massaging. Her breath quickened, and her eyes acquired a different kind of glaze. When he slipped his hand inside the elastic of her panties and moved lower still, her breath caught and her mouth opened, but her eyes didn't waver from his. Not until his questing fingers found the warm, pulsing center of her woman's body did her eyelids grow too heavy and at last flutter gratefully down.

That night it snowed. Jason and Sandy discovered it when they emerged from the shelter in the morning. Not much, just a dusting, enough to transform the valley into a silent, spun sugar fairyland, breathtakingly beautiful.

It was already melting in the first rays of the morning sun, because the storm had blown away in the night after dropping the snow—as a kind of promise, Sandy thought, like a kiss from a departing lover. The day was going to be gorgeous, one of those crisp, clear autumn days that smelled so good and always made her feel vaguely nostalgic for places she'd never been and times she hadn't known.

Sandy was excited, exhilarated, but worried about how the snow was going to affect her plan for trapping the horses—whether the herd would be in the meadow as usual, whether Jason would be able to get a hazing fire started in the wet grass. Just in case, they filled the picnic basket with dry kindling and gathered up an armload of firewood to take along.

Sandy was going to just stick the tube of antiseptic in her pocket, but then she realized that she'd probably need to clean the wound on the colt's haunches, which would require hydrogen peroxide and possibly a wad of gauze to use as a cloth. In the end, she decided to take the whole first aid kit, just in case.

They started off in a mood of excitement and anticipation, slipping and sliding on the melting snow. Sandy started to sing "Winter Wonderland," because it felt so appropriate, but Jason gave her such an incredulous look that she switched to "Back in the Saddle Again."

Down in the meadow the horses were acting nervous and edgy. Sandy thought they were probably a little confused by the snow, but she wondered, too, if perhaps they knew with some kind of sixth sense that something was about to happen. Rogue had often seemed to have an uncanny knack for anticipating her moves. This time, though, he seemed to be playing along with her. Whether by sheer luck, or whether the stallion had been driven by the snowfall to once again seek a familiar avenue of escape from the valley, he had his band gathered in a restless huddle near the foot of the mesa.

Leaving Jason to lay out the tinder for his hazing fire, Sandy shouldered the coil of rope and veered toward the trees to begin her circuitous route to the chopper.

Jason watched her go with feelings of excitement and dread. He had too much time while she was making her way around to the mesa to think about what could go wrong. He thought about doing something to spook the horses while she was out of sight of the meadow, sabotaging the plan. Then he thought about the look of appeal in her eyes and her confident grin when she'd said, "I'm pretty darn good."

In the end, he supposed, it came down to whether he had enough confidence in her, enough respect for her, not to get in the way of her doing what she felt she had to do. She wasn't a child. She knew what she was doing. Jason told himself that, but he kept having to fill his lungs full of air to ease the knots in his stomach.

It seemed a year before he saw her again, on the edge of the mesa near the listing helicopter. She waved the coiled rope over her head, giving him the go-ahead signal he'd been waiting for, then turned and sprinted for the chopper. Jason took his cigarette lighter out of his pocket and flicked it.

Nothing happened. His chest constricted. He shook the lighter, slapped it against his palm a couple of times, murmured, "Come on, baby, one more time," and flicked it again.

This time it produced a flame. Talking to himself, Jason knelt and touched it to the pile of dry tinder. When the fire was going well, he started adding little handfuls of damp meadow grass to it, until the smoke got to his eyes. Then he stood up and fanned the flames with his jacket.

By that time the horses were starting to get a little uneasy. Instead of milling around, they were all standing quietly, heads turned toward the drifting smoke, ears pricked forward, nostrils flaring. Jason never saw or heard a signal, but suddenly they broke to the left, heading straight for the mouth of the canyon. He caught a glimpse of the little red colt doggedly bringing up the rear, definitely favoring his injured hind leg.

Until that moment he didn't think he'd really believed the plan would work. He'd gone along with it for Sandy's sake, because he knew she'd never be satisfied until she'd given it a try, but he hadn't really thought they could pull it off. But as he watched those horses thundering into the canyon, just as Sandy had figured they would, he felt excitement grip him, along with a cold, belly-deep fear. After pausing just long enough to stuff the lighter into his pocket, he took off running.

For a terrible moment, Sandy thought the motor wasn't going to start.

"Damn," she muttered between clenched teeth, giving the engine all she knew how to give it. *"Damn."* She should have had Mike service it. She shouldn't have waited until after the roundup. She should . . . And then it fired.

Weak-kneed with relief, she nursed the engine until the vibrations evened out, then grabbed her rope and jumped out of the chopper. She hit the ground running.

The horses had disappeared around the bend in the canyon. Sandy could see their dust rising above the rim of the mesa, could hear the thunder of their hooves, their frightened whinnies, Rogue's piercing scream lifting above all the rest. The wind from the rotors blew dirt in her mouth and filled her eyes with grit, but she barely noticed. She went over the edge of the bank with one thought in mind—to get to a place where she would have a clear shot at roping that colt.

Jason, too, ran with one thought in his mind, and that was to get to where Sandy was before those horses decided to make a break for it. He ran as he'd never run before, unaware of his feet touching the ground, the breath knifing through his chest, or the desperate pounding of his heart. He ran like a man who was running for his life.

Chapter 13

He spotted her on the other side of the canyon, well inside the mouth, where she could catch the colt, as he brought up the rear, when the herd made its dash for freedom. She was in a good spot, he saw, near some boulders, so she could scramble for cover if she had to. Feeling easier in his mind about her, Jason looked to his own position.

Almost directly above his head, the helicopter was kicking up dirt and making an awful racket. He thought he must have gotten used to the quiet or something, because the motor seemed thunderous, and the unbalanced rotors made a terrible, eardrum-shattering keening. He gave the copter a worried glance, then moved past it, farther into the canyon, trying to get just opposite Sandy, so he'd be ready to help her cut the colt off when he came by.

He could hear the horses stamping and snorting around, just out of sight around the bend. Even above the din the otors were making, he heard the stallion's scream of challenge.

Here he comes, he thought, filling up with that special calm, that hair-trigger tension, that always came just before the moment of action. He looked across at Sandy, saw her grin, and wondered if she was feeling it, too. She looked calm and in control, lazily twirling the rope around her head.

The stallion's bugle sounded again. A moment later the horses came pounding around the bend, straight for the mouth of the canyon. Jason caught a glimpse of a wild, black mane and flashing teeth as the stallion drove his panic-stricken band toward freedom. And then they were thundering past, so close that he could feel the ground vibrate with their hoofbeats, taste their dust, smell their sweat, feel the heat from their bodies.

From the corner of his eye he saw the colt coming along, limping badly, and he leaped out just in time to head him off. He saw Sandy come walking up from the other side, still moving without haste, twirling the lasso with a sure and practiced hand. And then the loop hissed through the air and settled around the colt's neck.

When he felt the rope tighten, the colt jumped, went stock-still for a second, then uttered a terrified whinny and sat back on his haunches. Jason darted forward to help Sandy, who was running hand over hand along the rope, trying to keep it pulled taut. The colt was fighting in earnest now, bucking and shaking his head, so Sandy had her hands full; even though he was injured, it was obviously going to take both of them to subdue the little rascal.

Jason had almost reached Sandy when all hell broke loose and landed right on top of him.

Sandy heard, rather than saw what happened. She was busy trying to get the frantic colt over to the rocks where she'd left the first aid kit without getting kicked in the process. She'd seen Jason running toward her and, beyond him, the chopper's rotors flailing crazily against the sky. She knew that the horses must be just about at the canyon's mouth.

What happened next she only put together later, after the dust had settled and silence had come again to the valley.

Just as the last of the mustangs was approaching the mouth of the canyon, with a hideous screeching sound the helicopter keeled slowly over onto its side. Its rotors slammed into the ground, snapping off with explosions like rifle fire. Terror-stricken, the mares in the rear of the band wheeled and headed blindly back into the canyon. Like sheep, the others followed.

Half crazed with fear and rage, racing to regain control of his band, the stallion spotted Jason and Sandy struggling with the colt and veered straight toward them. Jason lunged, gave a mighty, desperate shove, and knocked Sandy and the colt back against the rocks.

Acting on blind instinct, Sandy threw her arms around the colt's neck and held on for dear life. When she looked up again, Jason had disappeared in a maelstrom of dust and moving bodies.

The noise was indescribable. Rocks and boulders loosened by the chopper's crash rumbled down the mountainside, their thunder mingling with the horses' screams. Dust rose in a choking, blinding cloud. Terrified, unable to see Jason anywhere, Sandy hung on to the colt and expected to die.

Instead, it was the noise that died, rumbling away not into silence, but into sporadic clatterings of falling scree. Now Sandy could hear the lesser thunder of galloping hooves. Raising her head, she was just in time to see the stallion hurl himself headlong at the side of the cliff. Horrified, expecting to see him batter himself to death on the rocks, she watched instead while he gathered himself, gave a mighty leap, and found a foothold where there seemed to be none. Front hooves scrabbling, powerful haunches quivering with the strain, the stallion scrambled across the slide, sending small rocks and gravel skittering down into the canyon. And then, trumpeting his triumph, he disappeared down the other side, leaving the echoes of his call rebounding through the canyon.

Slowly, one by one, the mares followed, picking their way step by cautious step across the treacherous rocks while Sandy watched in stunned disbelief. When the last one had disappeared from view, the furry body in her arms suddenly erupted in a desolate whinny, jarring her out of her shocked paralysis. Feeling stiff and shaky, she straightened and looked around for Jason.

When she didn't seen him, she called his name, hearing her voice as if it were someone else's, coming from a great distance. When he didn't answer, she felt a new kind of fear, a fear more terrible than anything she'd ever faced before, a great, yawning void so unthinkable that her mind could only reject it.

"No," she whispered. "Oh, no."

In despair she looked for somewhere to tether the colt, and finally managed to snag the end of the rope in a crevice between two boulders. Trembling violently, she scrambled out into the open, alternately screaming, "Jason!" and whimpering, "No, no..."

When she found him, he was lying on his back, staring straight up at the sky, his face chalk white, covered with dust. She thought he was dead. He *looked* dead.

Her mind still rejected the possibility. *"No,"* she bit out, tears of fury streaming down her cheeks as she dropped to her knees beside him. "Don't you dare be dead! Don't you *dare.*"

He blinked and turned his head slightly toward her. Relief knocked her back on her heels.

"Don't worry," he said in a strange, tight voice. "I'm not dead. You'll get your steak dinner." And with that he rolled away from her and was suddenly, wrenchingly, violently sick.

Still reeling from the emotional one-two punch she'd just been dealt, it took Sandy a minute or two to realize that Jason hadn't just had the wind knocked out of him. Exhilaration turned again to despair. She sat still, one hand clamped over her mouth, afraid to even think about how badly he might be hurt.

After a moment Jason said "Ah," in a disgusted-sounding voice and lay back down flat. With one arm covering his eyes he muttered thickly, "Can't be dead—hurts too damn much."

"Where?" Sandy croaked, and put out a hand, not daring to touch him.

"My leg. Left one. Definitely broken, I just don't know how bad."

It was bad enough; Sandy could see that even without a closer look. And anyway, under the circumstances, it didn't really matter. A sprained ankle would have been a disaster.

Suddenly overwhelmed, unable to say anything, just glad he was alive, Sandy touched his face with trembling fingers and said brokenly, "Oh, Jason..."

"Hey..." He caught her hand and held it pressed against his chest. Squinting at her from under his arm, he managed a ghastly smile. "At least you got the little guy."

She gulped and nodded. "Yeah, but his mother's gone. They all are. They went right over the slide."

"I know. I saw. The second slide must have opened up a route." He coughed, made a face and muttered, *"Damn."*

They looked at each other, not knowing whether to laugh or cry at the bitter irony of that.

"Well," Jason said, looking past her to where the colt stood, patiently now, at the end of his tether, "I guess it's too bad he's not a little bigger. As it is, it looks like I'm pretty well stuck. Listen..." He struggled to raise himself on his elbows. Sandy planted her hand squarely in the middle of his chest.

"Don't even *think* it," she said fiercely. "I'm not leaving you."

There was a long silence while his eyes, diamond bright, bored into hers. Her face felt stiff, frozen, her jaws clamped so tightly they ached. "Then I guess we're both stuck," he said finally.

"Yeah," Sandy said huskily. "And with another mouth to feed, too." She sat back on her heels and looked up at the sky. "Oh God, what do we do now?"

Jason cleared his throat. "Well, now that I seem to be through throwing up, you could see if there's anything in that first aid kit that'll fix a broken leg."

She'd forgotten all about the first aid kit. Knowing it was horribly inadequate, she ran to get it, amazed at how wobbly her legs still were. Shock, she supposed, realizing that Jason was suffering from it, too, and a lot more dangerously than she was. As she knelt with the kit beside his injured leg, she thought, Oh God, what now?

"Here," Jason grunted. "Cut it off—pants leg, not mine." He handed her his pocket knife. Just getting it out of his pocket had left his face gray and beaded with sweat.

Sandy took off her jacket and spread it over him. Then, with nausea hanging dangerously in the back of her throat, she set to work splitting the steams of the trouser leg. What she saw when she finally peeled it back wasn't reassuring. She knew enough about broken bones to recognize a compound fracture when she saw one, and enough to

know that if Jason didn't get medical attention for the leg
soon, he could lose it.

Trying not to panic, she poured hydrogen peroxide over
the wound and sat back while she tried to think what to do
next. She decided not to tell Jason how bad it was—at
least, not until he was feeling better. Right now he didn't
seem interested, anyway; he was lying very still with his
eyes closed, looking pale and clammy. She knew she ought
to try to immobilize the leg, but she had an idea that that
should wait until he'd stabilized a bit, too.

And she knew something else. There wasn't any way in
the world Jason was going to be able to make it back to
camp. Somehow, before dark, all by herself, she was going
to have to move the camp to Jason.

It was too much. If she stopped to think about it, she
knew she would never be able to do it. If she allowed her
mind to wander off the straight and narrow—away from
practical matters, like putting one foot in front of the
other—she was afraid she'd get lost in a swamp of despair
and never find her way out. So she didn't think.

Leaving Jason alone was unthinkable, so she didn't
think about that, either. She just did it.

First she went down to the meadow to get the picnic
basket Jason had left there. Then she went back to the
camp, where she gathered up everything and packed it into
either the sleeping bag or the basket. She took down the
lean-to, piled both basket and bag onto the framework of
pine branches and, dragging the whole thing like a tra-
vois, hauled it down the slope and across the meadow to
the slide. Don't think about how heavy it is, she told herself. Don't think about being tired. Don't think about
being scared. Think about Jason.

Oh, Jason, this is all my fault. I'm so sorry.

When she got back with the load of supplies, Jason was
looking much better. He'd gotten too warm, lying in the

midday sun, and had managed to drag himself back into the meager shade of the rocks. The effort had left him gaunt and exhausted, but his color was better and his skin warm. He told her that he'd been passing the time talking to the colt, who was watching their every move from the tightly stretched limits of his tether, ears pricked and eyes rolling.

"I think he's hungry," Jason remarked.

"I sure hope he likes grass," Sandy muttered, unscrewing the top of the thermos. Jason made a face when she poured water into the cup and lifted it to his lips.

"What's this? From the hot spring? What are you trying to do, put me out of my misery?"

"Hush up and drink it," Sandy purred, lowering her lashes. "For shock you need warm liquids. If you're worried, remember that we both swallowed quite a lot of this stuff the other day, and it didn't hurt us a bit."

Jason's smile and the light in his eyes went a long way toward restoring Sandy's spirits.

Jason smiled to hide the anger that burned in his heart. It was anger at fate, at nature, but most of all at himself. He'd felt the same anger fifteen years ago, when he'd dug Jared's body out of the snow and screamed in helpless rage at an empty sky. *Helpless,* that was what he was. Powerless to keep the ones he loved from harm. For fifteen years he'd been careful, kept himself covered, and it hadn't done any good at all. The minute he let his guard down, the first time he let himself care about somebody... The anger surged through him in waves, drowning thought.

He drifted through most of the afternoon, sleeping when the pain in his leg would let him. He knew how bad his leg was; while Sandy was gone he'd taken a good look at it. He'd even tried to tend to it himself, so Sandy wouldn't have to, but he'd gotten sick again and had to quit. He thought he might even have passed out again for a little while.

He woke up when Sandy came back with a basket full of grass for the colt. She'd brought him some water from the creek, too, carried in her hat. The colt sniffed at both, but wouldn't touch either one.

"I guess it smells too much like me," Sandy said sadly, trailing her fingers along the colt's dusty back. "He won't eat or drink."

Jason squinted up at her. "You doctor those cuts yet?" He'd been kind of glad to have the little guy around, in a way; the colt had kept him company.

Sandy shook her head and squatted down beside Jason. She picked at the blades of grass she'd brought and wouldn't look at him, but he knew very well what she was thinking: without his mother, the little horse wouldn't last long anyway. There wasn't much point in doctoring his wound.

"Funny," Sandy said, looking off into the distance. Jason could tell from the way her mouth twisted when she tried to smile, and the pale, set look on her face, that she was talking through pain. "I was only trying to help him, you know?" Her voice broke and became hushed. "I just thought...if I could get his wound healed, he'd have a better chance. And now..." She looked down, shading her eyes with her hand. "Now he doesn't have any chance at all."

Jason gave her braid a gentle tug. "Hey, lady, what are you trying to do, huh? Kick yourself for having a kind, compassionate heart?"

She threw him a startled look, then shook her head and turned away again. "Jason, if I hadn't interfered, that colt would be on his way to greener pastures right now with his mother and the rest of the band. And you wouldn't be—"

"If you hadn't interfered the first time, that colt would be *dead*." He waited for her nod, then touched her chin, compelling her to meet his eyes. Her mouth had a blurred look that wrung at his heart. Hating the look, hating her pain and guilt, he spoke with grit in his voice. "Look, don't blame yourself for what happened here, you hear me? You only tried to do something *good*. Other forces stepped in and messed it up, *you* didn't. This is not your fault! Understand?"

Again he waited for her nod, and then he pulled her to him and kissed her, tasting cool salty moisture on her mouth. He took it away from her with his tongue, bathing her lips as if he could somehow take away her sense of guilt along with the tears. He pulled back, looking into her eyes for a long time, until she sighed and whispered, "Okay." Then he kissed her again, briefly, and let her go.

Her hand touched his face, the lightest, tenderest of touches, like a butterfly landing and then moving on. Standing up suddenly, she muttered something about needing to get wood for a fire and moved away, walking with her head down and her hands in her hip pockets, with that special angular grace that was hers alone.

After she had gone, Jason sat for a long time, staring after her, thinking hard about what he'd just said to her, about himself, and some old and painful memories.

Sandy made three trips to the avalanche scar for firewood. By the time she figured she had enough to keep a good roaring fire going all night, the sun had gone down in the canyon and the cold was settling in fast, the way it does at high altitudes. She laid a fire in a sheltered spot between some rocks and the canyon wall, only a few yards from Jason. She didn't want to think about what it was going to take to move him close to the fire, but she knew he was too exposed where he was. They'd need all the

shelter they could possibly find. It was going to be col
tonight.

"Okay," she said, dusting her hands, "that should d
it. Let's have the lighter."

Jason was holding the lighter in his hands, along with hi
last cigarette in its flattened pack. He hesitated, the
handed it to her without a word. Sandy held it to the pil
of dry leaves and pine needles and flicked it. Nothin
happened. She flicked it again. Nothing.

Jason took it from her, shook it, whacked it against hi
hand, then clicked it several times. Finally he tossed i
down on the ground and uttered a single word of disgust

"Well," Sandy said, looking blankly at it. She fe
empty. She wanted to scream, *"Enough!"*

"What about the old campfire?" Jason's voice wa
calm. "Any life left in it?"

Sandy took a deep breath, trying to stir some life i
herself. "I don't know. I guess I'd better go and see."

They'd gotten in the habit of banking the fire wheneve
they left it, in order to save having to light a new one. Eve
so, once in a while they had come back to find the ember
cold in spite of their efforts. And they'd never left it un
tended for so long before.

Sandy stood up slowly, rubbing her hands on the front
of her thighs to keep them from shaking. She couldn't loo
at Jason, couldn't let him see how scared she was. "Wis
me luck."

"Here." He held out the pack of cigarettes. One las
cigarette. She stared stupidly at it. "Take it, you might b
able to use it." He shrugged. "You never know."

Nodding, not really understanding, but too numb t
argue, she put the pack in her shirt pocket and set out fo
camp.

She ran nearly all the way, though her lungs burned in the cold, thin air. Please God, she prayed silently as she ran. Please don't let the fire be out.

At first she thought it *was;* fine gray ashes sifted like dirty snowflakes across the cold stones. She almost burst into tears of relief when her desperate digging unearthed a few coals with lacy red edges—the last few precious sparks of life. In another moment, they, too, would be gone. How could she possibly revive them? How could she transport them back to Jason?

And then she knew. *The cigarette.* With clumsy fingers she shook it from the pack and put it between her lips. Kneeling, she bent low over the dying coals, trying to keep from inhaling the fine ash or blowing it into her own eyes while she located a tiny spark with the end of the cigarette. A precarious and potentially disastrous bubble of hysterical laughter rose in her chest. She fought it down.

Sandy Stewart, she thought, you really are something! The first cigarette you ever smoked in your life, and it's a matter of life...and death.

Acrid smoke poured into her throat. Gagging and coughing, she stared at the glowing end of the cigarette through tear-filled eyes; she had never been so happy in her life to be in danger of choking to death. Then, holding the precious ember cupped in her hands, she began the long run back to Jason.

Hoping he wasn't being overly optimistic, Jason moved himself close to the laid-out fire and wrapped the sleeping bag around him while he waited for Sandy's return. It was easier to move now that he'd lost most of the feeling in his leg, though that did worry him a little. At least the pain had let him know it was still alive. When Sandy got back, he'd see if maybe they could get a splint or something on it. With a splint, and some kind of makeshift crutch maybe...

Sure. And maybe that colt could fly.

The colt's hooves clattered restlessly on the hard ground. The little guy had been pretty quiet, but something sure had him spooked now. The way things had been going, Jason figured it was bound to be that mountain lion, come to get his long-delayed meal.

The colt danced sideways, pulling against the rope. His shaggy body shook with the force of his shrill, excited whinny.

Inside the sleeping bag, Jason's body froze. For a moment he thought it was his imagination, but then it came again—the sound the colt had already heard and answered. From beyond the slide came another whinny, just as excited, just as urgent, but deeper, lower pitched.

The colt was in a frenzy, throwing his head from side to side, fighting to free himself, erupting again and again in those sharp, urgent cries. The deeper ones replied, coming closer.

Hooves struck rock with a hollow sound; displaced pebbles skittered like hail down the mountainside. Jason waited, motionless, shrinking out of sight behind the rocks, straining to see into the purple dusk as hoofbeats pounded a galloping rhythm on the canyon floor. The colt's whinnies became continuous ripples of joy as a large, pale shape emerged from the twilight.

The buckskin mare had come back for her baby.

Chapter 14

Sandy was running as hard as she could, and when she heard the commotion she stumbled, nearly dropping the precious spark of heat and hope she carried cupped in her hands.

At first she thought all the horses had come back again, and she wondered why. Then she recognized the two voices, one high, one low, and wondered why she hadn't expected this. Good old maternal instinct! She should have known that mare wouldn't abandon her baby!

When the buckskin saw Sandy, she stopped short, veered and circled, calling to her colt in a series of whickers and grunts. The colt reared, tugging frantically at his tether.

"Sorry, old girl," Sandy muttered, scrambling over the rocks to where Jason lay beside the waiting firewood. "First things first...."

As she dropped to her knees, she took the crumpled cigarette pack from her shirt pocket and held it to the nub

of the cigarette she'd tucked between her lips. Eyes water
ing, trying desperately not to cough, she puffed until th
pack crackled and burst into flame.

"Bravo," Jason said softly.

Half laughing, half crying, Sandy touched the preciou
flame to the waiting tinder and watched the fire catch, then
eat hungrily into the little pile of dry leaves and pin
needles. It seemed like a miracle. She felt the way som
early human must have felt, creating fire for the first time.

"Oh God," she said, collapsing onto bare ground, onl
then realizing how near she was to complete exhaustion.
won't cry, she said to herself, though it would have felt s
good to do so. With relief, if nothing else. Things had bee
looking so hopeless. Probably, realistically, they were stil
pretty dismal, but they had a fire, and the colt's mothe
had come back. They weren't done yet!

"Hey," Jason said. She felt the warm weight of his han
on her head, his fingers burrowing through her hair t
gently massage her scalp. It felt so good. "Did you se
who's come back?"

Though it took every ounce of energy she had, Sand
roused herself and sat up. "I saw. I scared her away,
think." She peered over the rocks. The mare was still pac
ing agitatedly, torn between her fear of fire and man, an
her fierce maternal instincts. "I think she'll come to him
though, once she gets it through her head that he can'
come to her."

"You aren't going to turn him loose?"

Sandy settled back against the rocks. "No," she sai
flatly, shaking her head. If she turned the colt loose, th
mare would take him back with her across the slide. A
long as the colt remained here, the mare would stay clos
by. Nursing the embers of her hope in her heart, guardin
them the way she'd guarded the glowing end of the ciga

ette, afraid that if she exposed them they'd turn to ashes, Sandy didn't say any more.

Jason gave her a long look, but he didn't say anything more about the horses, either. If he had any hopes at all, he was guarding them as closely as she was.

With the fire burning brightly, keeping the cold and darkness at bay, Sandy turned her attention to Jason's leg. All the moving around he'd done couldn't have been good for it, and she knew she had to get it immobilized before any further damage was done. She wasn't looking forward to it. She wasn't squeamish; she'd dealt with injured animals before, and had even broken her own arm once, when she'd gotten pinned against a corral fence by a bucking mustang. But this was different. This was Jason. Her own pain had been much easier to bear.

He assured her that his leg was numb and he couldn't feel it anyway, but by the time she'd finished pouring more hydrogen peroxide in the wound, padding it with gauze and splinting and wrapping it, he was gray and sweating again, and had to lie down flat for a while.

"Numb, my foot," Sandy said brusquely, trying not to let the shaking inside her show in her voice. "It's a good thing I didn't feed you first, that's all I can say."

Jason managed a weak laugh. "That's a lovely thought. But listen, really—I'm not feeling very hungry right now. You go ahead and eat those fish."

"Not a chance, mister," Sandy said firmly. "You need to keep your strength up. You just wait a little while until you feel better. I don't need any fish. In fact, I'm sick to death of fish. If I eat another fish—"

"Sandy."

"Jason, I'm really not hungry, honest."

"Sandy..." He sighed. "All right, you give me no choice. If you want me to eat, you're going to have to match me fish for fish, you got that?"

"That's blackmail!"

"That's right."

So they shared the fish, leaving only one apiece for th
morning. And after that...

"I guess I'll have to go catch some more," Sandy said
with a confidence she didn't feel.

They slept in turns, tending the fire, listening to the mar
and the colt talking to each other in the darkness.

Sandy woke up to something soft and silky brushing he
face. Knowing what it was, she smiled sleepily and reache
up to touch Jason's beard.

"Shh," he whispered. "Don't move."

She opened her eyes. He touched a finger to her lip:
"Carefully now. Look...."

Raising herself by inches, she turned stiffly, lookin
where he pointed. A wonderful warmth poured throug
her, making her smile. A few yards away the buckski
mare stood quietly while her baby, still tethered securely t
the rocks, nursed to his heart's content.

"Oh," she whispered, "Jason..." It was more tha
she'd dared to hope for. For a wild mustang to come s
close, so quickly...

Something puzzled her. It was several moments befor
she realized the significance of the small, gray patches c
scar tissue on the mare's flanks and belly.

"Jason," she whispered, clutching his arm. "Th
mare's been ridden!"

How or why she could only guess, but it was unmistak
ably true. At some time in the fairly recent past, the buck
skin mare had worn a saddle. It must have been more tha
a year ago, because there was no doubt the colt wa
Rogue's, but probably not much more than that. Since th
mare was definitely a mustang and not a domestic hors
gone wild, Sandy surmised that she'd been rounded up an

dopted, and then had either escaped from her new own-
rs or been abandoned. It wasn't all that uncommon for
eople to underestimate the patience and expense in-
olved in adopting a wild horse. Maybe this mare's own-
rs had found they'd bitten off more than they could chew
nd simply taken her back to where she'd come from.
andy would probably never know.

"Jason, do you know what this means? That mare has
ad at least some handling—some training. Unless she was
nistreated, abused, I might be able to get a rope on her
airly easily."

"Hmm," Jason said, frowning. "The rope's on the colt.
f you cut him loose, they'll both be out of here."

"Yeah, I know." She chewed on her lip for a moment.
'Here, give me your pocketknife."

He fished it out and handed it to her without a word.

The mare gave a startled jump and clip-clopped away
vhen Sandy stood up, but she didn't go far. A short dis-
ance from the colt, she turned and stood, tossing her head
uspiciously, while her baby, deprived so abruptly of his
reakfast, snuffled disappointedly at the ground. When
andy took hold of the rope and began to reel him in, he
ame, prancing and balking.

Working quickly, Sandy sawed the rope in two, leaving
nly enough on the colt for her to resecure him. Using the
est, she hurriedly built a new loop and then, muttering,
'Wish me luck," stepped out into the open. Giving her-
elf no time to think, and the mare no time to suspect what
he was up to, she whirled the loop around her head and
et it fly. With the faintest of sounds it snaked through the
ir and settled over the mare's shaggy black mane.

Too late, the mare threw up her head and leaped side-
vays, but Sandy was already running to snub the rope
round a rock. The mare jerked and bucked a few times—
nd then stood still.

It really was that easy.

Cheeks flushed and eyes sparkling with triumph, Sand
turned to Jason, dusting her hands as if to say, "Wel
that's that!" She looked ready to burst.

Jason knew he was—with love for her and pride in her
and too many other feelings to name. When she droppe
beside him, laughing and breathless, he opened his arm
and gathered her close. He tried to think of something ligh
and clever to say, but he couldn't. All he could do was hol
her and kiss the top of her head and stroke the wisps o
hair back from her face. Inside, he felt very calm, almos
peaceful.

"Sandy," he said gently, "I want you to do somethin
for me."

"Sure." She sat up, smiling, brushing back her hai
"What is it?"

"I want you to promise me something."

Unsuspecting, she said, "Sure, what?"

"So that's a promise?"

Now she watched him warily, her eyes growing sultr
with suspicion. "I don't know. Maybe you'd better tell m
what you want me to promise."

Jason took a deep breath. "I want you...to promis
me...that as soon as that mare will carry you, you'll ge
on her and ride her out of here."

"The hell I will!" She pushed away from and went to si
on a rock some distance from him. The pink in her cheek
was from anger now.

"Sandy." He spoke slowly, trying to choose his word
carefully. "It's the only thing that makes any kind o
sense. I can't go anywhere with this leg. There's no sens
in us both sitting here, waiting to starve or freeze. You go
you get help, you send somebody back for me."

"Oh yeah? And what do you do in the meantime, huh? Freeze? Starve?" Her voice was constricted, as if she were holding her breath.

"So you leave me plenty of firewood, some camas—"

"How much is plenty? Who knows how long it'll take me to find help? What do you do if the lion comes back?"

"You leave me the hammer?" he smiled at her, but she wasn't buying it.

"No!" She made a violent, rejecting motion with her hand. Her voice was low, furious. "I'm not leaving you here. No way. Either we both go, or we both stay."

"Sandy, that's crazy. You—"

"*You're* crazy! That horse must have kicked you in the head! If you think I'd ever go and leave you . . ."

To his amazement, he saw that she was crying. "Sandy," he said gently, "why are you being so stubborn about this? Why do you insist on staying, when you know I'm right?"

"Why are you so pigheaded, so set on making me leave?" She stood over him, breathing hard, looking as if she wanted to drop a rock on his head.

"Look, Sandy . . ." His voice roughened. "It's the only thing that makes sense. Damn it, it's probably the only chance we've got! You're mobile, I'm not. You go, you get help. What's wrong with that?"

"Everything!"

"Tell me one thing!"

Her chest heaved. "I'd be afraid . . . I'd be leaving you here to die!"

She turned away from him, scrubbing furiously at her cheeks. He spoke very softly to her back. "So you'd rather stay here and die too?"

"*Yes.*"

"Sandy, that's crazy."

In a very small voice she said, "No, it isn't. I love you."

Jason stared at her rigid back, the bowed nape of he neck, and felt weighted down by helplessness and frustra tion. He knew he wasn't going to be able to make her go Because she thought she was in love with him, she wouldn' leave without him. She would die here with him, and h couldn't do anything to save her. The only two people he'(ever loved—outside of his parents—and he couldn't sav either one of them.

No! His mind rebelled, rejecting defeat. There had to b a way to make her go!

Hardening his heart, his voice, he said, "Hey, lister Sandy, I think you've got the wrong idea here."

She turned slowly. "What . . . ?"

He gave an embarrassed shrug, a little wave of his hand "Look, I know we've had a pretty good thing going her between us. I mean, it's been great, especially consider ing . . . everything. But I'm not the kind of guy to sta around long in one place, you know what I mean? Like told you, I've been all over the place. I've got a job wait ing for me in Hawaii right now. I like you a lot. I car about you, I really do. But . . ." He took a deep breath an(zapped her with the words he'd used on her once before "Don't make more out of this than it is, okay?"

She stared down at him, her eyes like sooty smudges When he couldn't stand the silence any longer, he added even more unforgivably, "Sandy, I don't want to hui you."

"Sure," she said. "Okay." She turned abruptly an(walked away.

Pain blossomed inside him, exploded through him Compared to it, the pain in his leg had been nothing *Nothing.*

"Where are you going?" The words ripped throug him.

She paused. "Fishing," she said, sounding almost sur-
ised. "I'm going fishing."

Once the blood had returned to her heart and brain,
andy knew what Jason was trying to do.

Though she knew there was quite a bit of truth in what
e'd just said to her, she also knew that he cared more for
r than he'd made it sound. She knew that his cruelty was
deliberate attempt to push her away. The only thing she
dn't know was whether it was because he really wanted
r to leave him and save herself, or whether it was to pro-
ct himself from loving, and being loved.

Either way, Sandy told herself, feeling bleak, it didn't
ake much difference. If Jason wouldn't admit or accept
ve, it didn't really matter what his reasons were.

And anyway, she couldn't think about that now. Only
ne thing mattered to her, and that was getting Jason out
' this valley alive and getting him to a hospital. She didn't
ow exactly when it had happened, but that big, gentle,
gged, lonely man had become more precious to her than
r own life. She had to save him, because the thought of
r own life without him in it was like an endless barren
sert, without water or shade, or any comfort whatso-
er.

First she'd save his life. After that she'd worry about
hether or not he could ever bring himself to love her.

First on the list of priorities, if she was going to save
son's life, was to keep him from starving to death, and
ings weren't at all well in that department. Sandy had
ver been much of a fisherman, and the damn fish just
eren't biting at all this morning. She supposed it was
ossible the little stream had been fished out; it wasn't very
g, and they'd been fishing it pretty heavily for the last
veral days. But the bottom line was that she wasn't

catching anything. Hunger burned in her belly, but t
frustration, the helpless anger, was worse.

She dug a few camas bulbs, but just the sight of the ug
brown things turned her stomach. Hungry and dejecte
she turned her steps toward the avalanche scar, hoping
find some rose hips, maybe a few shriveled berries. O
how she hated the thought of going back to Jason empt
handed, to watch the bones in his face becoming sharp
the hollows darker and deeper almost by the minute.

It was a cold, overcast morning, sharp and tangy wi
the smell of snow. As she stood at the edge of the meado
looking up at the treeless slope, Sandy could hear t
grouse calling to each other in the brush. Food. It w
there, if only she could find a way to catch it. Ang
flooded her, and then a calm, cool resolve.

The "sling" and the pebbles she'd stuffed so hurried
in her pocket to hide them from Jason were still there,
bulge so insignificant that she'd forgotten about the
Thinking, Why not? What have I got to lose? she pull
them out and swung them experimentally. With her jaw s
in lines of determination, she began walking through tl
brush.

A hush fell over the hillside. Small, unseen things scu
ried away through the scrub, while overhead a hawk ci
cled silently, waiting his turn.

Something flew up, too small to be a grouse, and too f
away to hit, in any case. Sandy paused, her heart knoc
ing in her throat, awash with adrenaline. She took a de
breath and moved on. And then suddenly, almost und
her nose, the brush exploded. Birds shot out in eve
direction; the air was full of the creaky beat of their wing

Sandy's breath hissed between her teeth. The sli
whipped through the air; the pebbles flew. She clapp
both hands over her mouth and froze in total disbelief

one of the birds fluttered and tumbled down into the brush.

"Oh God," she said in a high, squeaky voice. "I hit it!" Her heart was beating so hard, her legs shaking so badly, that she could barely stand up. As she ran jerkily toward the spot where the bird had disappeared, she had only one thought in her mind, a prayer: Oh please God, let it be dead!

She didn't know what she would do if it was only stunned or injured. She'd never killed anything in her life—fish didn't count. She'd never believed she would actually hit one of the stupid birds. She hadn't thought beyond the point of "shooting" at it at all.

Now, though, the terrible reality was staring her in the face. Literally. She found the bird without any trouble, lying half on its side, blinking at her. Once again she put her hands over her mouth and whispered, "Oh . . . God."

Jason's knife was still in her pocket. Shaking violently, she dug it out and held it clutched tightly in her hand while she sniffed and brushed away tears. At her feet, the bird fluttered and was quiet once more, waiting. Crying so hard that she could barely see, Sandy thought of Jason and opened the knife.

Jason had been listening for her footsteps. She'd been gone a long time, and he'd been getting a little worried about her. Once again he'd passed the time talking to the horses, and he thought they both seemed to be getting used to the sound of his voice. When the mare began to snort and dance restlessly at the end of her rope, he knew Sandy was coming back.

He watched her come toward him, surprised at the way his heart had jumped into high gear at the sight of her. He didn't call to her, just waited for her, feeling a little uneasy about how she'd be, after the things he'd said to her.

She looked...different, somehow, very pale, smiling, but...different. He couldn't say why, but there was just something about her—a kind of quietness.

"Well," she said, letting her breath out as she set the picnic basket on the ground and stretched her hands toward the fire, "I didn't catch any fish. I'm sorry, I told you I wasn't much good at it."

"It's okay," Jason said, touching her pants leg. "I was tired of fish anyway."

"Good," she said, dropping to her knees and opening up the basket, "because I found this instead." She took something out of the basket and, without looking at him, laid it on the ground.

Jason stared at the bird, then at Sandy. She still wasn't looking at him. "Where in the world did you find that?"

"I killed it."

"You killed—*how?*"

One of her hands lay on her thighs, curled into a fist. Without a word, she opened her fingers. Jason stared in total disbelief at the crumpled scrap of soiled nylon that tumbled onto the ground.

"With *that?*"

"Uh-huh." The affirmation came on the crest of a sound somewhere between a sob and a giggle. Jason reached for her. She resisted him at first, then came into his arms, shaking, he wasn't sure whether with laughter or weeping.

"It was an accident, I think—a fluke," she said in a hushed voice, muffled against his chest.

Jason growled, "I don't believe that for a minute."

"I hit it with a rock. It only stunned it. I had to—"

"Shh," he said, stroking her hair, feeling her body's shaking in the depths of his own.

"I can't believe I k-killed a bird with my *bra.*" Her laughter exploded against his neck. He tightened his arms around her, knowing it wasn't laughter that trembled inside him, wondering how long he could keep it from erupting. "Jason," she gasped, "nobody is going to believe this. It's too ridiculous. If you ever tell anybody about this, I swear I'll kill you."

"Are you kidding?" His chuckles felt like rocks in his chest; his voice was a husky growl. "This is the stuff family legends are made of. It's something we'll tell our grandchildren about—that, and the one about the mountain lion—"

She pushed herself away from him and sat up, wiping her eyes. "Our grandchildren?"

Skewered by her steady gray gaze, Jason shrugged and muttered, "You'll tell your kids...."

"Our. You said we'll tell *our* grandchildren. I heard you."

Silently, he watched her while the world fell away, leaving only her eyes, her face, and the clasped hands she brought to press against her trembling mouth.

"Jason Rivers, you are a coward and a fraud." Her voice was low and rough-edged. "You *love* me. I know you do. Don't even try to deny it!"

He shook his head slowly. "I won't."

"You won't?"

"No."

"Then *say* it, damn it!"

He opened his mouth, but no sound came.

"It won't kill you," she rasped. "It won't even hurt much," she rasped.

He smiled at her, aching so badly. "It isn't saying it that hurts, Sandy. It's doing it."

"But," she whispered, "not saying it doesn't keep you from doing it—or from hurting. Does it?"

He shook his head. "No." The word was a fragment, torn from his soul by an explosion of emotions. So were the ones that followed it. "And I do...love you."

She went on looking at him, and he at her. The silence flowed between them like a river. Finally Sandy cleared her throat and said, "And that hurts you?"

He nodded. "And scares me."

"Why?"

How could he explain the way he felt at that moment? As if his body and soul had been flayed, laid wide open, raw and unprotected. The terribleness of his vulnerability overwhelmed him, and he couldn't speak.

Sandy's eyes darkened. Unclasping her hands, she laid one of them on his arm. "Jason," she whispered, "please don't be afraid to love me. I know...you lost someone. Someone you loved very much." He heard her swallow as she struggled with the words. He looked down at her hand—her fine, strong hand, now rough, dirty, blood-stained—and he picked it up, clasping it between both of his and bringing it to his mouth.

"Oh, Jason," she said brokenly, "I can't guarantee nothing's ever going to happen to me. You can't give me any guarantees, either. Nobody can. An awful lot of the time, you can't keep things from happening to the people you love. All you can do is just love them as much as you can, while you have the chance."

He closed his eyes and let his breath out slowly. After a while he nodded and said hoarsely, "Okay, lady, you asked for it. As much as I can, I do, and I will." He didn't add, "While I can," but it resounded loudly in the space between them.

They sat still for a long time, looking at each other, listening to the echoes of everything that had been said, and not said. And then Sandy pulled her hand from his grasp and stood up. When he asked her where she was going, she gave him a bright, fierce smile.

"We're going to have that chance," she said. "Both of us."

While Jason cleaned and cooked the grouse, Sandy worked with the mare.

She began by standing quietly, just talking and talking, while the mare listened with her ears pricked forward, her nostrils twitching. She kept that up until the mare's natural curiosity got the best of her and she stretched out her neck and blew her warm, moist breath against the front of Sandy's shirt.

The mare shivered her dusty yellow hide and tried to sidestep when Sandy touched her, but Sandy just went on rubbing her neck and back with long, quieting strokes, communicating in ways that transcended the boundaries separating humans from other living things. She had a special kinship with horses; her hands told them so, and they understood.

When Sandy took off her jacket and laid it across the mare's withers, the animal flinched, but stood still. When Jason called her to come and eat, Sandy left the jacket there. The mare stood patiently, watching and wondering.

Just as Jason and Sandy finished the last of the grouse, the first snowflakes began to fall like feathers from the slate-gray sky.

After the meal, Sandy rolled up the sleeping bag and threw it over the mare's back.

"Okay, old girl," she murmured as she unwound the rope from the rock she'd snubbed it to. "This is a big step. Don't let me down...."

Docile as a lamb, the mare followed Sandy down to the creek, took a drink of the icy water and followed her back again.

"She's definitely broken to lead," Sandy said to Jason, breathless with excitement. "I just know she's been ridden. I'm going to give it a try."

He gave her a long, steady look, then nodded. "Be careful."

The mare grunted when she felt Sandy's weight, and danced nervously, her hooves clattering on the hard ground. Sandy stroked and calmed her, speaking gentle reassurances, bestowing lavish praise.

A moment later she slid to the ground and turned to Jason with her heart a throbbing weight in her stomach. "Well?" she said, squinting up into the lazily swirling snowflakes. "What do you think?"

"I'm ready to go," he said quietly, "if you are."

They looked at each other for a long time in silent communication, leaving all their fears and hopes unspoken.

Sandy took the colt across the slide first, knowing the mare might need some extra incentive to make it over with the added burden of Jason's weight on her back. It wasn't easy, and it was made more perilous still by the rapidly accumulating snow. She had to coax and cajole, push, pull and at times half carry the trembling colt over the rocky trail, then leave him snubbed to a rock, crying piteously while she went back for Jason and the mare.

An eerie quiet had fallen. The snow sifted down, muffling the colt's distant whinnies and the sounds of their preparations. Jason and Sandy hardly spoke at all. They moved in silence, in a silent world.

While Sandy gathered the few things she thought they might need and put them in the picnic basket—the flashlight, emergency road flares, the few camas bulbs that were

eft—Jason crawled laboriously onto some rocks. Sandy
maneuvered the nervous mare into position and calmed her
while Jason made the awkward transition to her back. She
arranged the sleeping bag around him, jammed her hat on
her head, picked up the basket, looked around one last
time, then gave the lead rope a tug. At last, like silent, stoic
refugees, resigned, but with hope in their hearts, they
moved off into the swirling snow.

Sandy never know how they made it over the slide. The
only sounds were the scrapes and thuds and clatters of
hooves on slippery rock, the mare's grunts and labored
breathing. Sandy's own breath came in desperate, throat-
burning gasps that sounded like sobs.

Safely across, she took off her hat and rested her forehead on Jason's thigh while the mare whickered softly to
the joyful colt. She felt Jason's hand on her head, his fingers gently massaging her scalp, telling her that he was all
right. Straightening her shoulders, she put her hat back on
and tilted it forward over her eyes, then once again moved
out into the snow, carrying the basket, leading the mare,
while the colt gamboled along at his mother's heels.

They walked the rest of the day, until the darkness and
the snow forced them to stop. They took shelter of a sort
in a stand of heavy timber, under a jumble of rocks, fallen
logs and the roots of great, brooding pine trees. Huddled
together in the sleeping bag, with the mare and colt tethered nearby, Jason and Sandy passed the long night singing all the songs they could remember, talking about their
childhoods, and planning what they were going to do when
they got out of the mountains.

Jason told Sandy about his family's ranch in the Stan-
ley Basin, the one he'd left so long ago, that waited for him
till.... "In the shadow of the Sawtooth Mountains," he
told her, "with meadows full of wildflowers and grazing
cattle."

"And horses?" Sandy asked.

"Yes," Jason said, kissing her. "And horses."

"We can adopt mustangs," Sandy said happily. "A whole bunch of 'em."

Jason's soft laughter stirred the wisps of hair on her forehead. "Sure, why not? Starting with Little Rogue over there, and his mother."

"Rascal," Sandy murmured. "His name is Rascal."

The snow was a blessing in a way. There were no blizzard winds, and the air actually seemed warmer than it had during the nights they'd spent in the valley. The cloud cover helped to hold the heat, but when the snow stopped falling and the skies cleared, *then,* Jason knew, the temperature would fall....

All the next day they plodded on. Time no longer had any meaning. Sandy measured it in footsteps, one at a time.

About midafternoon, by her rough estimation, the snow stopped falling. A bitter wind sprang up, clearing the clouds away, and the sun came out on a wilderness of stunning beauty. The cold brilliance hurt Sandy's eyes, making her long for the sunglasses she'd left in the valley.

The valley. Rogue's Valley. It seemed unreal to her now, like Shangri-la. The only reality was pain and cold, and the fear that Jason would pass out and fall off the mare's back. If he did, she knew she would never get him back on again.

It was nearly sundown when Sandy first heard the helicopter. It never came close, staying out of sight beyond a ridge of mountains on her left, but she was too exhausted to feel anything, even despair. All though the long autumn dusk she kept thinking she heard it, until after a while she didn't believe it anymore.

She kept walking, even after dark, trusting the mare's instincts, knowing that if they stopped, even for a moment, they would stay forever.

They had just crossed a wide, snowy meadow and were entering another stand of timber when the mare suddenly began to snort and dance.

"Whoa, old girl," Sandy murmured dully, automatically stroking the mare's neck.

Jason straightened and muttered, "What is it?"

The chopper burst upon them suddenly, erupting over the ridge just ahead with a racket that shattered the snowbound silence of the night. Flying low, it clattered out across the meadow they'd just traversed, its searchlights stabbing at the ground like silver knives.

Hope poured through Sandy like a powerful drug, clearing her mind and bringing warmth and strength to her half-frozen arms and legs.

"It's too dark!" she cried, cursing bitterly at her stiff fingers for being so clumsy as she tried desperately to get the mare's rope lashed to a tree. "He'll never see us!"

Jason croaked, "The flashlight..."

Scrabbling in the basket for the flashlight, Sandy found the emergency flares instead. Sobbing with effort, her throat and lungs on fire, she raced through ankle-deep snow, popping the flares and dropping them in a wide circle.

"Please," she prayed, not even knowing whether she spoke out loud. "Oh, please, come back. Please come back...."

At the far end of the meadow the helicopter made a wide, sweeping circle and started back. Sandy stood still in the ring of sputtering pink lights, her head thrown back, the bitter wind blowing her hair. She was standing like that when the chopper's searchlights found her.

"I can't leave the horses," Sandy said.

She was sitting in the Forest Service helicopter, wrapped in blankets, drinking hot coffee. It was making a delicious pool of warmth inside her. If she let herself sit still too long, she'd fall asleep.

The pilot snorted. It was Larry, her forest ranger friend. Sandy couldn't believe it—she'd thought she must be dreaming, or hallucinating.

From behind her on the floor, Jason's laughter sounded like dry leaves. "She won't, you know. Stubborn as a mule."

"I know," Larry said, shaking his head. "Believe me." His voice sounded hollow with wonder. "I can't believe I found you. Everybody'd just about given you both up for dead. But I just didn't want to give up, you know? I was just going to make one last run...."

"Larry..." She tugged at his arm. Only two things were important enough to her now to penetrate the fog that was settling over her. "Leave me here. I'll be okay. Leave me some blankets and some matches. I'll build a fire. Take Jason to a hospital. You can send somebody back for me. With a sling for the mare."

"I'll send somebody back for the *horses*," Larry said grimly. "But you're not staying here. Right now, I'm taking the both of you to a hospital!"

"Larry!"

He swore explosively. "Will you quit worrying about the damn horses? For God's sweet sake, here we all thought you were dead, and all you are is *nuts!* Those horses will be all right until we get back with a sling. Now, will you shut up and fasten your seat belt?"

"No," she said. "I'm going to ride in back with Jason. But you promise you'll take care of—"

"They'll be back at headquarters before you are," Larry said with a sigh as they lifted off.

With her face pressed to the chopper's window, Sandy watched the mare and her colt until they were swallowed up in darkness. Then she curled up beside Jason, put her head on his shoulder and fell sound asleep.

"Sandy's a friend of yours, is she?" Jason asked the Forest Service pilot as they streaked across the snowy, moonlit wilderness.

"Yeah," Larry said. "I'm pretty fond of her."

"Known her long?"

"A few years. How about you?"

"Couple of weeks," Jason said. And then, firmly "I'm in love with her. I'm going to marry her."

The forest ranger turned around. He and Jason exchanged long looks across Sandy's head; then Larry nodded, held out his hand and said, "Congratulations."

"Thanks," Jason said. Smiling, he kissed the top of Sandy's head and closed his eyes.

It was June, and a sweet spring wind from the slopes of the Sawtooths was blowing across the corral, stirring the wisps of hair around Sandy's face.

"Hey, lady, somebody here needs you."

She turned to smile at Jason, who was coming toward her carrying a tiny bundle cradled in his arms, limping only slightly now. Love and joy flooded her as she went to him and kissed the top of her brand-new daughter's head.

"Hungry, is she?" she murmured, touching the baby's silky auburn curls with a wondering finger. "Oh, Jason, I still can't believe how beautiful she is. I can't believe she has red hair!"

Laughter softened the rugged lines of his face. "I guess I forgot to mention that Jared had red hair. And my mother's was red, before it turned snow white."

"I guess you did!" She lifted her face for his kiss, leaning across their daughter's waving fists.

"Mmm," Jason said, frowning suddenly. "Are you sure you should be up and around so soon? Shouldn't you be—"

"Jason," Sandy said, laying her hand on his face and pressing her thumb to his lips. "Hush. Don't fuss over me. I'm fine."

She took the baby from him, and he slipped his arm around her waist. "More than fine," he growled, hugging her close. And then, jerking his head toward the other end of the corral, he asked, "How's that little red rascal's halter-breaking going?"

Sandy laughed. "Well, he's got his father's temperament, all right, but he's coming along. He ought to be well broken by the time Jenny's old enough to learn to ride."

"Jenny, huh?" Jason paused thoughtfully as he held the corral gate for her. "You like that one best?"

"I think so. Yeah. Jenny Rivers. I like that a lot."

"Jenny it is, then. What about a middle name? Jaimison?"

"Good grief!" Sandy said in horror, settling herself down on a sunny patch of new grass beside a sumptuous picnic basket. "Jenny Jaimison?"

Jason stretched himself out beside her and opened the picnic basket. "Okay, how about Stewart?"

"That's not quite as bad."

"Look at this—Mrs. Clancy's outdone herself," he said, laughing as he held up a bottle of champagne tied with a pink ribbon.

"Oh—too bad I can't drink it," Sandy said, smiling at her squalling daughter. "I don't think it would agree with either Jenny or me."

"She's thought of that, too. Look." Jason pulled a bottle of sparkling cider from the basket.

"Bless Mrs. Clancy," Sandy murmured, feeling the prickle of tears. "And Harvey, too. I'm so glad Jenny arrived in time for the wedding."

"That's next week, isn't it?" Jason asked, frowning. "When are we expecting the Senator?" He watched with a kind of awe as she unbuttoned her shirt and guided the baby's frantically searching mouth to her nipple.

"Ouch," Sandy said as the tugging produced a familiar melting tingle. She smiled at Jason, giving him the look he always called "smoky." "Mom and Dad will be here tomorrow. Think you can handle the crowd?"

Jason drew one finger slowly across the pink streaked skin of her more-than-adequate breast, touched his little girl's velvety cheek and shook his head, for a moment too full of wonder to reply.

"Lady," he said fervently, when he could speak again, "after what we've already been through together, I think we can handle anything, don't you?"

"Yes," Sandy Jaimison Stewart Rivers whispered. "Anything."

* * * * *

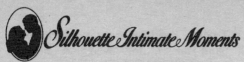

Silhouette Intimate Moments

Rx: One Dose of

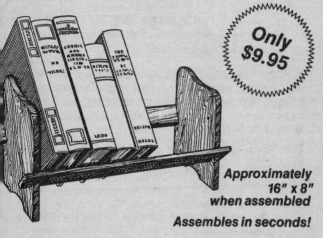

Silhouette Special Edition

NORA ROBERTS'S 50TH SILHOUETTE NOVEL

In May, SILHOUETTE SPECIAL EDITION celebrates Nora Roberts's "golden anniversary"— her 50th Silhouette novel!

The Last Honest Woman launches a three-book "family portrait" of entrancing triplet sisters. You'll fall in love with all THE O'HURLEYS!

The Last Honest Woman—May
Hardworking mother Abigail O'Hurley Rockwell finally meets a man she can trust...but she's forced to deceive him to protect her sons.

Dance to the Piper—July
Broadway hoofer Maddy O'Hurley easily lands a plum role, but it takes some fancy footwork to win the man of her dreams.

Skin Deep—September
Hollywood goddess Chantel O'Hurley remains deliberately icy...until she melts in the arms of the man she'd love to hate.

Look for THE O'HURLEYS! And join the excitement of Silhouette Special Edition!

SSE451-1